P9-DEB-398
3 6015 00129 5803

THE BELL TOWER

Recent Titles by Sarah Rayne

TOWER OF SILENCE
A DARK DIVIDING
ROOTS OF EVIL
SPIDER LIGHT
THE DEATH CHAMBER
GHOST SONG
HOUSE OF THE LOST
WHAT LIES BENEATH

PROPERTY OF A LADY *
THE SIN EATER *
THE SILENCE *
THE WHISPERING *
DEADLIGHT HALL *
THE BELL TOWER *

* *available from Severn House*

THE BELL TOWER

Sarah Rayne

This first world edition published 2015
in Great Britain and 2016 in the USA by
SEVERN HOUSE PUBLISHERS LTD of
19 Cedar Road, Sutton, Surrey, England, SM2 5DA.
Trade paperback edition first published
in Great Britain and the USA 2016 by
SEVERN HOUSE PUBLISHERS LTD

British Library Cataloguing in Publication Data

Rayne, Sarah author.
The bell tower.
1. West, Nell (Fictitious character)–Fiction. 2. Flint,
Michael (Fictitious character)–Fiction. 3. Bell towers–
England–Dorset–Fiction. 4. Horror tales.
I. Title
823.9'2-dc23

ISBN-13: 978-0-7278-8559-3 (cased)
ISBN-13: 978-1-84751-668-8 (trade paper)
ISBN-13: 978-1-78010-722-6 (e-book)

All Severn House titles are printed on acid-free paper.

Severn House Publishers support the Forest Stewardship Council™ [FSC™],
the leading international forest certification organisation.
All our titles that are printed on FSC certified paper carry the FSC logo.

Typeset by Palimpsest Book Production Ltd.,
Falkirk, Stirlingshire, Scotland.
Printed and bound in Great Britain by
TJ International, Padstow, Cornwall.

AUTHOR'S NOTE AND ACKNOWLEDGEMENT

The lyrics for 'Thaisa's Song' were created from a mixture of old ballads and ancient death songs. The main inspiration, however, came from the eerie and hauntingly beautiful 'The Unquiet Grave', which is thought to date to around 1400.

'The Unquiet Grave' can still be heard today, more than 600 years after it was written. It has been recorded by many contemporary musicians and singers. Sadly, the original composer's name has been lost.

Sarah Rayne

ONE

Corby & Sons
Solicitors
Oxford

To: Mrs Nell West,
Nell West Antiques, Quire Court, Oxford
cc: Dr Michael Flint,
Oriel College, Oxford.

Dear Mrs West and Dr Flint
QUIRE COURT SHOP
Enclosed is a copy of the new lease for your present shop and the adjoining shop, which is being assigned to you.

Could you read through this carefully, with particular attention to page three, which sets out the work you are proposing to carry out, to make the two shops into one unit.

This isn't the full lease, which goes back over several hundred years and is fairly lengthy. This is more in the nature of an abstract; however, these are the relevant extracts.

Do please let me know if there's anything that isn't clear.

Kind regards,
Yours sincerely,
J. L. Corby

'I didn't realize,' said Nell West, studying the lease sent by Corby's, 'that Quire Court was so old. But according to this, four of the shops – including this one – date back to the early fifteenth century. It was known as Glaum's Acre then.'

'And,' said Michael, turning over the pages, 'in the sixteenth century it was apparently owned by a monastic order.'

Nell watched him, thinking this would be exactly how he looked when he was about to lecture to a group of students. Serious and absorbed, and utterly endearing.

'In those days,' said Owen Bracegirdle, who was having supper with them, 'the monasteries and the Church owned half of England between them. Is there any more chilli con carne, Nell? Thanks.'

'It's difficult to tell the age of a place like Quire Court,' said Nell, spooning chilli on to Owen's plate. 'All that stonework and the mullioned windows and whatnot.'

'And the stone arch that leads through to Turl Street.'

'Can I see the reference to the monastery?' asked Owen.

'It was in Dorset. A place called Rede Abbas.' Michael passed the relevant page across the table. 'I should think this whole document would originally have been in Latin, wouldn't it?'

'Yes, but they'd translate it for the benefit of later leaseholders. Probably modernized the language a bit at the same time.' Owen bent over the photocopied page. 'Did you see this clause?' he said, after a moment. 'I don't know how it got into a document dealing with Quire Court, but the oddest things were sometimes interlinked. It says the monks asserted their right to hold what they called St Benedict's Revels – "exactly one month after Michaelmas Quarter Day".'

'Revels sound quite lively for monks,' said Nell.

'It'd hardly have been sex, drugs and rock and roll, but I daresay a bit of frivolity went on. I'll look it up when I get back to College,' said Owen. 'I think it's time I wended my way back to Oriel, anyway. I've got an early tutorial tomorrow morning with an anxious final year, and I suspect I've had about half a bushel of wine tonight. Michael, you've probably had the other half, so are we sharing a taxi back, or . . .? Oh, wait, is it one of those "What's for breakfast, darling?" nights. Yes, I see it is. Nell, you're blushing.'

'I'm not,' said Nell, who was.

'A nice, old-fashioned custom, blushing,' said Owen. 'But, in any event, I'll say, "Bless you, my children," and wend my way back to my solitary bed.'

'So Quire Court's got Tudor roots,' said Michael, some considerable time later. He was sitting on his favourite window-seat in Nell's bedroom, looking out over the shadowy old stonework. 'I didn't know that.'

From the bed, Nell could just see the old arch that led to Turl Street. The stones were bleached to silver by the moonlight.

'You've occasionally talked about it being haunted,' she said.

'I've never been entirely serious, though. And I was only meaning a very mild, gentle kind of haunting, anyway.'

'The serenity of undisturbed ghosts,' said Nell, half to herself.

'Did I say that?'

'Once or twice.'

'But before tonight, if I did think there were ghosts here, I saw them as vague, and even scholarly,' said Michael, still staring out at the darkness. 'Amiable, absent-minded old gentlemen searching for a mislaid fragment of a book. Or craftsmen lovingly fashioning silver objects. And writers and poets, scratching away with quill pens by candlelight.'

'Isn't that what you think now?'

'No. It's as if reading that lease – even the few pages that Corby's sent – has opened up a deeper level.' He looked across at the bed. 'Am I romanticizing?'

'Yes, and in rather a dark way. It's not like you to do that. Come back to bed and romanticize in a different way.'

Hi Michael

I'm assuming you'll pick up this email today – that you're back in your rooms at Oriel by now, it being ten in the morning.

I've found St Benedict's Revels. The idea was to celebrate the life of St Benedict by holding a two-day fair with music and pageantry – mummers and musicians and jugglers, and a performing bear as well, I shouldn't wonder. Then a feast to round it all off. It does strike a slightly peculiar note, considering Benedict himself was a hermit, much given to preaching and practising strict discipline and obedience, not to mention chastity; in fact on one occasion the old boy is said to have thrown himself into a briar patch to banish tempting visions. Still, as somebody said since (John Lennon?): Whatever gets you through . . .

Reports say that on one occasion the monks caroused so enthusiastically most of them became 'myse-dronck'. I love that expression – I might try to reintroduce it into common usage, possibly starting in the Senior Common Room after the Dean's Christmas lunch.

But to return to our muttons. After one of the feasts, several of the monks reportedly treated the company to several rousing songs with the most astonishingly irreligious titles. 'Cuckolds All Awry' seems to have been the mildest, and there was another called, 'The Knight's Lusty Lance'. There's apparently an eyewitness account somewhere, written by one Brother Cuthwin, so I'm going to try to track him down.

It seems, though, that the present-day council (Arts, Rural, or even Privy for all I know) have recently decided that it was a pity the Revels had ended and the insubstantial pageant had faded, and there's to be all manner of Tudor caperings at the end of next month. The date is vaguely around Michaelmas, so it sounds as if they're trying to keep to the monks' original requirement of providing 'feasting of roast meats and mead'. I daresay only a cynic would wonder if they have an eye to the tourist trade as well.

Have you found out, yet, that Wilberforce wrought havoc in that flowerbed near the Senior Library last night? I don't know the details, but I believe a newly planted rose bed was involved, and somebody said Mr Jugg – who I always think sounds like a character from Happy Families; not that he is, for a more glum individual I've yet to met – anyway, Jugg is plotting revenge in his potting shed, because he doesn't think cats should be allowed in College, and certainly not cats who dig up newly planted rose bushes that were presented by somebody from the Ben Jonson Society, and were the first set of cuttings (shoots? saplings?) to be named for him.

'Ruined, Dr Bracegirdle,' he said to me this morning. 'Shredded all over the quad as if a flock of wild beasts had rampaged everywhere.'

I believe Jugg is currently fashioning lengths of wire hung about with wind-chimes to crisscross the bed in question and thwart any future feline mayhem. There were, however, worrying rumours in the SCR this morning about dishes of fish laced with arsenic being put out. So I think you'd better keep Wilberforce incarcerated until Jugg has calmed down.

Owen

Michael, having read this, forwarded it to Nell, who would enjoy hearing about the Rede Abbas revels. He thought the rose-bed disaster might make a good episode for the current Wilberforce book he was writing, so dashed off an email to his editor at the children's publishing house with the idea, then set out on a pacifying mission to the affronted Jugg. This last took far longer than he had expected, and he supposed that somewhere between writing Wilberforce's fictional adventures for seven- and eight-year-olds, soothing injured gardeners, and writing an apology to the Ben Jonson Society – as well as paying for a new consignment of rose bushes – he would find time to tutor a few students.

'I've found the website for the Rebe Abbas Revels,' said Nell, the following evening. 'And it looks quite interesting.'

'Street stalls, dancing, music, and drama,' said Michael, reading the printed list of events. 'And a couple of morality plays – that's a nod to the days of the original monks, presumably. It looks as if they're staging a jazzed-up version of the Seven Deadly Sins. That was a common theme in those medieval romps. I should think they'll play down Lust, don't you?'

'It coincides with Beth's half-term and also her birthday,' said Nell, 'so it could make a good birthday treat for her. She's keen on the idea – in fact, her teacher is keen as well, and they might make a school trip out of it. They can book the kids into a local Ramblers' Hostel, apparently. They're already planning a midnight feast in the dormitories to celebrate Beth's birthday.'

'God help the ramblers. How far is Rede Abbas?'

'About two and a half hours – right on the Dorset coast. It looks quite an easy drive, though. Could you come with us?' said Nell, eagerly. 'We could book into a local B&B or a pub for a couple of nights.'

'I'd like to if I can,' said Michael. 'I'd certainly like to see what today's performers make of a medieval morality play. I'll see what I've got on at College. What about the shop?'

'It looks as if it'll be around the time when the builders will have reached the most disruptive part, so I'll have to close the shop for about a week anyway. It might be a good idea to be completely out of the way.'

Beth was entranced at the prospect of the Rede Abbas Revels.

'The programme says they might be performing something that hasn't been heard for nearly five hundred years.'

'The operative word is *might*,' said Nell. 'That sounds more as if they're trying to find stuff that nobody's heard for hundreds of years. It's most likely a marketing ploy.'

'Still, it'll be a really good weekend, won't it?'

'It sounds very good. I'd like to research the history of Rede Abbas while we're there if I can. But I'll probably be staying at one of the pubs with Michael, which means I won't be around too much while you're with your friends. So you won't be embarrassed by the presence of a parent.'

'Um, you don't embarrass me,' said Beth, in an awkward mumble. 'Michael doesn't, either. Most people at school think he's pretty cool. Good-looking and stuff like that, I mean.'

'Well, yes,' said Nell, momentarily disconcerted.

'I think,' said Beth, reaching for the programme again, 'that the Dusklight Concert with the five-hundred-year-old song will be the coolest, wickedest thing of the whole weekend.'

'So do I. And isn't it time you were in bed?'

Having chased Beth up to bed, Nell stood at the downstairs window looking across at the rear of her shop. She was looking forward to having the new premises and to living in the huge flat that was being created across the first floors of both buildings, and she was looking forward to arranging antique weekends and workshops in this house as well. She liked this house. She liked looking out of this window late at night, seeing the moonlight silvering the old stonework of the shops. It almost made it possible to subscribe to Michael's views about gentle, inquisitive ghosts. Nell did not really believe in those ghosts, but if they were to appear they would be soft, blurred figures, their outlines slightly fuzzy because they had lived their lives by flickering candlelight and lamplight.

Lamplight . . .

A light was showing from under the eaves of her shop. It was probably just the reflection of a streetlight from beyond the Court, although streetlights had never reflected on the windows before. She leaned forward, to see better.

The light was reflecting because one of the upstairs windows of her shop was open. There was no doubt about it; it was one of the small attic rooms. It was not much of a security risk to leave it open – the shop had a good alarm system, and any enterprising burglar would have to set up a very long ladder to get up to that window. Even so . . . She glanced at the time. Quarter to ten. Not so very late. She went up to Beth's room.

Beth was reading by the bedside light. Nell said, 'I've just seen there's a window open at the shop. It's one of the attics, so I expect the builders left it open – they were up there earlier today. But I'd better close it – it might rain or birds could get in. I'll only be ten minutes – will you be all right?'

'Mum, I'm not going to vanish in ten minutes,' said Beth.

'I'll lock the door.'

'Well, all right, but don't *fuss.*'

'I'm not. But put the bedroom light on, and sit on the windowsill where I can see you from the garden,' said Nell, and Beth sighed with exaggerated emphasis, and said, Oh, well, she s'posed so.

Nell ran down the stairs, snatched up the keys, and sped along the garden. Halfway along she looked back at the house. Beth was sitting in the windowsill; she had switched on the bedroom light, and she waved to Nell and made a goldfish face and swimming motions with her hands, which was something she did in traffic jams to disconcert other motorists. Nell grinned, waved to her, and unlocked the shop door, reaching for the panel to deactivate the electronic alarm.

The faint light was in the main part of the shop as well. Quire Court had several Victorian-style wrought-iron streetlamps, and one was immediately outside. But as she went up the stairs, the light flickered and then dimmed, as if a lamp was being quenched. The narrow stair began to feel slightly scary, and the shadows seemed to be filling up with sounds and movements. Nell reminded herself that the sounds would be nothing more than birds scrabbling in the eaves, and traffic and people in the streets around the Court. Someone nearby was even singing. It was a bit early for raucous songs or drunken revelry from students, although this did not sound very raucous, and it did not sound drunk either. It was a single voice: a girl's, high and cool and quite sweet. The words did not sound English and Nell did not recognize the language, which had an unusual cadence. It could be anything, though; Oxford teemed with all races and creeds.

She was about to continue up to the attic, when she realized that the singing was not outside the shop at all. It was inside. She stood still, listening. Was it coming from the attic floor, with that open window? No, it was downstairs. Had someone followed her in? Or had someone already been in here, crouching in the darkness? The alarm had been on when she came in, but could someone have climbed through the open window? But it was on the second floor, and it would have meant using a long ladder and squeezing through an impossibly tiny space. And where was the ladder now? And what burglar would sing like this?

Nell began to make her way back down the stairs as quietly as possible. The open window would have to wait until tomorrow. There was someone in here, hiding somewhere in the dark corners of the empty building, and she was going to get the hell out of here and beat it back to the house and to Beth, then call the police.

As she reached the foot of the stairs, the light flared up, casting moving shadows across the walls, and this time Nell realized with new horror that a faint smell of oil was coming from Godfrey's half of the shop. A new image scudded into her mind – of papers being crumpled together, then doused with oil or petrol before a match was struck. This was so alarming she forgot about burglars who sang strange, sad songs and went towards the sounds, trying to remember where the fire extinguisher was, and if it had remained inside the building while the work was going on.

The singing was nearer now and there were other sounds as well, as if something was being dragged across the floor. There was the harsh ring of metal against stone, then the rhythmic slap of wet mortar on brick. Nell edged towards the outside door but, as she did so, something moved in the shadows – something that resembled the blurred pencil sketch of a human figure. Nell gasped and shrank back, but the figure had vanished. The burning-oil scent faded, and the old building settled back into its normal near-silence.

Nell, no longer caring if an entire army of drugged or drunk vagrants were camping out in here, tumbled through the partition into her own part of the shop. Her hands were shaking, but she reached the outer door and managed to tap in the security code and drag the door open. She locked it, and heard with relief the security system click back into place. Anyone inside would be trapped.

She ran along the garden path, relieved to see that Beth was still curled up on the window-seat. Nell waved to her as she ran along the garden path, and Beth waved back. Reality returned slightly. It was unlikely that anyone could have been inside the shop, but it might be as well to phone the police to report a possible intruder.

The night-duty officer at the police station was reassuring and efficient, and a patrol car was sent out with remarkable speed. Nell handed over the keys and the alarm code.

'Nothing to be found,' said the sergeant, having made an inspection, and returning the keys. 'We made a thorough search of both shops. You were sensible to call us out, though. Here's a crime reference number in case you need to phone us again, and here's my direct number. Ring if you need to, but everywhere looks fine. We've re-set the security system using your code, but maybe you'll feel happier if you change the code in the morning.'

'If I can't trust the police force, I can't trust anyone,' said Nell, nevertheless making a mental note to change it.

When finally she got to bed, the strange, sweet singing was still trickling through her mind as she drifted into sleep. But it would be just a rogue echo from beyond the Court, nothing more.

TWO

Email from: Olive Orchard, Organizing Committee, St Benedict's Revels
To: Daniel Goodbody, Local Historian and Revels Chair

Dear Daniel
Sorry to report we still haven't found the elusive 'Thaisa's Song' for the Dusklight Concert.

However, Gerald is doggedly going on with his search and insists it isn't just a vague legend. He says something is telling him there's a copy in existence somewhere, and you know Gerald. When he becomes convinced of a thing, there's no gainsaying him.

He spent the entire weekend exploring the library's archives – by which I mean those ancient, mildewed bundles of newspapers and documents he keeps squirrelled away in the half-cellar that opens off the Crime Fiction section. It was a pity you couldn't accept my invitation to supper while he was out of the house, particularly since Gerald had inadvertently locked himself into the cellar and we had to call a locksmith. He says it's not neurotic of him to lock the cellar, because an inquisitive child once found its way in there while its mother was absorbed in the latest Richard and Judy recommendations. The child shredded every copy of the *Abbas Advertiser* for 1939, which means future generations will never know how Rede Abbas reacted to the outbreak of WWII. (I don't know if the mother borrowed any Richard and Judy books.)

Regards,

Olive

To: Organizing Committee,
St Benedict's Revels,
c/o Council Offices
Rede Abbas

Dear Sirs

I hear with concern that a search is being made for the music known as 'Thaisa's Song', and that, if found, it will be sung at the forthcoming St Benedict's Revels.

I do beg you to abandon this search. The music is thought to have been lost for almost five hundred years, but it would be better for it to remain lost.

I realize you will probably put my letter down to the ramblings of a crank or the fantasies of an eccentric, but I should be very grateful if you would abandon this search for 'Thaisa's Song'.

Sincerely

Maeve Eynon

Email From: Olive Orchard, Organizing Committee, St Benedict's Revels

To: Daniel Goodbody, Local Historian and Revels Chair

Hi Daniel,
Here's the letter from Miss Eynon, which personally I should consign to the wpb. Gerald says Miss Eynon should be consigned there with it, because she drifts into the library and upsets everyone by talking about ancient tragedies and pointing out how many mistakes there are in books on local history (one was your own *opus*, I'm afraid). But Gerald hasn't the heart to ban her from the Reading Room, and says she's probably only mad nor-nor-west anyway.

However, a polite note with your name on it (and all the letters after your name you're entitled to), might reassure the lady. I shouldn't think there's anything peculiar about the music, should you? But perhaps you and I should get together to discuss it? I'm available almost any night this week. Or next week.

Kind regards,
Olive Orchard

From: Mr Daniel Goodbody, Local Historian and Revels Chair
To: Olive Orchard, Organizing Committee, St Benedict's Revels

Dear Olive
Angels and Ministers of grace defend me from Maeve Eynon and her Cassandra-like prophecies of doom!

Of *course* there isn't anything peculiar about 'Thaisa's Song'. I have no idea who 'Thaisa' is, or was, or how she came to be associated with the ballad – most likely she was the romantic focus of some medieval troubadour. But, whoever she was, it would be a nice tribute to Rede Abbas's past if we could find and perform the song at the Dusklight Concert, because Rede Abbas's past is what the Revels are about.

I'm so sorry that at the moment I can't accept your suggestion for a drink one evening, but with the Revels coming up there's so much pressure of work. Perhaps when all that's over . . .

D.G.

The strange singing heard in the shop was still in Nell's mind next morning, but she pushed it away, let in Jack Hurst, whose building firm was dealing with the renovations, and focused on the day ahead.

This involved signing the new lease, which would effectively make Nell and Michael joint owners of the two shops. Nell had resisted any definite or official kind of link for so long that the prospect of this new arrangement, in which Michael would have a financial involvement, was starting to assume symbolic significance. More than once she wondered if she would end in feeling disloyal to her dead husband – which was absurd because Brad would have been genuinely pleased that she was being so adventurous. But as she and Michael drove to the solicitor's office, Nell wondered if she would recoil from actually signing when it came to it.

As if he had picked this up, without taking his eyes off the road, he said, 'Are you nervous about endowing me with half your worldly goods?'

'It feels like a massive step into unknown country.' Nell deliberately ignored the oblique reference.

'You aren't going to back out at the last minute, are you?'

'No. Are you?'

'No. It's a bit of a Rubicon-crossing moment, though,' he said. 'Well, it is for me. But I'm glad we're crossing it together.'

He took her hand briefly, and Nell suddenly knew it was going to be all right, and that of course Michael understood about them stepping into an unfamiliar place.

In fact, far from being unfamiliar, the sight of her signature and Michael's on the lease looked reassuring and familiar, and as if the two names belonged together – as if they ought to have been written like that long since. She glanced at him, and saw that he was regarding the signatures with an expression of satisfaction.

'All dealt with,' said the solicitor at last, handing them their parts of the document and stowing his own in a box file. 'And your ex-neighbour, Mr Purbles, has signed the counterpart, so everything is nicely in place. Oh, and the change of use for the house at the back has been approved. Residential to business use for the antique workshops. My wife's rather keen to come to one of those, by the way.'

'I'll send you a brochure,' said Nell, pleased. 'I'm having some printed.'

'Are there any questions you want to ask?'

'I don't think so. In essence, the lease is the one I've had for the last few years – except everything's doubled. All the repairing obligations and insurance liabilities are the same, except for the clauses allowing the two shops to be knocked into one.'

'And the lateral conversion on the first floor for your new living quarters,' nodded the solicitor. 'The freeholders are Christchurch College, as you know. They've put in several stipulations about the adaptations, but on the whole I think they've been fair. They want to make sure you aren't doing anything that might damage the overall structure, and that you'll be keeping to the original character of the Court.'

'Which I would anyway,' said Nell.

'Quite. You'll let me have the building guarantees and electricity certificates, will you? I see you're extending into the area immediately under the roof, as well.'

'Yes. That will be part of the living quarters. Godfrey – Mr Purbles – hardly used any of the upper rooms, and I don't think he ever used the attic floor at all.'

'No forgotten Old Masters likely to be discovered up there?'

'If there had been any, Godfrey would have found them and sold them,' said Michael.

As they got up to go, Nell said, 'I was intrigued by the references to the original owners.'

'The monks,' said the solicitor, smiling.

'It seems odd that a monastic house in Dorset owned property as far away as Oxford.'

'In those days the Church owned large swathes of the entire country, Mrs West. But I agree that it's a bit odd in this case, because as far as I've ever been able to make out, that particular monastery was quite a small one and not particularly rich.'

'What happened to it?'

'I don't know its eventual fate, but it was still in existence in the late 1800s, because that was when the freehold of most of Quire Court was transferred to Christchurch.'

'So the monastery survived dissolution,' said Michael, thoughtfully.

'It seems so. Probably it was too insignificant – and too poor – to attract much attention. Rede Abbas must have been a very tiny place – it's barely more than a speck on the map now.'

It was not possible to be away from Quire Court for all of the work, and Michael and Beth spent a companionable evening speculating on the fate of the Court's various ghosts. Michael drew vivid word pictures for the enraptured Beth, involving indignant spooks tumbled from their beds by twenty-first-century machinery, the ghosts scrambling untidily into doublet and hose, their wigs askew as they scurried hither and yon. After this, the two of them embarked on a discussion for a new Wilberforce the Cat book, in which Wilberforce moved into an old house, only to find himself at the mercy of an entire family of resentful ghosts, who objected to his presence and went to considerable lengths to dislodge him.

Nell, watching the two dark heads bent over notebooks and sketch pads, hearing Beth's sudden giggle of delight and seeing Michael's absorption, thought: Brad would have been pleased with this. He would have known he could trust Michael. I can trust him as well, she thought. How have I been so lucky?

'The idea for Wilberforce being plagued by comedy spooks is pure Oscar Wilde, of course,' said Michael, later. 'It's straight out of *The Canterville Ghost*. I must look out a copy of that for Beth – I think she'd enjoy it. But I emailed my editor about the idea, and she loves it. She says sales are doing very well in the current quarter, and the Wilberforce website they set up is being bombarded by eager seven- and eight-year-olds. So I'm going to take a swing at the ghost idea.'

'I love the sound of Wilberforce pursued by irritable ghosts. Uh – did you say you could be here tomorrow to help with the wall-demolishing? Only if you can be free, of course.'

'Nell, there's no need to sound defensive. I've kept the afternoon free, and I'd sweep out the Augean Stables for you. All three thousand of them.'

'Never mind the Augean Stables – as long as we get that pair of Regency desks back on display without too much delay, because I paid well over the odds for them and I need to sell them as soon as possible. Can you be here at two?'

'Neither flood nor fire nor the scalding winds that rive the knotty oaks shall keep me from you at two tomorrow.'

'If we get any scalding winds, Hurst's men will probably abandon ship until next week.'

But there were no winds, scalding or any other kind, and Michael helped Jack Hurst's two sidekicks to carry the Regency desks and the other larger pieces of Nell's current stock into the little house at the end of the garden, then went back to drape everything else in dustsheets. One or two inquisitive customers wandered in while this was going on, despite the large notice explaining that both shops were being temporarily closed for renovations. They prowled around, not appearing to mind the mess, and several wanted to know if Godfrey Purbles's antiquarian bookshop service would be continuing. Two of them joined in the cleaning operations, during which Nell sold a hand-painted filigree fan, a pair of Victorian miniatures painted on silk, and one of the Regency desks.

When the sledgehammers finally smashed into the dividing wall, they did so with a crash like the crack of doom, and for a split-second the whole of Quire Court seemed to freeze. There was a moment of extraordinary stillness before clouds of stone-dust and shards of rubble flew upwards. Nell, standing at a safe distance with Michael, had the sudden disconcerting impression of something that was neither brick nor stone splintering. Or was it more as if something had been cracked open?

She was relieved when Jack Hurst peered out from the dustsheet draped over the door, like a Victorian showman behind a camera lens, and gave the thumbs-up sign. 'All done, and a more beautifully behaved wall you never saw. It came down like a collapsing pastry case.'

'I'm glad I apologized in advance to the other residents,' said Nell, surveying the dust-strewn Court in some dismay. 'There's a lot more mess than I thought.'

'Don't worry about it,' said Hurst, cheerfully. 'We'll use a pressure hose to sluice everything away. Bright as a new pin this time tomorrow.'

Michael was studying the Court and the stone-fronted shops, and Nell said, 'I suppose you're visualizing the ghosts fleeing in disarray.'

'Not exactly. But if you look across at the stone arch – no, not the one on the front of the shop, the big one over the Court's main entrance . . .'

'Yes?'

'Doesn't it look as if a couple of figures are standing there? As if they're hovering between two worlds – trying to make up their minds to step into the twenty-first century.'

'All I can see,' said Nell, 'is a whopping great crack in the plinth on the left-hand side. If that isn't cemented soon, it'll widen and the whole thing will crash down.'

'You're a heartless wench. Didn't you realize that arch is the portal through which the Quire Court ghosts come and go?'

'Well, if the arch does fall down, I hope the ghosts are on their own side of the portal and that there aren't any customers directly underneath at the time,' said Nell.

Jack Hurst arrived promptly the next morning, full of plans to finish the plastering so it could dry out over the weekend.

'It's all looking good, Mrs West. Make a nice flat for you. And that rear stairway means it'd be completely self-contained, so you could rent those upper floors if you ever wanted to live anywhere else.'

'So I could.' Nell had not thought of this aspect.

'Make a good office suite,' he said. 'Good central location – you could charge a nice rent for it. How about we put a main door by those stairs with a five-lever lock, just in case. Make it separate and more secure. Speaking of which, were there any more signs of that intruder you had the other night?'

'Thankfully, no.'

'You sometimes get prowlers when a place is being renovated,' said Jack. 'People looking to see if any valuable equipment's been left around. Matter of fact, we thought we heard someone wandering around late yesterday afternoon after that wall came down. We'd been in the attics chipping off the old plaster. Shocking condition, that plaster, but the fabric underneath is sound. But Darren swore he'd heard footsteps up there, didn't you, Darren? No one around, though, but we'll keep a weather eye out.'

'I'd appreciate that,' said Nell.

'Mind, one look at Darren this morning, and any self-respecting burglar would take to his heels and run. On the beer last night,' said Jack, grinning; at which Darren, slightly red of eye and pasty of complexion, was understood to mumble something about a beer contest and to add, a touch resentfully, that you had to keep up.

Nell provided Darren with a couple of paracetamol, then drove Beth to school, during which they discussed the forthcoming journey to Rede Abbas and the transportation of Beth's birthday cake, which had been ordered from her favourite patisserie in the High, and was to be discreetly smuggled into the Ramblers' Hostel for the midnight feast.

'But you're not to tell anyone,' said Beth, anxiously. 'On account of we don't think it's allowed.'

Nell promised to maintain absolutely secrecy, and returned to Quire Court to find lights blazing from the portable generator, and Jack Hurst plastering a wall. His second-in-command was threading electricity cables behind a section of trunking, and the hapless Darren was handing round bacon and sausage baps on the grounds that everyone knew you had to mop up a hangover with substantial food.

'When he's finished scoffing that,' said Jack, 'I've told him to clear out the rest of the stuff in Mr Purbles's storeroom. Chock-full of papers that is.'

'Ask him to carry everything out to my house, would you?' said Nell. 'I promised Godfrey I'd leave all that stuff for the recycling collection on Saturday. There's a couple of cardboard boxes somewhere. Darren can tip everything into those.'

With thin morning sunlight filtering in, the rooms appeared innocuous and ordinary, and if anything scrabbled or sang or burned oil lamps today, Nell could not hear or see it. She went up to the attics. Beth loved the idea of a bedroom with a sloping ceiling, and of having a tiny sitting-room-cum-study of her very own. The bedroom would be large enough to take twin beds so that she could have a friend to stay sometimes. In a few years there would presumably be boyfriends who would stay overnight, as well; Nell tried to think how she would cope with this, then wondered if they would still be living here by that time.

The sunlight came politely into the attics, filtering through the small windows, which had the same lead crisscross strips as the lower floors, lying in diamond-shaped patterns across the floor. Dust motes danced in and out of the light, and Nell's spirits rose. She walked round, thinking Beth could have a deep, squashy armchair in this corner, a TV in the other, and a desk beneath the window overlooking the garden.

The window overlooking the garden.

As Jack had said, they had stripped a good deal of the old plaster away, and beneath the window it had fallen away in large sections, revealing the original bare stones. The sunlight slanted across this part of the wall, and written across the old stonework – written so deeply that in places the letters were slightly indented – was a name and a date. *Theodora. October 1850.* Intrigued, Nell bent down to see it more clearly.

Under the name and the date, written in what was obviously the same hand, were more words. They were faded, but they were perfectly legible: *If anyone finds this, please pray for me, for it will mean the dead bell has sounded and I have suffered Thaisa's fate . . .*

Nell sat back on her heels. The writing was old enough for the words not to matter any longer, and Theodora and Thaisa, whoever they had been, were long-since dead. Even so, she found herself shivering slightly, and when she put out a finger to trace the words, she felt as if she was touching cold, dead flesh. This was absurd, of course. Any fate that had overtaken Theodora and Thaisa was long ago. At least a hundred and fifty years. She repeated this several times.

The rest of the day was spent in sorting out the remaining details for the trip to Rede Abbas, but several layers down, Nell kept seeing the scribbled message on the old attic wall.

Theodora, thought Nell. Who were you? What were you doing at Quire Court and what was the dead bell that might sound? Above all of that, what was 'Thaisa's fate' that frightened you so much?

THREE

From: Olive Orchard, Organizing Committee, St Benedict's Revels
To: Daniel Goodbody, Local Historian and Revels Chair

Daniel –
Well, rehearsals for the concert are going smoothly, and the Morality Play sequence is shaping up to be nicely robust, but in perfectly good taste.

Gerald is very busy setting up a display of the archived documents he's unearthed. He's found some interesting stuff – old photos and lithographs, and a few odds and ends of documents from St Benedict's Monastery. He's currently disinterring those glass-topped cabinets we had for the centenary. Fortunately, only a couple are actually broken.

Annoyingly, though, Gourmet Snacks can no longer supply

the food, having been declared bankrupt last week, so we shall have to use Street Food Inc instead. Gerald is inclined to be suspicious of them and thinks they are too cheap and you get what you pay for. On the other hand, he says he always thought Gourmet Snacks were the wrong choice – Tudor monks were unlikely to have celebrated the Revels with langoustine pâté or passion-fruit panna cotta. Personally, I would prefer pâté and panna cotta to Street Food's burgers and kebabs, but life is full of compromises. Gerald also points out that the monks traditionally had roast meats and mead at the Revels, and he thought we had agreed to follow that theme as closely as possible, although he does agree that burgers and kebabs might be regarded as a modern-day equivalent.

I have asked The Fox & Goose about outside lighting and the car parking, and will report.

Looking forward to having our drink together before much longer.

Olive Orchard (Hon. Sec.)

From: Daniel Goodbody
To: Gerald Orchard, Librarian

Dear Gerald

I was sorry not to have seen you earlier today, but I was very impressed by the library's display for the Revels – you have certainly disinterred some exciting-looking material. I'm intending to take a closer look when I'm less busy with the Revels arrangements.

I'm also grateful to you for agreeing to keep the library open until seven each evening during the four days.

Kind regards,

Daniel

From: The Fox & Goose
To: Olive Orchard, Organizing Committee, St Benedict's Revels

Dear Mrs Orchard

No, we will not allow the lighting for the Dusklight Concert to be linked to our electricity supply, since we do not trust temporary electricity meters.

We will loan out our car-parking signs for use in Musselwhite's Meadow, which we feel is entirely in keeping with the meadow's history. It was once common land and has been a stopping place for gypsies for many centuries, so we feel it very suitable that travellers coming for the Revels should be allowed to park there. We propose making a charge of £10 a day for this. What fee the committee levies to individual motorists is, of course, its own affair.

We cannot undertake to staff Musselwhite's ourselves, on account of having quite sufficient to do, with all the folk who will be staying here for the Revels, most of whom will be wanting decent wholesome meals rather than convenience food from street stalls. The Fox & Goose has always provided good plain cooking to its customers, and would have done so for the entire festival, if asked. Roast meats would have been simple to prepare and serve, and we have a very good selection of local ciders which would have replicated the monks' mead.

Kind regards,

p.p. Fox & Goose.

From: Daniel Goodbody, Local Historian and Revels Chair
To: Gerald Orchard, Librarian

Dear Gerald
Herewith a catalogue index number to a volume of the Victoria County History, which refers to 'Thaisa's Song' and might assist your search. It's one of the VCH's earliest editions – a 1900 volume in fact – and according to the entry the song is an old Welsh ballad, probably dating to the thirteenth or even the twelfth century. It first appeared in Dorset around 1530, although how it got from Wales to Dorset no one seems to know, and who sung it in 1530 is anybody's guess. The entry says that over the centuries the original words and meanings became corrupted (their word, not mine!), to say nothing of losing a fair amount in the translating.

It's to be hoped that if you do find the music, the lyrics

will be in English, because I shouldn't think the choral society would be able to sing or even pronounce the original Welsh, and I don't suppose the current library budget allows for the purchase of twenty Welsh dictionaries.

Daniel

Organising Committee, St Benedict's Revels,
Council Offices
Rede Abbas

Dear Miss Eynon
Thank you for your latest letter about our Revels Dusklight Concert and the current search for 'Thaisa's Song'. I am so sorry the possibility of including that piece causes you concern, but I promise you that if we do find it, it will be sung with as much accuracy as possible, and will, we think, form a very pleasing tribute to the history of Rede Abbas.

Perhaps I could call on you at your home to set your mind at rest on any particular anxieties you may have? If you could let me know when that would be convenient, I will be very happy to do so.

Kind regards,
Daniel Goodbody
Chairman, St Benedict's Revels

Cliff House
Rede Abbas

Dear Mr Goodbody
I am afraid it is not convenient for you to visit me and will not be so at any time in the future.

'Thaisa's Song' has a sad and troubling background, and should be left in the dark silence in which it has dwelled for several centuries. There are parts of the past everywhere that have been sealed off, and in Rede Abbas's case it would be better if they remained sealed.

I am surprised that you, with your knowledge of the past and your years of studying history, do not appear to understand or even acknowledge the power that can sometimes lie hidden within ancient music.

Sincerely,

Maeve Eynon

Email from: Olive Orchard, Organizing Committee, St Benedict's Revels

To: Daniel Goodbody, Local Historian and Revels Chair

Daniel –

Gerald was very pleased to have that VCH reference you sent – he will thank you himself when he isn't so busy. He's just made another intrepid expedition into the library cellars in case he's missed anything that might be lurking down there. He says if you stand very still in that cellar and concentrate, you can sometimes glimpse the past and you can certainly smell its aura. Personally, I've only ever smelt mildew or Jeyes' Fluid if the cleaners have been in, but when I said so, Gerald replied in an injured tone that it was a sad day when history and romance were quenched and smothered by disinfectant.

He still hasn't found 'Thaisa's Song', but he's continuing to search.

I'm sending the programme proofs for you to approve. Can you believe that the printers have called the Saturday night concert 'Dust Light'! Wretched computer spell-check.

If you care to bring the marked proofs back, any night would be fine, or I could call at your house for them. Gerald usually has his supper at The Swan on Fridays when the library stays open until seven, so Fridays are always particularly convenient for me.

Olive

Daniel Goodbody's letter, suggesting he visit her, had generated such nervous fear in Maeve Eynon that she had gone all round Cliff House bolting the doors and checking the locks to make sure no one could get in without her knowing. In the downstairs rooms she closed the shutters as well. She did this every night and every morning anyway, but it would not hurt to make sure at midday.

The shutters, when closed, made the rooms very dark, but once they were in place, she felt able to make a cup of tea, which she drank while writing her reply to Daniel Goodbody's letter. He could not be allowed to visit the house, of course. No one could, not ever. In all the years Maeve had lived here, there had never been what other people called guests. Once or twice workmen had had to be allowed in to deal with the plumbing, which was old and clanky, or to mend a bit of guttering if it fell off, but Maeve always stayed with them and made sure they did not go into the other parts of the house.

It was unlikely that her letters to Daniel Goodbody and his precious festival committee would do any good. Daniel Goodbody, for all his pretence at knowledge, and for all the books he had written about local history, would not understand how the past could be dangerous; and that stupid Olive Orchard, who had somehow got herself appointed as festival secretary, would only laugh. Maeve did not like Olive Orchard and she did not trust her. Also, it was very unbecoming for a woman of Olive's age and size to simper and flutter over Mr Goodbody as Olive did, and behave as if she did not have a husband. Still, Olive Orchard's husband was only silly, wittering Gerald from the library, whom Maeve could not believe would rate very highly as a husband on any scale.

When she had heard about the search for 'Thaisa's Song', she had thought for a long time before writing to ask that the idea be dropped. She did not like drawing attention to herself – Aunt Eifa had never done so, and Maeve, who had only been ten when her parents died and she came to live at Cliff House, had grown up imbibing Aunt Eifa's rules and precepts. It occasionally surprised her when she realized it was forty years since she had come to this house – and that it had been forty years since she'd first heard 'Thaisa's Song'.

Her parents had died within a couple of weeks of one another, which was why Maeve had been brought to live with her mother's cousin, who was called Eifa Eynon. It had been dark and raining when she'd been brought to the house, and she had stared up at it, and hated it. It seemed to her to be so much a part of the dark rainy night and of her own misery that she had wanted to run away from it. But there wasn't anywhere she could run to; so she had to go into the house and meet her mother's cousin, who said she was to call her Aunt Eifa.

The house was bleak and uncomfortable and everywhere smelled damp because of being so near to the sea. Aunt Eifa herself was thin and severe and her clothes smelled of stale bread. Maeve hoped she would not find her own clothes smelling of stale bread if she lived here.

Aunt Eifa said Maeve would take her own family's name from now; she would be Maeve Eynon, which was what her mother had been before her marriage. It was a good name and came from an old family, and Maeve should be proud to use it. Maeve was too miserable and too bewildered to care what she was called, so she nodded and agreed.

She would have liked to have something that had belonged to her parents during those first weeks at Cliff House, but their house and all the furniture had been sold, and there did not seem to be anything. Aunt Eifa said there would be some money from the house sale which Maeve would have when she was eighteen, but Maeve would rather have had something now – something her mother and father had owned and that would feel like a link to them. She did not think there could be anything, but several weeks later a couple of boxes were brought to Cliff House. Aunt Eifa took them up to the spare bedroom and said Maeve could look at them when she wanted. She did not know what was in there, just a few personal possessions, she thought. Some pieces of jewellery maybe, and odd papers and photos. She was not much of a one for photographs herself – the past, once gone, should stay gone – but Maeve might like to look through the boxes, or even make up a scrapbook or a photograph album of her parents.

The spare bedroom, which was never used because no one ever came to stay, was quiet when Maeve eventually went into it. It felt somehow removed from the rest of the house. Dust motes danced in the thin autumn sunlight, and the oak-framed swing mirror over the old dressing table had a mist across it. Most of the mirrors in Cliff House had that mist because of the damp, so that when you looked in them, you thought it might not be your own face looking back, but strange, ghost-creatures, who had crept up from the sea and got into the house.

The spare room was neat and bleak, and the window looked out towards an old graveyard. The graves were all very old, and most of the headstones were lopsided, because the ground had slipped underneath so that they leaned against one another as if they might be drunk. Maeve hated seeing these lopsided stones, because it made her wonder if the dead people could sleep peacefully underneath.

The boxes were pushed against the wall, and as Maeve sat on the floor to investigate, the feeling that this room was shut off from the rest of the world was strongly with her. A hard lump of sadness came up in her throat, but she was not going to give way to crying because it would not bring her parents back, and crying always gave her a blocked-up nose and a snuffly headache. So she swallowed very hard several times, and the lump of misery eventually dissolved sufficiently for her to open the box.

It contained a jumble of things, most of which did not look very interesting apart from a large envelope containing photos. Might they be old family photos? Neither of her parents had seemed to have any family, except for Aunt Eifa, who had been her mother's aunt or second cousin or something. There had not been anyone else. Maeve had sometimes wished she had cousins and aunts and uncles like people at school, but her mother had often said that families were nothing but trouble and they were better without them.

There were only a few photos in the envelopes and they did not tell Maeve anything she did not already know. Some of them showed her parents looking happy and with their arms round one another, and Maeve put out a tentative finger to trace the smiling faces, and with her other hand curled her fingers, as if she was expecting to feel her mother or her father clasp her hand. Stupid, of course.

There was a small beaded evening bag, which her mother had sometimes used for dressed-up parties. Inside were a handkerchief and a comb. Maeve pressed the handkerchief to her cheek, smelling the scent her mother had used, which was called Intimate. There were a few pieces of jewellery – one was a narrow string of corals, which Maeve thought her mother had been wearing the night of the car crash. She let the bright, hard beads fall between her fingers, thinking she would never want to wear it herself, but that she would keep it. There were some cufflinks of her father's, as well, and the leather strap of his watch. This was starting to be dreadfully sad and she was beginning to wish she had not looked.

She was about to close the box and go back downstairs when she saw a small oblong of something that had slipped into a corner. A cassette. Maeve lifted it out. The plastic cover was scratched, but the tape itself looked all right. There was no label of any kind, and

Maeve thought it was not a pre-recorded cassette – her parents had liked music, all kinds of music, and they had had a lot of cassettes which they played. But this was the kind of cassette that people bought as a blank, so they could record their own music.

She sat on the floor holding the cassette for a very long time then, moving slowly and quietly so that Aunt Eifa would not hear her, she took it along to her own bedroom. Music did not form any part of life at Cliff House, but Maeve had a small cassette player and radio and there was a slightly battered piano in a small downstairs room, which Aunt Eifa said had belonged to her grandmother or her great-grandmother, she was not sure which. She thought music a waste of time, though, and she was apt to stomp around the room loudly and intrusively if Maeve played any of her cassettes. She did not like the radio, either – nothing but a lot of caterwauling noise, she said – so Maeve only played her cassettes and her radio in her bedroom, keeping the volume low.

She waited until Aunt Eifa went on one of the long walks she took at least twice a week, then she shut herself in her bedroom and took out the cassette from her parents' box. She sat on the edge of the bed, looking at the tape for a long time. There was probably nothing of any interest to hear. But supposing there was one of those messages people recorded to be played after they were dead? Maeve did not know if she wanted to hear that, but then she thought she could not bear to wonder about it and not know what it was.

Before she could change her mind, she slotted the tape into the player and pressed the Play button firmly.

FOUR

At first there was only the whirring of the tape, then, startlingly and clearly, her mother's voice, blurred with laughter, said, 'I'll only do it if you promise not to laugh and put me off.'

It brought Maeve's mother back so vividly that for a moment she thought she could not listen to any more. But her mother sounded happy, and Maeve would like to have this previously unknown, happy memory of her, so she left the tape running.

Then her father's voice came. He said, 'I can't promise I won't laugh. But I'm going to record you singing. You can take it to your lunch party tomorrow and play it to the twinset-and-pearls brigade. It'll liven them up a bit.'

'I don't think it's that kind of music, Rufus. I think it's sad music.'

'Then we'll jazz it up. Let me see it properly . . . Good God, what language is it, for pity's sake? It looks like best-quality gibberish.'

'Or Elvish,' said Maeve's mother, and she suddenly sounded perfectly clear and sober. 'Like *Lord of the Rings*.'

'It looks more like *Lord of the Flies*,' said Maeve's father. 'And they're spattered all over the paper as if they've been swatted.'

'It's not spattered flies, it's just very old,' said Maeve's mother. 'It's called "Thaisa's Song" – it says so on the score. But it's no use you trying to join in, because you won't be able to pronounce a quarter of the words, especially not in your current condition. How on earth much have you had to drink this evening?'

'How on earth much have you, if it comes to that?'

'I haven't been counting, but let's have another one before we start.'

There was a pause, filled with rustlings and chinkings of glass. Maeve understood her parents had been a bit drunk and giggly, which would have been embarrassing if she had been there at the time, but was not, somehow, embarrassing now.

Then her mother's voice said, 'All right, I'm ready. Are you going to try picking out the notes on the piano?'

'Yes, it looks simple enough – I ought to be able to sight-read it.' There was the sound of old, brittle paper being rustled.

'Switch the Record thing on,' said Maeve's mother.

'I have. It's been running for the last five minutes. Stop pissing around and get on with it.'

There was another of the pauses, then the singing began. And at once Maeve, sitting cross-legged on her bed, felt as if she had been plunged into black, icy water.

Her mother had had a good voice – she had taught Maeve songs from her own childhood, and they used to sing them together. She often sang to the radio or records as well. But today her voice on the cassette sounded different. It was almost as if something outside of her was trying to break through and make itself heard.

Maeve's father was picking out the tune on the piano – a note, a chord at a time. He was quite a keen pianist, although Maeve sometimes thought he was not very good. He was not very good now; he had said the music looked simple enough to sight-read, but he kept stumbling and missing the notes so that it sounded as if the music was splintering. Then quite suddenly he seemed to understand it, and to play more confidently.

The music made Maeve think of freezing winter mornings when the frost traced patterns on the windows and your fingers burned from the cold if you forgot your gloves. Despite that, it was the most beautiful music she had ever heard.

She understood what her father had meant when he called the words gibberish, because they did not form any pattern she recognized. They were certainly in a foreign language, although she had no idea what it was. She had just started French at school, but this was not French. The words were like thin glinting silver, coiled tightly on a spool, unwinding because the music was forcing them to unwind. But her mother seemed at home with them, and as Maeve listened, she began to feel at home with them as well. In an extraordinary way, they were familiar – she even thought that if she tried hard enough she might be able to grasp that coiled silver string, and understand what the song was about . . .

And then something deep within her mind did grasp it – not all at once, but in frayed fragments, a shred at a time, and the shreds and the fragments tumbled around in her brain like the coloured shards of a kaleidoscope. At first they did not make any sense. Then the colours fell down into their right places and she knew what the words were.

Who is this, knocks on my tomb?
Asks where and what I am,
Who is this who calls to me?
I cannot see nor hear.

I cannot see, I cannot hear
Who knocks upon my tomb.
I cannot speak, I cannot reach
The one stands by my tomb.

Maeve was starting to feel pleased at having understood this – so pleased that it was almost blotting out the dreadful sadness at hearing her parents' voices again – when something happened that drove all pleasure and all grief out, and left a cold, clamping fear.

There were two voices on the recording. One was her mother's, singing in that high, unfamiliar way, but there was a second voice: a voice that was thin and distant, and that struggled to form the words or understand the tune, so that it was just a half-beat behind. Was that because this second singer could not see or hear – could only sense that someone knocked upon his – her? – tomb? But there was no one else in the room with her parents – that had been obvious.

Then her mother stopped singing, and the tape whirred for another few seconds. Maeve's father said, a bit uncertainly, 'It's a dreary old dirge, whatever the words mean. I didn't think you'd be able to pronounce any of it, but you did.'

'Did you understand any of it?'

'No. Did you?'

'I'm not sure,' said Maeve's mother, slowly, and Maeve knew at once that her mother had understood it all, just as she had understood it herself, but that she did not want to say so.

Her father said, 'Where on earth did you find it?'

'I told you. It was in that box of stuff from Cliff House. That weird cousin I've got down there – Eifa Eynon. I helped her clear out an attic when I went down there last summer – and getting into the house was a miracle in itself, because she hardly ever lets anyone in. Don't you remember? There was a fusty old box that had been my grandmother's, or maybe even my great-grandmother's. Somebody ages back, anyway. There was some marvellous old jewellery, and Eifa said I could have it and welcome, because she never wore jewellery. So I brought it home. And there, inside an old jewel case, was this music. "Thaisa's Song". Only—'

'What?'

'I'm not sure it's such a good idea to let the lunch crowd hear it, after all.' She paused, and Maeve knew again that her mother had understood the words but was not going to tell her father. Then she said, 'I think what I'll do, I'll listen to it again in the car on the way there, and decide if it's really too dreary.' There was the sound of the piano lid being closed.

The next day Maeve's mother went happily off to her lunch, taking the recording with her to play as she drove.

'Enjoy yourself,' said Maeve's father.

But Maeve's mother never reached the lunch. On the way there her car crashed and she was killed outright in a tangle of crushed metal. Maeve's father had to do something called 'identifying the body', and he came back to the house grey-faced and shaking and *old*. There was a bad moment when Maeve did not recognize him – she thought he was somebody else, because her father could not look old and grey and as if everything inside him had been cut out and thrown away.

Two weeks later, still apparently stunned with grief and shock, he was found dead in his bed, an empty bottle of antidepressant pills on the bedside table, together with an empty bottle of whisky. Several of his wife's belongings were scattered over the bed. Among them were a cassette and a sheet of music.

The coroner said it was impossible to know if Maeve's father had accidentally taken too many of the pills that had been prescribed to help him through the bereavement, or if it had been deliberate. He could not, though, believe that a good family man would commit suicide, leaving a small daughter alone in the world. His verdict, therefore, was Accidental Death.

People said it was all appallingly tragic, unbelievable, a devastating loss to the nine-year-old Maeve, the poor mite. But what a mercy there had turned out to be a cousin in Dorset – somebody on the child's mother's side – who could take her.

Maeve never told Aunt Eifa about 'Thaisa's Song' – about how her mother had found the music in Cliff House and recorded it, or how Maeve herself had found the cassette and played it. She did not tell anyone about it, because she wanted to keep it for herself. It was a link to her parents – it was their voices on the tape. The strange thing, though, was that she found she did not want to play it again – not for a very long time; perhaps not ever.

She had been at Cliff House for five months, and she was starting to become interested in school things. She was particularly interested in a project in the art class.

'You're all going to make a montage this term,' the art teacher said. 'It can be on any theme you like, but try to use lots of different things – different textures, scraps of fabric, photographs, pressed flowers, newspaper cuttings. Make it interesting and vivid, and unusual, and we'll have an end-of-term display of the best ones.'

At first Maeve could not think what to do for the montage, and Aunt Eifa was not very helpful; she thought projects and montages were nonsense. In her day people had been taught to read and write and do sums and that had been good enough. Maeve tried not to think that her mother would have been interested in the project, and made suggestions for it.

But gradually she started to think that there was something in Rede Abbas that might make a really good project – something she could photograph and find out about. Something no one else might think about using.

The ancient bell tower on the cliff ledge. The dark, ugly tower, from which the long-ago monks had tolled an immense bronze bell to call everyone to prayer.

It had once been part of a long-ago monastery – somebody had come to school to give a talk about it – and Maeve had been interested in the story of the monks who had lived in a small house on the cliffside until the cliff began to crumble from the constant pounding of the sea. The monks had abandoned the place then, they had silenced the bell and made themselves a safer home a mile or so inland, but even after hundreds of years, a few fragments of that first monastery remained – there were traces of the walls. And there was the old bell tower.

Maeve could see that stretch of the cliff from her bedroom. On some mornings she could see the tower jutting up from its shelf of rock like a decaying black stump, but there were other days when it was surrounded by sea mist, and evenings when the dusk hid it, so that it vanished altogether. Her mother would have spun stories about it – she would have said it was one of the darkly enchanted towers in fairy stories; somewhere that was not always there.

Her father, wanting to interest his daughter in poetry, had read to her Robert Browning's dark, menacing poem, *Childe Roland to the Dark Tower Came.* He said she was too young to appreciate it entirely, but he would read it anyway and some of it might stick.

Maeve had not understood very much of it, and she had shuddered over the lines about the hoary cripple with the malicious eye, waylaying travellers with his skull-like laugh, but she had loved listening to Dad reading it to her and explaining parts of it.

When she came to live with Aunt Eifa and saw the bell tower for the first time, fragments of the poem came back to her. Of how no footprint had ever led into or out of it . . . How it was a squat turret, blind as a fool's heart, and how the soil around it broke into substances like boils . . . Rede Abbas's tower was not Childe Roland's, Maeve knew that, but she thought it must be very like it. And making it the subject of her school project would be making a memory of her father, just as the cassette recording was a memory of her mother.

She waited until Saturday afternoon when Aunt Eifa was busy in the garden, then put on her coat and fetched the camera her parents had given her on her last birthday. It had its own case with a strap and Maeve hung it around her neck and set off.

Here was the path that wound past the old graveyard and then down to the cliff. She had never gone this far along the path before, and it was a bit scary, because it was like the darkling path Childe Roland had taken. She went past the graveyard, not looking in at the lopsided graves today. The path dipped steeply here because of the sea's erosion, so she had to walk carefully. There were warning signs, telling people to be watchful, and sections of railings had been put on the seaward side to stop people falling over the cliff's edge.

At any moment she would see the tower. She recognized the curve in the path she could see from her bedroom window, and the stunted tree that was like a signpost pointing the way to the sea. Then she rounded the curve, and there it was below the path, stark and black against the cliffs, mist clinging to its wizened walls. Even from up here it looked remote and unreal, as if it might have been spun from black cobwebs. Maeve reminded herself that it was only a pile of black stones, with openings left at the top where the monks' bell had clanged out.

But it might still be Childe Roland's Tower. It might be other things, as well. They were currently reading and discussing *The Hobbit* in English at school, and Maeve could see that Rede Abbas's bell tower might easily be one of Mordor's black turrets. It might stand directly over the entrance to the goblin tunnels, or be the disguised portal to the black dungeons.

She went down the path that brought the seaward side of the tower into line. She had never seen the tower from this angle before, and for the first time she saw there was something that neither Mordor's spires nor Childe Roland's ogre-ridden lair had. A stone figure had been fastened to the tower, or carved into one of its walls – a jutting-out figure like the horrid, leering faces you sometimes saw on the edges of old buildings and even churches. But those were usually just faces, and this was a complete figure, a bit bigger than life-size. It was worn and weathered, but it was easy to see it was meant to be a woman. The face was pitted and the head was flung back as if defying the sea. Blind stone eyes stared out to the grey wastes of the English Channel.

This was something Maeve had not known about and she repressed a shiver. People in Rede Abbas said the tower was not as high as it had originally been, because the crumbling cliff was causing it to sink, a little each year. Parts of the foundations had already been washed away, and one day the whole thing would break away from the cliff and tumble into the sea as the old monastery had done.

She could see the high-tide marks. They came halfway up the tower, which meant the sea would wash into the tower itself, and the stone figure would be under water for several hours. The stone eyes would stare into the green underwater world, and fish would swim in and out of the empty eye-sockets when the tide was in.

It was all a bit spooky, but it would be pretty good if she could get photos of the figure. She went as close to the seaward side as she could, angling the camera upwards. She was not sure how well the shots would come out, but at the third attempt she saw a small window halfway up the side of the tower. It was narrow, and it was barely wide enough for a bird to fly in, but if you were inside the tower you would be almost exactly in line with the figure. If you could lean far enough out, you might even get a close-up of the face.

But to do that, Maeve would have to go inside the tower, and she felt a lurch of nervousness in her stomach at the idea. Still, it would be brilliant if she could get that close-up, and even some shots of the sea from up there. It would make her project the best of them all and it would be in the end-of-term display.

She would do it. She would not think that this was Childe Roland's squat turret surrounded by poisoned earth, or Mordor's menacing citadel. She would just think about the monks who had come here to sound the bell for prayers.

There was a small door on the side of the tower. It was battered and scarred, and there was a massive black iron ring handle on one side. It was firmly shut, and for a moment Maeve thought it was stuck or even locked. She had no idea whether she was pleased or disappointed. But then there was a teeth-wincing screech of old metal against even older wood and the ring handle turned. Maeve put her hand on the door's surface, not liking its hard, harsh feel. It shivered, and for a moment it seemed as if it was refusing to move, but when she pushed against it, it swung inwards.

Maeve stepped inside.

FIVE

It was like entering an old black cave with the thick stench of things gone bad inside it – ancient sea worlds washed up and left high and dry to slowly decay.

But it's only dead fish and seaweed, thought Maeve, fumbling for her handkerchief and putting it over her mouth and nose. I'll only be here a few minutes, and it will be worth it if I can get photos.

As her eyes began to adjust, she saw that threads of red sunlight trickled down from a narrow stairway and lay across the floor, like bloodshot veins in a diseased eye. There were coils of seaweed like wet snakes on the ground, and the walls were shiny with damp and crusted with salt. It was much smaller inside the tower than she had expected, but she understood this was not a room in the ordinary way, but a kind of hallway for people to walk through on their way up to the bell chamber. The stairs faced the door; only the first three steps were visible, then they twisted around out of sight. The window she had seen from the ground would be up there. It would be pretty scary to go up those stairs, but Maeve was not giving up now. As she crossed the room to the stairs, she deliberately stomped her feet hard down to prove she was not frightened.

Iron staves were driven into the stair wall at intervals, and there was the remains of a rope, which must have been looped into them to act as a banister. Not much of the rope was left, but it was rather a friendly thing to see, because it made those long-ago monks suddenly real. Maeve thought they might have found climbing these stairs to perform their bell-ringing a bit of a struggle, so the rope had been put there to help them.

The staves were cold and a bit slimy, but holding on to them made climbing the stairs easier. Maeve could still hear the gulls screaming and the sea washing in, and it reminded her that the ordinary world was not far away.

Or was it? The sea was starting to sound different. Was that because of the thick walls, or the enclosed stairway? Was the sea coming in? She was supposed to be careful about the tides – Aunt Eifa and all the teachers at school had told her over and over that it was important to always carry an up-to-date tide table so she did not get caught. She would not get caught now, though; she glanced at her wristwatch and saw it was not yet four o'clock. She thought at this time on a Saturday the tide would be coming in, and when she pulled the tide table from her pocket she saw she was right. The tide would have turned around midday, but the evening high tide was not until seven thirty. It was a bit shivery to realize that in three more hours the room downstairs would be under water. Still, she would be gone long before then.

The sea really did sound different up here. Maeve could almost imagine she was hearing singing inside the waves – wild, beautiful music that made you want to go towards it. There were legends about creatures who lived beneath the sea, and who sang to lure sailors on to the rocks and wreck the ships. She did not really believe those stories, but standing here it was easy to think she could hear a single, clear voice. It was even easier to think it was singing the song Maeve's mother had recorded the day before she died.

She listened for a moment, and this time made out some of the words, and the beginning of a new fear started up, because it really was the song her mother had sung that day. It was 'Thaisa's Song'. There was the line about not being able to see or hear, and about someone knocking on the tomb . . . The words were still in that strange, unknown language, but Maeve was sure it was the same.

But now the voice was singing lines that she did not remember being on the cassette – or if they had been, she had not heard – or perhaps simply had not understood – them.

The one stands by my tomb, my love,
Can never save me now.
For the sea will be my grave, my love,
And you will be my own.

The singing could not be real, and yet the singer's voice sounded exactly like the second voice she had heard on the tape – the voice that had echoed her mother's. Maeve glanced uneasily back down the stairs, imagining how the stairway would look when the water came slopping and trickling in. *The sea will be my grave, my love . . .* That meant drowning. It would be a bad thing to drown in here – to be trapped inside this tower and to see and feel the water pouring in and know you could not get out. But it was ages before high tide, and she had plenty of time to get her photos and go safely outside.

She started up the next spiral. She could see the window now, and she could see the outline of the stone figure, the shape of the nose and lips and chin outlined clearly against the cliff immediately behind. The window was not as narrow as it had looked from the ground, and Maeve thought she could squeeze on to the sill and hold up the camera.

The stairs widened out a bit here, and opposite the window, on the right of the stairs, was a doorway. Maeve hesitated, then stepped over to it, nervous but curious to know why there was a room up here. It was smaller than the room on the ground and there was a ledge all around the sides. Odd strands of rope lay on the ground. Light came from the window outside, and Maeve could see that there were two square holes in the ceiling far above her. She leaned back, craning her neck, and gasped, because directly above her was the bell itself. She could see straight up into its innards – she could see the torn, twisted metal stump where the tongue had been removed. The pieces of rope must have been attached to the bell in some way. Maeve could see how they would have hung all the way down into this room, and how the monks would have pulled on them to tilt the bell back and forth so that it chimed.

Did she dare go all the way up to the bell room? It would be fantastic to be able to tell everyone about it at school on Monday, and when the photos had been developed she would be able to show them as proof. She came out of the ringing chamber and went up the last spiral of stairs, hardly daring to breathe. It was bitterly cold up here because the bell chamber had openings all round the walls. The wind blew strongly in, making her eyes sting and snatching at her hair. And now she was at the very top of the stairs and she was looking straight into the bell chamber.

It was terrifying. It was like staring into a nightmare. Maeve had never been so frightened of anything in her life. The bell took up most of the room and it was huge; it was the hugest thing imaginable. It was like an ogre's head made of bronze – and it was a head that might suddenly throw itself back and begin screaming with dreadful, iron screams.

All ideas of going in fled, but Maeve made herself stand in the doorway for long enough to take a photograph. It might not come out, and it would probably be blurry and horrible because her hands were shaking so much, but it was worth trying.

The bell was clamped between two massive wheels. Maeve did not understand how they worked but, as she stood there, a faint thrum of sound came and something stirred within the massive bronze depths. The thick copper lip lifted very slightly, and Maeve's heart leapt. At any minute it would start to scream at her and then she would die of fright. She backed away to the stairs, but the first step was there before she was ready, and she missed her footing and fell backwards. The world wheeled all around her, and for several crowded seconds she thought she was going to tumble all the way down to the ground, and that the bronze ogre's head would laugh as she did so.

She grabbed blindly at the wall, and her hand closed around one of the iron staves. It broke away with a shower of stone dust, and Maeve grabbed at the next one, not caring that it tore into her hands, only grateful that this one held firm and stopped her tumble. She had landed on the wide section of stair between the narrow window and the ringing chamber, and although her heart was racing and her hand was bleeding slightly, she was not hurt. She wrapped her handkerchief round her grazed hand and got up. What she really wanted to do was to run out of this place as fast as she could and leave the bell to crouch up there for ever, but she had come up here to get photos for her school project, and it would be really great if she could still do that. She glanced back up the stairs, but no further sound came. She was starting to feel slightly better. And if the bell really had moved, it had probably just been the wind nudging it. It might be something that happened quite often. This was so reassuring a thought that she looked back at the stone figure.

The wall here must be very thick, because the sill of the window was a good two feet deep. Maeve could not reach out far enough to touch the stone figure, but to touch it was the last thing she was going to do. But, having got this far, she would not give up, so she positioned the camera until the figure was lined up in the viewfinder. It was a clear shot of the head and shoulders, and it would make a brilliant photograph. Maeve was so pleased she almost forgot about the bell. She pressed the shutter, and waited for the camera to whirr itself forward so she could take a second one.

But before she could do so, something happened that was far scarier than the faint hum of sound from the bell – something that was so terrifying Maeve almost cried aloud.

At first it was only a flicker of movement coming from the blind stone eyes – a movement so slight it could not have happened. It's the sun going behind a cloud, or a bird flying past, she thought, staring at the figure, not wanting to keep looking at it, but afraid to look away.

Then the stone eyes swivelled round and looked straight at her, and they were real; they were living, *seeing*, eyes.

This time Maeve did cry out, and her cry echoed around the enclosed space. As she half ran, half fell down the stairs, she could hear the echo of her own voice. It was not until she got through the door leading to the safe outside world that the echoes died away.

She had no memory of the walk back to Cliff House, although she thought afterwards that she had probably run most of the way, sobbing and terrified. But when she got back to the house, Aunt Eifa was still working in the garden, and it did not seem as if Maeve had been particularly missed, or even as if she had been away for very long. She took off her coat, and carried the camera up to her bedroom.

She closed the curtains very firmly so that she could not see the bell tower. She would never look at it again – she would even ask if she could move to the bedroom on the other side of the house where there was no view towards the tower. Then there would be nothing to remind her of it.

Except that there was something.

It had been when she had fallen down the stairs. As she'd fallen, she had clutched frantically at the walls – the iron staves – anything that might save her. She had managed to grab one of the staves, but although it had stopped her, it had come partly away from the wall, and Maeve's hand had slid into a cavity behind it. She had snatched her hand back at once, because there was no knowing what scuttly creatures might lurk in such a place, but she had registered the feel of something in the old stones that was not spidery or beetle-like.

A book. It was scarcely believable, but at some time in this place's history, someone had put a small book into the crevice behind the iron stave on this part of the stairs. For a moment Maeve had been sufficiently intrigued to almost forget the dead bell overhead. As she had drawn the book out, she had had the oddest feeling that it was not her hand that was holding the book – that it was a hand from a long time ago, and that it belonged to someone who wanted Maeve to know what had happened.

It was probably nothing more than an old tide table or somebody's abandoned tourist guide. It felt cold and slippery, which was a bit shudder-making, until Maeve realized there was a wrapping around it. Polythene? Plastic? She thrust it into her coat pocket, and forgot about it in the panic-stricken scramble to get away from the terrible stone eyes.

Later that night, as the clock downstairs was chiming half past eleven, Maeve opened the wardrobe very quietly and reached into her pocket for the book she had found. The cold, slippery wrapping turned out to be oilskin – Maeve recognized it because fishermen along the coast wore oilskin macs and hats as protection from the sea and the wind. It kept things safe for years and years. How many years had oilskin kept this book?

Still moving stealthily so as not to wake Aunt Eifa, she switched on the bedside lamp. Then, with extreme care, she unwrapped the layers of oilskin from the book taken from the bell tower.

There were several pages of handwriting. It was slanting and it was not the kind of writing people did these days, so it was not very easy to read. Maeve frowned and concentrated. At first she could not make out many of the words, then she suddenly saw the pattern and how the letters were formed, and the first line jumped out at her.

'*I think I have about three hours left before I die . . .*'

Something seemed to trail dank, cold fingers across her face and across her neck, and all around her Cliff House seemed to have plunged into a deep silence. Maeve pulled the blankets around her and began to read.

I think I have about three hours left before I die.

There's no means of telling the time in here, but there's still some light coming in, so I know that dusk has not fallen altogether.

I've struggled to break down the boards they nailed across the doorway –

I've dragged at them until my knuckles are bleeding and my nails torn, but I'm a musician, for pity's sake, and the strength in my hands isn't the kind of strength that can smash oak planks. They nailed the planks very firmly indeed, and it would take seven giants with seven hammers the size of Thor's to tear them down. My gaolers – my executioners! – did a thorough job. I watched them do it, their faces greasy with sweat from exertion, their eyes mean and greedy in the light of the candle flares.

I have to accept that I'm trapped here, inside the bell-ringing chamber. It's a terrible place. The stench is like the rotting carcasses of a thousand fish or the putrefying souls of all the sinners who ever lived. I make no apology for the extravagance of that description, for surely a man is entitled to extravagance when facing death, and anyway I have been sick twice already from the smell, and will probably be so again.

Darkness is closing down and the tide coming in. The sea will wash into the tower below me and, inch by inch, it will come up into this room – the level will gradually rise until it reaches the ceiling above my head. Even in this uncertain light I can see exactly the level the sea will reach – it has left its salted print all around the walls, near the ceiling. So I can see that the sea will reach a level that's a good three feet over my head. If I could get out of this room and go up to the bell chamber itself, I should be above the sea's level, but I can't get out, so I shall drown.

Before they dragged me up here, they nailed more of the oak planks over the floor downstairs. I fought them with every ounce of strength I had, but it was no use. If I start to think about what they nailed under those planks, I shall succumb to real madness. Oh, let me not be mad, not mad, sweet heaven, Keep me in temper . . .

And now I am quoting from the Bard, and surely a sane man would not do so, even when facing his own certain death? But the thought of what lies beneath the floor far below me is enough to send the sanest man into madness.

But if God wills that I am to become mad, let it not be until the end – that hour when the sea starts lapping and seeping through the stones . . . Will it be quick? They say drowning is an easy death as deaths go, but how can anyone really know?

I believe the madness may already have begun to take my mind. As I write this – using a charcoal stick and one of the notebooks I always carry for my work; even as I write these words, I can hear the sound of soft, sweet singing quite close to me.

I know it cannot be real. I know it will be part of the madness. But it's so clear, so near.

It will be a terrible irony if my madness takes the form of hearing music that can't exist. Music has been my life – is it to accompany me to my death?

And yet the people here delighted in the music I arranged for the choir in our monastery – and the music I played for our High Masses and feast days. The villagers had even started to walk up to our chapel to listen, which pleased Father Abbot.

'Andrew,' he said to me, 'you are bringing these people to God through music.'

The singing is louder now. I can hear the words and I understand them. I understood them on that night I first heard this music. I heard it emerge from its cobwebbed dimness, and I felt the life breathing into it. The music is known as 'Thaisa's Song', although I have no idea if that is its real name. I made copies of it so that its beauty and its strangeness could be heard once more. I thought I was doing something good and useful.

> I didn't know, not then, what the music really was. Now I do know.
>
> It's a death song. 'Thaisa's Song' is a dread lament that always brings a tragedy.

Maeve laid the book down on the bed, her mind teeming with images.

She had not understood quite a lot of what she had read, but what she had understood was that Andrew, whoever he had been, whenever he had lived, had been imprisoned in the bell tower – in the ringing chamber just off the stairway; the room where she had stood that very afternoon. People had nailed up the doorway to the room so he could not get out. Why? What had he done? Whatever it had been, it was dreadfully easy to visualize him huddled in that room, waiting for the sea to come in and drown him. Before he died had he managed to reach up and push his diary into the crevice behind the loose iron stave? Maeve tried to remember exactly where the book had been, and thought it had been quite high up, certainly above the water marks, although not far above them. Inside the ringing chamber or outside? She could not remember. Or had someone found the book after his death and left it there in his memory, like people left flowers at the roadside when somebody died in a car crash?

She looked back at the pages, wondering how old Andrew had been. He sounded quite young. A monk. And a musician. He had not been able to break down the planks across the door and the stairs, but that was not because he was feeble. Maeve suddenly did not want him to be feeble. She would read just a very little bit more, then she would stop. She did not want to read Andrew's fear and panic as death came to him. But just another two pages . . .

> A short while ago, the singing grew fainter, and I thought someone was moving around in the bell chamber overhead. That is impossible, but a little while ago I made a new attempt to get at the stairs. It was no use, of course, and this time I tore one of my hands on a nail. I've wrapped a fold of my sleeve around it to staunch the bleeding. It doesn't matter. It wouldn't matter if I bled to death, and perhaps that would be a kinder death than the one that's approaching . . .

So now I'm back in the same corner, hunched on one of the ledges against the wall. The light is fading and I can't be sure I'm writing as clearly as I would wish. I could have hoped for a few threads of moonlight at the very least. It will be hard to drown in the dark. But it's a moonless night. And I'm more alone than I've ever been in my life – more alone than anyone has ever been, I think. As they brought me up here I thought there was a shiver of sound or movement from beneath the floor, and I fought them all over again. Nothing had moved, of course. What's beneath those planks could not possibly have moved, and never will do – not now, not ever.

I believe the madness I feared is with me now.

It has come in three guises. No one tells you that madness can be splintered in such a way. But don't all important things come in threes? The Wise Men, the Holy Trinity, the three gods of the Hindu pantheon . . . And let's not forget Satan's own trinity – the devil, the beast and the false prophet.

All those threefold hierarchies are woven throughout myth and religion and life. But where does myth end and religion begin anyway? Oh, God, what if religion is all simply a myth and there's nothing beyond death save black blankness, stretching out into an empty eternity . . .? What then, all you believers, all you philosophers, all you preachers and healers and prophets . . .?

The first of the three harbingers of my madness is the singing – a voice singing that accursed 'Thaisa's Song'. The music I copied that night. If I could find those copies I would burn them – I would tear the words to unreadable shreds.

There is not one voice singing now, but two. Or is it an echo? No, it's a second voice, trying to join in.

But it isn't the only sound in here, for the second harbinger is at hand. It's immediately above me, crouching in cold, silent darkness. The dead bell. The ancient bell that those long-ago monks used to sound as their call to prayer. They rendered it dumb many years ago, tearing out its tongue – I don't know why they did that. It's one of the things I always meant to try finding out. But now it's too late.

I can hear the bell stirring and I can feel it waking. There are little shivers of sound, and there's the sensation of an old mechanism clawing its way into life again. It's like the Brazen Head of myth – the sorcerous creation that once was supposed to encircle all England. The Head that spewed out those words about Time. 'Time is . . . Time was . . . Time is past . . .' It was benign and protective, that creature, but the Brazen Head that is above me tonight is malevolent and greedy.

As for the third harbinger . . . I scarcely dare write of it, for it's the maddest of all three.

It's the stone figure. This room is almost immediately opposite its window. As the villagers were nailing up the doorway, I could see the figure that clings to the tower's side – it was in sharp relief against the night sky, the face black and forbidding and impossibly old. No, that's the wrong word – it's not old, that face, it's *timeless.* And whatever age it is, its eyes moved. *They moved.* They swivelled round in their dead, cold sockets, and watched as I was imprisoned in here. Did they watch with pity, with triumph, with approval? I can't stop thinking about it. I swear it happened. I swear it by the vows I took when I entered St Benedict's earlier this year. Poverty, chastity, obedience . . . That's yet another trinity – but a sterner one. Have I obeyed that trinity? I thought I would manage poverty and I thought most of the time I would manage obedience. As for chastity – well, always knew that would be the most difficult of the three.

Far above me, I can feel the dead bell, the Brazen Head, stirring.

And I can still hear a voice – or is it two voices? – singing 'Thaisa's Song'.

Maeve shut the journal with a snap that was shockingly loud in the quiet bedroom.

She was not going to read any more – not now, perhaps not ever – because she could not bear to know what Andrew had written at the end. Instead she got out of bed and hid the book inside an old shoebox, which she put at the back of the wardrobe under some folded blankets.

Had Andrew died in the tower that night? Had he drowned when the sea came slopping and gushing in? He had used words and expressions she had never heard in his journal, but there were some things Maeve had understood very clearly. One of those things was that he, too, had seen the ancient bell as an ogre's head. The Brazen Head, he had called it. Maeve would look up the word 'brazen' in her school dictionary tomorrow.

What was even clearer and what was the most frightening thing of all was that Andrew had seen the stone eyes watching him, exactly as Maeve had. And he had heard someone singing 'Thaisa's Song'.

'Thaisa's Song'. Andrew had known about it – he had heard it played and sung. 'A death song,' he had written. 'A dread lament that always brings a tragedy.'

As Maeve tried to sleep, she knew that it was not reading about Andrew's fear that had upset her so much – or even reading how he, too, had seen the stone eyes move and felt the dead bell stir.

It was reading what he had written about 'Thaisa's Song'.

She was finally tumbling over into sleep, when she remembered that Andrew had written about copying down the song, and this brought her fully awake. Did one of those copies still exist, or had they all been burned, the words torn to unreadable shreds as he had wanted?

SIX

From: Olive Orchard, Organizing Committee, St Benedict's Revels
To: Daniel Goodbody, Local Historian and Revels Chair

Daniel –
Gerald is capering around the house in high glee because your Victoria County History reference has led him to another entry about the fourteenth-century monks singing 'Thaisa's Song' at a Requiem Mass to mourn Elizabeth 1's death (1603?). It was part of the general lamentations, which I should think was very appropriate, because as far as any of us know, it's one of those gloomy dirges, all graveyard yearnings and willowy bodies draped over tombs, and mournful voices from the deep.

So Gerald has declared his intention of spending the evening sorting through the boxes brought out of the monastery when it was demolished (1970s, I think that was), in the hope that among the reams of turgid Victorian records and letters, there might be a few Tudor remnants. One of the Victorian monks apparently made a life's work of transcribing some records left by a Brother Cuthwin from the 1500s, so Gerald is hotfoot on the trail of that.

He says the search could take some time, so it will best if I don't wait supper. If he's late, he will be perfectly happy with something on a tray – perhaps some soup, but not tomato which always gives him acid indigestion, and not leek and potato which upsets other areas of his system, and he doesn't want to fall victim to *that*, not with all the Revels activity going on.

It was a pity you had to cancel the little lunch I had arranged for us last week, but I entirely understand that you had to remain at home to deal with the blocked drain at your house. However, with Gerald closeted with his archives, you would be most welcome to come along this evening to make up for that. The smoked salmon and Chablis are still in the fridge (Gerald doesn't care for smoked salmon and would rather have a pint of beer than a glass of wine any day). The Brie has three days to go before the sell-by date expires.

The run-up to the Revels is going smoothly, although it was a pity that the tractor got bogged down in Musselwhite's Meadow while towing in the generator. You wouldn't have thought it would take an entire afternoon to un-bog it, would you? I couldn't help thinking of all those generations of gypsies who are said to have rested their wagons there, some of whom must have got stuck at times.

It was a pity the rope snapped just as they were hauling the tractor through the gate, but I am glad you think we can claim the cost of dry-cleaning Gerald's suit from Festival expenses.

All best,
Olive

From: Daniel Goodbody,
To: Olive Orchard,

Olive – So that's why Gerald wasn't at his usual post in the library when I called in earlier, and why there were alarming thuds coming from under the floor.

I did look at the display in the museum section, though. Those notes from the mid-1800s look very enticing. I shall read them very thoroughly after the Revels kerfuffle is over.

We can certainly plunder Festival funds for the dry-cleaning, even if I could privately wish Gerald had donned anorak and wellingtons for the tractor rescue like everyone else.

I'm so sorry I won't be able to come to supper this evening. It is very kind of you to ask, but I have to attend a Parish Council meeting to discuss the new sewage pump for Puddleston.

Daniel

Cliff House,
Rede Abbas

Dear Mr Goodbody,
I have just seen the programme for your Dusklight Concert, and see that despite my warnings, you are including 'Thaisa's Song'.

May I enter one last plea that you remove this from the schedule. It has always trailed a wake of tragedy with it.

Sincerely,
Maeve Eynon

From: Daniel Goodbody, Local Historian and Revels Chair
To: Gerald Orchard, Librarian

Dear Gerald
I was very impressed by the library's display, and grateful to you for staying on duty until seven each evening. I'm sure you will find the Kalms helpful, although it wasn't a good idea to take them at the same time as the Scotch. I hope your migraine has blown itself out by now.

As for Miss Eynon and her Cassandra-like prophecies, I'll see if I can smooth her over. Of course we'll go ahead with 'Thaisa's Song' if you find it.

Kind regards,
Daniel

Michael had spent a reasonably productive day. The morning was taken up with tutorials, and the afternoon was devoted to finishing the latest Wilberforce book, which was, it appeared, already notching up enthusiastic pre-sales. Michael's editor had emailed twice to say they did not want to push him – in fact, heaven forfend that they should do such a thing with any author – but it would be really useful to know when they might expect delivery of the final MS. In fact, if they could possibly have even a draft within the next week, that would mean they could put out some advance information for their sales team to use. But she was really not pushing him.

Michael, in a rash moment, had agreed last year to a deal for a series of books that worked their way through the tapestry of England's history, written in a format suitable for seven- and eight-year-olds. A different Wilberforce cat character starred in each one. He had thought that signing the contract might prove to be a triumph of optimism over experience, but in fact he was rather enjoying writing the series. He was especially enjoying the final one, which had an Elizabethan setting and was going to end with Wilberforce being knighted for capturing pirates and given a house and lands as an expression of the Queen's gratitude.

College was relatively quiet this afternoon, and mellow sunlight lay across the small courtyard outside Michael's windows. The real Wilberforce was snoozing on the windowsill; Michael did not trust him not to be plotting further mayhem, but at least he knew where Wilberforce was, and that in itself made for an untroubled working environment.

With the memory of Quire Court's original owners, and also the impending Rede Abbas Revels in his mind, he was going to close the Histories series on a note of revelry. He accordingly caused Wilberforce to join clumpily in a maypole dance on a village green, during which Wilberforce became hopelessly entangled in the trailing ribbons, and had to be rescued and revived with copious draughts of mulled wine, the quaffing of which resulted in him leaping into the centre of the festivities and entertaining the assembled company with a spirited rendition of a lively ballad. Michael allowed the revellers to join gleefully in the chorus, and supposed his editor would expect him to dig out a suitable verse or two to reproduce at this point. It was to be hoped he could find something that was not too bawdy. He re-read Owen Bracegirdle's email about the Rede Abbas monks and the ballads performed during the first

St Benedict's Revels, and thought it a shame that Brother Cuthwin's 'Cuckolds All Awry' was not likely to be suitable for seven- and eight-year-olds.

He saved the scene to the hard drive for polishing later, then phoned Nell.

'I'm guessing you'll be too busy with getting ready for tomorrow's journey to link up for supper tonight?'

'Well, we will, really,' said Nell. 'We're bundling up all the old papers from Godfrey's storeroom at the moment. He didn't have time himself, and he said he'd be eternally grateful and for ever in my debt if I could do it for him.'

'That sounds like Godfrey.'

'I don't know about him being grateful; what I do think is that he owes me a very lush lunch when I next see him,' said Nell. 'There's far more than I thought. Jack Hurst's men cleared most of it out because they're fitting some new flooring over the weekend, but there's still masses of it. Beth and I are tying it in bundles for the recycling lorry on Saturday.'

'Godfrey's part magpie, part squirrel,' said Michael.

'Yes, but he's a very canny squirrel and he never misses anything, so we aren't expecting to find a first-folio Shakespeare or an undiscovered Chaucer in the baked-bean carton.'

'What time are you setting off in the morning?'

'Around half eight, I *hope*.'

'Have a safe journey.'

'You too. Don't miss the train on Saturday, will you?'

They had decided that as Michael would only be at Rede Abbas for Saturday night, he would travel by train on Saturday morning, then he and Nell, with Beth, could drive back to Oxford on Sunday in Nell's car. As Nell said, the train took three hours, but it was nearly that time by road anyway, and they could share the driving coming home.

'I won't miss the train,' Michael said. 'I'll be with you even if I have to travel on the ship of fools, and cross hills whose heads touch heaven, or—'

The ship of fools might be more reliable than National Rail on a Saturday morning,' said Nell, somewhat caustically, to which Michael replied equably that he would check for any delays before setting off.

'In any case, I'm looking forward to The Swan's four-poster.'

'So am I,' said Nell, and he heard the smile in her voice.

Michael dined in Hall that evening, after which he was swept up by Owen Bracegirdle and hauled along to a meeting of the Whatley Society, where two of Owen's more promising final years were leading the evening's debate. The topic was, 'How free is the free press today?' and it turned out to be so voluble and so lively a session that discussions were animatedly continued in the bar afterwards.

As Michael was crossing the quad back to his rooms later, he was greeted by the doughty Mr Jugg, who had been lying in wait for him, and who imparted the information that Wilberforce, still enamoured of the rose garden with the Ben Jonson Society plants, had become entangled in the trip-wires cunningly placed across the soil by Jugg's own hands. Finding himself enmeshed, Wilberforce had fought furiously to get free, setting the wind-chimes jangling with, said Jugg, as much noise as if it had been a rehearsal for the Last Trump.

'How did he get free?' asked Michael. And then, 'Oh God, he isn't still there, is he?'

Wilberforce was not, however, still there. A second year, who had been climbing into College through the buttery window, had run out to see what the rumpus was, and had discovered Wilberforce and managed to extricate him.

'After which the wretched animal shot off like a bat escaping hell,' said Jugg. 'I couldn't tell you where he is now, for we haven't seen hide nor hair nor whisker of him since. As for the student who rescued him . . . well, Dr Flint, I didn't ask what he was doing climbing through a window at that hour, because it's nothing to do with me if students behave like house-breakers. What I did think, though, was that we might have to fetch out the medics, because there was blood all over the Archduke Josephs we planted in spring, and you never saw such a—'

'Wilberforce's blood?'

'The second year's. Bleeding hands like you never saw, and that isn't swearing, it's a statement of fact. And me with only a bit of sticking plaster in my first-aid kit.'

Michael passed over a £20 note for the replenishing of the first-aid kit, expressed the hope that the Archduke Josephs would survive, and suggested the donation might also stretch to a couple of large whiskies to steady Jugg's shredded nerves. He then established the identity of the second year and, on reaching his rooms, wrote a hasty note, apologizing profusely for Wilberforce's behaviour, hoped the student's scratched hands were not too troublesome, and promised to stand him a large drink at The Turf after the weekend by way of recompense. About the illicit entry through the buttery window he did nothing, other than make a mental note to ask the Bursar to ensure the catch was secure in the future. It was all very well to be a don and in a position of some responsibility, but Michael could remember nights when he, too, had climbed through a buttery window after being locked out.

As he let himself into his own rooms, he thought it would be something of a rest cure to get to Rede Abbas and partake in a series of revived Tudor bacchanalia.

Nell and Beth finished tying up the bundles of old folders and papers by eight o'clock that evening.

Godfrey had left two large boxes: one had originally contained tinned tomato soup, the other cheese biscuits; but both were now crammed with wodges of papers, books whose covers were too eaten away with damp or mould to be sellable, and partly disintegrated folders. Some of the folders bore remarks in Godfrey's writing, identifying them as bills or income tax correspondence. The thickest file bore a firmly written legend, saying, 'Receipts for payments 1990–2000, and every last one copied to the tax inspector may he succumb to the Seven Curses of Egypt.'

Nell grinned, then contemplated Beth, who was brushing dust from her jeans. 'You look like a chimney sweep's boy. Have you finished? Good, so have I. Shall we each have a shower then order in a pizza?'

'I'd utterly love pizza,' said Beth, surveying the boxes. 'Godfrey had mountains of rubbish, didn't he? Did you know there'd be all this?'

'I thought there might be. Michael says Godfrey's a magpie.'

'He's a musical magpie,' said Beth. 'Did you know there're music scores in one of those boxes? They must have been crumbling away for years and years. Ought we to make sure they aren't valuable before we throw them out? Because you always say—'

'Make sure rubbish really is rubbish before throwing it out. I know I do,' said Nell, 'but if there was ever anything valuable among all this, Godfrey would long since have found it, and sold it for a disgustingly large sum of money. And the whole of Quire Court – in fact the whole of Oxford – would have heard about it. Why? Have you got visions of an undiscovered Mozart sonata or something?'

'Um, well, not exactly, because I don't think this is a sonata,' said Beth, kneeling down and peering into the smaller of the boxes. 'It's just an old song. It's really old, though. Oh, and there's a spider that's got in between the pages – ugh.'

There was a short rustling interval as the spider was routed, then Beth cautiously reached down into the box.

Nell came over to see what she had found. It would not be anything valuable, because Godfrey really was unlikely to have missed anything. And at first sight it did not look valuable, or even particularly interesting. It was two sheets of music score, handwritten, the edges curling, the paper badly foxed. The writing at the head of the paper was a rather elaborate copperplate and in places sheer age had faded it to pale brown, so that it was difficult to decipher. Then, quite suddenly the letters fell into place, and Nell could read it. A graceful slanting hand had written: *Thaisa's Song. Copied from the original.* There was a squiggle of initials alongside.

But she hardly saw the initials. It was the name that was exploding in her mind. 'Thaisa's Song'. *Thaisa.*

If anyone finds this, please pray for me, for it will mean the dead bell has sounded and I have suffered Thaisa's fate . . . Thaisa's fate . . .

How often did you encounter the name 'Thaisa' in the space of three days? As if from a long way off, Nell became aware of Beth saying something about the words of the song being in a foreign language.

'The writing's pretty clear, but I don't know what it says, d'you? It isn't French, I don't think, or Italian.'

'No,' said Nell. 'It isn't either of those. I don't know what it is, Beth.' She tried to focus her mind, but the words strung out beneath the musical notation did not seem to have any root she could recognize. Could it be something Middle Eastern? No, the letters would be formed differently, surely?

'The music's pretty simple, though,' Beth said, still studying it. 'I bet I could play it by sight.'

Nell was instantly aware of two warring compulsions. Half of her wanted to tell Beth to play this strange old music with the unreadable lyrics, and to know more about Thaisa who had suffered an unknown fate and who might have left this music behind. The other half wanted to tear the music to shreds and bury them under the discarded papers, so that the pieces could never be joined up again, and the music itself could never be played . . . From what strange, unacknowledged depths of her mind had that last thought come?

'It'd be pretty cool to play an old song somebody threw out, like, a hundred years ago,' Beth was saying.

'Why a hundred years so precisely?'

'Don't know. I bet it is, though. See, it's all musty and splodgy, isn't it?'

'Foxed.'

'Uh, well, OK, foxed. Can I try it? I mean, can I try to play it? I'm getting really good at sight-reading. It'll be part of the Grade Four exam, so this'd be extra-good practice.'

'It's a bit late,' said Nell. 'And the pizzas will be here any minute. Go up and have your shower. We'll have a toasted marshmallow in some hot chocolate afterwards. You can try the music before we leave in the morning.'

SEVEN

Thin sunlight lay across the music of 'Thaisa's Song' next morning, showing the discoloration and the spidery notes and words. Beth had left it on top of the cottage piano, which Nell had bought two years earlier. It had not been a very expensive piano, but the tone was good and Beth loved it with a passion.

Nell hesitated, turned the score face down, so only the blank reverse sides showed, then went into the kitchen to make an early breakfast.

The kettle had just boiled, and the scrambled eggs were

coalescing creamily, when she heard hesitant piano notes from the sitting room.

Beth was seated at the piano, frowning with the intense concentration that made her look heartbreakingly like her dead father. 'Thaisa's Song' was propped up on the stand. She played a series of notes, then a chord, then stumbled. Nell started to speak, but Beth began to play again, and this time seemed to grasp the music's pattern.

At first Nell thought it was rather beautiful in a silvery kind of way. Then, in some way she could not pinpoint, it changed, as if something had twisted it with a deep, hurting wrench. It was like running very fast, and suddenly turning your ankle on an uneven bit of ground, so that you got a sickening pain.

'Beth – stop there, please.' She had not meant to speak, but the words came out almost of their own volition.

'Don't you like it?' Beth looked round, puzzled. 'I'm doing really well, and it's pretty easy to read. I wish I could sing the words as well.'

'I don't like it very much,' said Nell, managing not to actually shiver. 'No, I don't know why – it's just one of those things. Come and have some breakfast.'

'Only half an hour late,' said Beth, as they got into the car. She grinned at Nell, and Nell smiled to see her brimming with such delight at the prospect of the three days ahead.

'Half an hour's good going,' she said. 'And I don't even think we've forgotten anything.'

'The laptop,' said Beth suddenly. 'You didn't put the laptop in.'

'I don't need it just for two days.'

'You might. You might want to make notes about – um – all the history stuff you're looking for. And what if somebody wants you to sell something hugely valuable or find – um, I don't know – a Chippendale desk or something, and emails you. Oh, and the leaflets for the antique weekends – the printers said they might email the draft of those.'

'I've got the mobile—'

'The laptop'd be better.'

She was already halfway out of the car and Nell bowed to the inevitable. Beth was a modern child, who did not think it was possible to move ten yards without at least one electronic communication device. And the laptop might well be useful. She was hoping to track down that link between Rede Abbas and Quire Court – she could make notes more easily on the laptop.

As they drove away from Quire Court, she said, 'I think I'll go through the side roads. They'll take us a mile or so out of our way, but the traffic in the city centre will be solid at this time of the morning, so it'll probably be quicker in the long run.'

The side road wound around the city's outskirts, and Nell pointed out a corner of Oriel College between two other buildings.

'Pity we haven't got time to whizz up to the front door and surprise Michael,' said Beth.

'Yes, but we'll see him on Saturday.'

It was more by guesswork than calculation that Nell turned down a tree-lined street with houses set back from the road. It was still in sight of Oriel, and she was reasonably sure it would lead through to the motorway network.

'These are nice houses,' said Beth, looking out of the window approvingly. 'Look at that one with those trees in the garden and the gate with all the scrolly stuff on it. I love that one, don't you?'

Nell slowed down to look. Everything seemed to stand still. The house was familiar from a dozen – a hundred – dreams. A tall old house, indistinct until now, slightly misty until today, but a house where she had sometimes thought she and Beth, with Michael, might one day live – doing so contentedly among books and music and a comfortable untidiness. She had always pushed the image away, because she had never known how well it would work in reality. But now, here the house was. Unmistakable. It looked as if it had been built in the early 1900s; it was redbrick, but with white roughcast rendering in places. There was a deep porch and large bay windows on each side of the front door. Bookshelves would line the walls of one of those rooms, and there might be books on the floor as well, because the room would be a study and the shelves would long since have overflowed. There would be another room somewhere for a piano as well . . . The main sitting room – it would be large enough almost to warrant the dignified term of drawing room – would be at the back of the house, overlooking a garden with flowers that had old-fashioned names: gillyflowers and snapdragons and delphiniums. The afternoon sunshine would slant through the windows, and there would be an immense sense of companionship and safety everywhere . . .

Nell snapped off these thoughts before they could develop any further, and, forcing her voice to sound ordinary, she said, 'It is a nice house, isn't it? I think that's a maple tree in the garden – the leaves will be beautiful in autumn.'

'Hold on a minute, I'll take a photo,' said Beth, scrabbling for her phone. 'Well, I don't know why, just because I want to. OK, got it. Drive on *now*, Mum, the man behind's really cross. He's saying "Women drivers" and waving his hands. He'll get out and thump you in a minute.'

Nell put up a hand in apology to the irate motorist, and drove away from the house. It was annoying to discover it took an enormous effort to do so.

They reached Rede Abbas just after lunch. There was a straight drive along a coastal road and Beth rummaged for her phone again to take some photos.

'We'll send them to Michael, so he can see what everywhere's like before he gets here,' she said, enthusiastically. 'Can you slow down a bit – well, can you even stop, because I'd really like to get a shot of that house up on the cliff. It's double-spooky, isn't it?'

'It's a bleak-looking old place,' said Nell, stopping the car and looking towards the clifftop house. 'It'd be pretty lonely to live up there in winter.'

'Michael would say it was gothic or something, wouldn't he, and start remembering people who wrote stuff in old rectories and poems in graveyards and things.'

'You'll run out of battery,' said Nell, as Beth aimed the phone's camera.

'I won't. Michael will love all this. Oh, and look over there – Mum, do look, isn't that the creepiest thing you ever saw! No, not the house, the *tower*,' said Beth in exasperation, as if it ought to be obvious. 'Down there – on a kind of ledge.'

Nell looked to where Beth was indicating, and felt a faint chill. The cliff house had been bleak and gloomy, but the ancient stone tower, visible from the road, jutting up from a ledge partway down the cliffside, seemed to belong to some dark, lost era of its own.

'It's utterly horrible, isn't it,' Beth was saying, bouncing in her seat with delight. 'Those gaping holes near the roof, like staring eyes – they're really spooky.'

'I don't know about Michael talking gothic – you're definitely doing so,' said Nell. 'But it is spooky, I'll grant you that. I should think that part of the cliff slipped away over the years – it must once have been a lot higher up. The tower looks like an old bell tower – that'd be the reason for those open bits at the top.'

'Would the bell have been inside that bit with the holes?'

'Yes. A massive bell it'd have been, from the look of it. People would have heard it chime for miles around through those open sections.'

'Would it still be there, the bell?' Beth was photographing the tower delightedly.

'I shouldn't think so. Or if it is, it'll have been silenced.' A dead bell, thought Nell. *If the dead bell sounds, it means I have suffered Thaisa's fate . . .*

'What would it be rung for?'

'Prayers, I think.' Nell pulled her mind back to the present. 'Calling the faithful to worship – it probably belonged to the monastery that used to be here. Or it might be even older than that. Maybe it was originally built to give some kind of warning to sailors or fishermen on this stretch of coast.'

'It's not for fishermen or prayers, it's a vampire's tower,' said Beth, happily. 'It's a *Twilight* place. If you went inside there you'd come out as – um, what it is when you're changed to something else?'

'Transformed? Transplanted? Transmitted to another TV channel?'

'I'd like it to be a vampire tower,' said Beth, ignoring this levity as Nell drove on. 'And it'd be really good if we could have our midnight feast there. I'll bet if you went in at midnight, you'd come out all different and vampire'd up.'

Nell stopped the car again and turned to face her daughter. 'Beth, I know you didn't actually mean that, but if you and your friends do go out to that horrible tower tonight or at any other time, I'll take you straight back to Oxford and there'll be no music lessons for a month.'

Beth stared back, and for a moment Nell thought she was going to rebel. But then her small face crinkled with amusement, and she said, 'I won't, really, I won't. I didn't really mean it, anyway, 'cos it'd be too spooky.' She looked back at the tower, then gave a melodramatic shiver, made a cross-eyed face at Nell, and stuck out her tongue.

'You were winding me up, weren't you, you horrible child?'

'Yes,' said Beth, and returned to her phone and the absorbing task of emailing her photos of the bell tower and the clifftop house to Michael.

Beth was safely deposited at the Ramblers' Hostel as soon as they arrived. Nell was pleased to see she was greeted with squeals of delight from several of the girls who fell on her with glee, swore they had been lying in wait for her for at least two hours, and demanded to know where she had been. Somebody had been sick on the coach, which had been utterly gross, and they were all sleeping in a dormitory like one of those old school stories, and if Beth had not brought the unmentionable thing as she had promised, the you-know-what was going to be cancelled.

Beth grinned, and brandished the large cake box bearing her birthday cake, which was greeted with whoops of joy, then hastily covered up with somebody's jacket. Beth gave Nell a quick hug, and plunged into the giggling mass of schoolgirls (there were a few boys as well, Nell noticed), all of them discussing their planned midnight feast with loud shrieks that could probably be heard all over the hostel. The teacher who was trying to instil a vague semblance of discipline waved to Nell, made a semi-despairing gesture that still managed to indicate she was in control, and shepherded them inside the hostel.

Nell unpacked in The Swan's bedroom, which had chintz curtains and oak beams, had a quick wash and brush-up, then went out to explore. Walking through the sharp, clean, autumn afternoon towards the market square was invigorating, and if any spirits threatening to sound dead bells walked anywhere, they did so politely and invisibly. What on earth was a dead bell, anyway?

The square was efficiently signposted and was only ten minutes' walk from The Swan. It was clearly going to be the centre of the activities that weekend, and it was crowded with people setting up stalls or carrying crates and boxes. Participants in the festivities were wearing an astonishing mix of costumes and wandering around, like film extras waiting for their scene. Most of them had outfits approximating the Tudor and Elizabethan eras – Nell counted four Henry VIIIs, three executioners with hoods and cardboard axes, various court ladies, several cowled monks, a possible William Shakespeare and a sprinkling of wandering minstrels.

Three men in overalls were hammering into place a dais for that evening's performances, and a large notice requested people please to be prompt if they wanted to sit down for the Seven Deadly Sins at 7.30 p.m., since a large attendance was anticipated. Nell wished Michael were with her to appreciate the irony of this polite request.

A large lady with a commanding voice and an important presence appeared to be directing most of the operations. Nell got close enough to see she had a name badge, which proclaimed her to be Olive Orchard, Organizing Committee. She was berating a wispy little man who had a ginger moustache and an armful of books, and who was arguing plaintively that Olive might issue her orders until hell froze, but he, personally, did not give a tuppenny hoot if they were short of seating; in fact Olive might recall he had warned the committee about that at least twice. If you must needs advertise a performance of the Seven Deadly Sins, you should expect to be oversubscribed, said the wispy man firmly. In the meantime, the library would not open itself, not if the Seven Deadly Sins and the Five Cardinal Virtues mounted open warfare in the market square – and, that being so, he was off to unlock the doors that very minute.

The reference to the library attracted Nell's attention, so she followed the wispy man at a discreet distance. Sure enough, through a stone alley with small, bow-fronted shops on both sides, there was the library, and the man was unlocking the door and going inside. Nell gave him five minutes, then went in.

The library was larger than she had expected, and it looked well stocked. Several shelves were labelled 'Local History', and there was even a small room through an archway leading off the main area, which bore the legend 'Museum'. Nell could see glass cabinets and glass-topped display tables containing old documents and books. Surely there would be something on the Rede Abbas monks in there?

She smiled at the wispy gentleman who had arranged himself behind the central desk, which had a card proclaiming him to be

Gerald Orchard, Librarian. Husband of the formidable Olive? There had been unlikelier pairings. She asked if she could look in the museum.

'Certainly you can.' He was clearly delighted to be asked. 'It's all local history, a lot of it the genuine original material, and we're rather proud of it.' This was not said boastfully or self-consciously, but with a genuine pleasure in the subject. Nell thought he was rather an endearing little man, and hoped Olive did not henpeck him too much.

For a moment she thought he was going to accompany her into the museum, but he only said, 'Go straight through the arch over there. Are you here for the Revels?'

'Yes, with my daughter.'

'Oh, that's nice. We're getting a lot of visitors for it. So gratifying, because everyone's worked very hard. Let me know if you want any more information about any of the exhibits.'

EIGHT

As soon as Nell stepped through the archway, she was glad Gerald Orchard had remained in the main part of the library. There were display cases and cabinets, each one containing a fragment of Rede Abbas's past, and also old photographs and sketches of people and buildings. There were even several costumes on life-size dummies. Some of the cabinets held pottery and glass, but others had old documents, and Nell went towards these at once.

There were several photographs of the stone tower she and Beth had seen on the coast road, and a neatly typed account of its history.

> *The Rede Abbas bell tower is a famous and very ancient local landmark. It's thought to date to pre-Christian times, and although it's not known what its original purpose was, during the Early Middle Ages the first St Benedict's Monastery adopted it for the monks' use.*

[It was a frequent ploy of the early Christians to make use of pagan symbols – their maxim being that if you put new wine into old casks, eventually the wine would come out tasting of the cask.]

However, over the centuries the sea gradually eroded the coastline, and parts of the cliff collapsed. The monastery, by now severely unsafe, was abandoned, and the monks moved inland. The original monastery was finally lost altogether, with only the bell tower remaining, and, in fact, still used for some years. Gradually, though, it too became unsafe. The cliff slipped further, and the sea began to encroach on the tower, to the extent that the lower levels were – and still are – flooded at high tide.

It's believed there was an earlier bell, but the one that still hangs in the belfry dates to the sixteenth century and was donated by Edward Glaum. The Glaums were wealthy local landowners, and although the line has died out, the name can still be found attached to various buildings and local charities. [See articles about St Mary Abbas almshouses and Puddleston schoolhouse.]

The Glaum bell is a massive, half-ton bronze structure. [See photo D]. Research suggests it was rendered mute – i.e. its tongue removed – around 1540, possibly at the order of the Abbot of the time, Seamus Flannery, although this cannot be verified. However, it is known that around that time St Benedict's Monastery came under threat of suppression by King Henry VIII's Commissioners.

[See sketches D to G of the bell's mechanism and a woodcut of local workmen removing the tongue, with the monks and the Abbot looking on.]

A fragment of an anonymous sixteenth-century document, written during Seamus Flannery's time as Abbot, has this to say about the tower:

'There is a local belief that the Rede Abbas tower was originally built as a tomb and that, at times, in the deep and vasty darknesses of the night, the lonely chime can be heard, as if whatever lies buried there is calling to be rescued from its dark, silent grave . . .'

Even today, there are those in the area who insist that the bell's dead chime is sometimes heard.

Nell read this account twice, enjoying it even more the second time. It was a pity that the sixteenth-century chronicler's name had been lost; she would have liked to know the name of the person who had penned such a beautifully gothic sentence. But it was all grist to the researcher's mill, and she made notes of everything, including Seamus Flannery's name in case he came in useful as a research springboard. The account had apparently been compiled by a Daniel Goodbody, whose designation was given as 'local historian'. This was a title that might mean anything, from an enthusiastic amateur to the head of some scholarly department for the entire county. Either role might be useful, though, so Nell added Mr Goodbody's name to her notes, and moved along the displays, hoping the monastery would reappear.

It did reappear, in the form of two pages headed, 'Curious Cures from our Past', taken from the records of a Brother Cuthwin, who apparently had been the monastery's infirmarian in the mid-1500s. Nell had not realized that St Benedict's had been a hospital order, and she thought Cuthwin might be the same brother whose robust account of the St Benedict's Revels Owen had found. He might even be the person who had left that fragment of detail about the stone tower and the dead bell's disconcerting habit of occasionally sounding in the deep and vasty darknesses of the night.

The sixteenth-century script was virtually illegible to the untrained eye, but the helpful Daniel Goodbody had made a transcript, which was set out in clear modern print. Nell was grateful to Mr Goodbody, but she liked seeing Cuthwin's actual writing on the page, even though she could only make out a few words of it.

Several of Cuthwin's remedies were set out, among which were his own cures for troublesome digestion. He had held by the efficacy of a mixture containing agrimony, which he wrote was, 'Particularly good for the bowel, especially after an over-indulgence of rich foods.' He had also believed that cytisus scoparius (common broom, he was careful to explain), was an excellent purge for the same indisposition, and that gooseberry jelly was sovereign for bilious humours. At the end of this last entry, he recorded, with innocent pleasure, how several of the local farmers' wives had sought him out for this recipe, since it had been found helpful for calming morning sickness in pregnant ladies.

At this point the present intruded in the form of the phone ringing in the main library. Gerald Orchard snatched it up, and plunged into an acerbic discussion, during which he pointed out that giving the Revels' catering contract to Street Food Incorporated had never had his support in the first place. They were a cheap, catchpenny set-up; what you sowed, so you did reap, and Gerald was not in the least surprised that the reaping had included an outbreak of sickness among some of the festival helpers after partaking of Street Food's idea of crab salad. Clearly the crab had been off, and the 'Freshly Caught' slogan on the table was very likely a blatant infringement of the Trade Descriptions Act. In fact Gerald considered the festival committee had been lucky to get off with 24-hour attacks, because the entire population of Rede Abbas, not to mention incoming tourists, could well have ended up in the nearest A&E departmento.

So if Olive had any sense, she would persuade the Organizing Committee to swallow its pride, and Olive herself would go cap in hand to The Fox & Goose to ask, as politely as possible, if they would lay on platters of suitable food. Sausages, chicken drumsticks, and plenty of jacket potatoes, served on long tables in Musselwhite's Meadow would be Gerald's recommendation, and exactly the kind of plain, easily managed food people would expect and enjoy on such an occasion, although he did not suppose anyone would take any notice of him. And now, if Olive did not mind, he was very busy, in fact he was in the process of scouring school registers from 1946, and yes, he was still in pursuit of that probably apocryphal chimera, and no, he had not banged on about it all through breakfast. He took it very unkindly of Olive to say so. And yes, he would be on time for the Seven Deadly Sins, and he was very sorry if Gluttony's costume was the wrong size, but there was not much that he, Gerald, could do about it, and probably nothing anyone else could do about it, either. There was the sound of the phone being crossly put down.

Nell smiled, and moved back to the display cabinets, still hoping to find a link to Oxford and Quire Court. She was pleased to see the next display still focused on the monastery, and there were three pages, written in an elegant, slanting and more or less legible hand. There were no actual dates, apart from the year at the head of a couple of them, but the typed label (Mr Goodbody again, presumably), explained that the pages were from the journal of Brother Andrew, OB, who had been at St Benedict's during the mid-1800s.

After a moment Nell identified 'OB' as Order of St Benedict and, with a feeling of pleased anticipation, started to read the nineteenth-century Andrew's notes.

> My first November in the monastery – and a wild and unfriendly month it is. The days are filled with storms and glowering skies that press down like flat irons. The sea is being churned into a perpetual cauldron, as if Lucifer himself is stirring up broth for the sinners, and if this is Dorset in winter I shall begin to wish I had entered a Spanish monastery where it would at least be warm.
>
> I had assumed when I entered St Benedict's that the rooms would be infused with incense and laden with serenity – dammit, I *wanted* serenity and incense! But everyone is preparing for winter, gathering and storing apples and quinces, and the kitchens are boiling blackberries and damsons for jam, smoking huge hams, and chopping tomatoes and herbs for chutney. The entire monastery is starting to smell like the scullery of a none-too-grand restaurant. As for the silence of a religious house – the cellarer dashes around the corridors, his feet pounding the stone floors, making anxious inventories of store cupboards and larders, pressing various people into service, and discussing financial calculations with the Bursar at meals.
>
> However, we gather serenely enough in our common room each evening after supper and before Compline, when it is our recreation hour. Most of us spend that hour studying or reading. Brother Egbert, the scholar among us, sits at a high sloping desk, with an oil lamp for illumination. The lamp casts a warm, comforting glow, which helps dispel some of the spiteful winds that sneak in through the ill-fitting windows.
>
> Egbert is working on papers left by a sixteenth-century Brother Cuthwin. He found a box containing the documents in a corner of an old still-room and is hoping that, once he has deciphered the pages, his translation can be bound and added to the monastery's library – or perhaps even printed and given wider circulation. He has mentioned, with a modest air,

a long-standing friendship with the Reverend Doctor Bulkeley Bandinel, Librarian of the Bodleian Library in Oxford. I have no idea if the Reverend Doctor would be interested in Cuthwin's chronicles, but Egbert seems hopeful.

Tonight he asked, with a pleased chuckle, if we would be interested in hearing the section he had been working on.

'It's an account of a lively sounding night celebrating St Benedict's Revels,' he said. 'It seems Cuthwin and the Brothers had a somewhat robust evening.'

We all wanted to hear it. Egbert is making a splendid job of Brother Cuthwin and we have become quite fond of him.

'I'm paraphrasing everything a good deal, as you know,' Egbert reminded us. 'Transposing it into today's phrasing and terms. But I hope I'm retaining the essence.

'We performed a part-song after our supper of roasted meats and mead,' Cuthwin had written, and even across three centuries his innocent delight reached us. 'The first song was *The Knight's Lusty Lance,* which is always a favourite. I played the Knight, and Brother Francesco took the part of the maiden. There was much cheering, which encouraged us to then embark on *The Tinker's Trusty Rivet.* Father Abbot had said earlier this was not an appropriate ballad, but he was not in the room (he seldom joins any kind of festivity or frivolity), so, slightly flown with success (also our own mead), we sang it lustily and well, and everyone joined in the chorus. We kept a weather ear out though, for, as Brother John says, when Seamus Flannery was appointed Father Abbot, he became extremely stern. Most of us feel that, considering Seamus's past life, this is a clear case of poacher turned gamekeeper, although it's said there is no prude so great as a reformed libertine. (I would never dare call Seamus Flannery a libertine to his face or, in fact, to anyone else's face, but I believe it's perfectly true that his women were legion before he found God.)'

'A libertine,' said Brother Ranulf who had been listening to Egbert's reading from his seat by the fire. 'Dear me, I never knew that about any Father Abbot in Rede Abbas.'

'The actual term Cuthwin originally used to describe Seamus Flannery was somewhat stronger,' said Egbert. 'I thought it was better not to make a literal translation of that—'

'Indeed no.' Ranulf was shocked.

'Go on,' said several voices, and Egbert resumed reading Cuthwin's words.

'I have to confess our song was not, perhaps, entirely seemly in certain places. When we reached the verse in which the tinker's trusty rivet became doubled and the maiden cried for shame, many of the brothers cheered and banged their tankards on the table, and Francesco, much encouraged, leapt on to the table, and began capering along the spilled remains of our meal. I daresay it was inevitable that he should skid in a patch of grease from the roasted meats, but it was unfortunate that he should then tumble headlong into the window at the far end of the refectory – an illustration of St Barnabas, which I have always thought very gloomy, but it did not deserve to be shattered by Francesco while he was portraying the troublesome complexities of the tinker's rivet.'

'It's Rabelaisian, isn't it?' observed Ranulf, as Egbert paused to look round the common room.

'Beautifully so.'

'Yes, but I don't think we could allow that section to be printed,' said Ranulf.

'I don't see why not.' Egbert, who is somewhat unworldly, turned a puzzled look on Ranulf.

'Well, if you think our own Father Abbot would approve of—'

'I wish I had known Cuthwin,' I said, hastily. 'Have you found what happened after the Revels that night, Brother Egbert? Can you read it to us?'

'I have managed a little more,' said Egbert. 'So if anyone really does want to hear some more—'

'Yes, please,' said several voices.

'Three days after our merry-making,' Cuthwin had written, 'the Bishop arrived for a Visitation, and there was no concealing the damage inflicted during the entertainments. St Barnabas's shattered window was there for all to see, proof black and damning as the devil's hoofprint. Father Abbot had already set a number of penances – the Bursar later said, crossly, that it was a singular experience to hear Seamus Flannery speaking so severely about extravagance and wanton behaviour. However, he has asked local craftsmen to make a repair, and Job Orchard, the local stonemason, is to create a whole new window frame in stone.

'And now we hear that Thomas Cromwell's Commissioners are to come to Rede Abbas. This may be a direct result of the Bishop's Visitation but, whatever it is, it has thrown us into turmoil. Master Cromwell is said to be compiling a survey of the country's monasteries and their wealth at the request of the King – listing all the gold and silver and valuable possessions some of the monasteries harbour so jealously and acquire so greedily. We believe the Commissioners seize on the smallest excuse to close any monastery and take its valuables for the King's coffers. There are also shocking tales of laxity and laziness among other monks, although it is whispered that many of these are untrue, and simply excuses to swell the King's – and Cromwell's – coffers.

'We are all very worried, although I am sure we are a very temperate House (St Benedict's Feast excepted) and, in any case, quaffing a few tankards of mead surely could not count as outright debauchery.

'Seamus Flannery goes about with a look in his eyes I should not care to encounter in the night watches. Francesco, always one for a colourful phrase, says there are demons in his soul that he constantly fights.'

Seamus Flannery again, thought Nell. And also an Orchard. Gerald's ancestor? It seemed a long way back, but it was an unusual surname, and families did sometimes stay in the same place for hundreds of years.

She re-read the account, rather liking the sound of Andrew, then saw there were several more pages under the two on display. Presumably someone had simply turned up the documents, thought the deciphered sixteenth-century letter might be of interest, and laid the pages out with that section uppermost. Was it worth trying to read the pages beneath? Nell went back into the library, where Gerald Orchard was frowning suspiciously at what looked like a sheaf of school registers, presumably still in pursuit of the chimera, whatever it was. He looked up, and Nell said, 'You have some fascinating documents in there.'

'I found most of them in the old cellars here,' said Gerald, eagerly. 'A lot of stuff was brought from the old monastery when it was demolished in the 1960s – the contents of the monks' library, I think – and everything was left here. There's never been time to make a proper catalogue of it all, but every so often one of us goes down there to see what we can find. What's there is in fairly good condition.'

'I'd love to have a closer look at one of the documents in your display,' said Nell. 'The one written by Brother Andrew in the 1800s. There's a report of how the monks transposed a much older document, but it looks as if there are other pages underneath.' She saw him hesitate, and said, 'I have an antiques business in Oxford, so I do understand about treating old things with care – hold on, I've got a card somewhere.'

Gerald Orchard, presented with the business card which Godfrey Purbles had helped Nell design, beamed. 'I'm sure we could let you loose on the rest of that exhibit for half an hour,' he said. 'I don't know what's in there, although I'm intending to read it all as soon as I find time. But I'll unlock the cabinet for you. Only – would you mind very much if I asked you to—'

'Wear white cotton gloves? Of course not.'

'You have no idea,' said Gerald, getting up from the desk, 'how refreshing it is to talk to someone who understands. Hardly anyone does, you know. I'll fetch some gloves for you, Miss – sorry, Mrs West.'

'Nell.'

'Nell. I'm Gerald.' He shook hands solemnly, provided her with the gloves from a box in a nearby drawer, then unlocked the cabinet and drew out the papers.

'I'll put them over here in the reading section, shall I? It'll be more comfortable.'

'Thank you,' said Nell, as he carried the pages to a small table and chair in an adjoining alcove, after which he returned to his own desk, where he again became absorbed in the school books.

Nell, grateful for the ease with which she had been given access to Andrew, pulled on the gloves, and prepared to step back into the monastic world of the nineteenth-century monk.

With the first few lines of the now-visible pages, it became obvious that Andrew had been the monastery's Precentor. The music master.

Friday
Created an arrangement for a Bach cantata to celebrate the Feast of St Cecilia next week. As patroness of music, it seems fitting we should have a really splendid, fully choral Mass in her honour. The Bach is quite complex, but I think with some practice we can achieve a beautiful tribute. After some thought, have added the *Caritas pater est*, which will make a good contrast and is just as beautiful, along with one of Handel's solo recitatives . . .

. . . A local landowner by the name of Adolphus Glaum is to attend our St Cecilia's Day service, in company with his two daughters. Father Abbot says Mr Glaum, who is a Justice of the Peace and regarded as the local squire, comes to many of our services, and we must make him welcome. However, Brother Ranulf tells me Father Abbot only suffers Glaum because his family has always contributed generously to the Order, and our hospital is always in need of funds. He adds that he knows this to be an uncharitable remark, but says Glaum is two-faced and double-tongued and well able to afford the donations, being richer than Solomon and all his sultans put together. According to Ranulf, the Glaum family have all been much the same, all the way back to the sixteenth century. Drink and women, says Ranulf, gloomily . . .

Father Abbot has asked if I could re-arrange the music for St Cecilia's Feast Day so that it is simpler. We do not, he explains anxiously, want to overwhelm our guests with pageantry – Squire Glaum in particular prefers simpler worship – and do I not think Handel can be somewhat *theatrical?*

Have said I will consider his suggestion.

Have not said I have absolutely no intention of pandering to the preferences of this man, Glaum, who is clearly the guest Father Abbot means. I do not at all like the sound of Adolphus Glaum, and the music will remain as I have planned it; in fact if I thought I could coach the Brothers sufficiently well to sing

> *Israel in Egypt,* complete with battle sounds and all the effects, I should do so.'

This page of Andrew's notes ended halfway down, and for a moment Nell thought there was no more to read. But when she turned the page over, using extreme care, she saw that the journal continued, as if Andrew had deliberately left the blank half page to indicate a pause. As she began to read again, she had the sensation that she was stepping into a darker segment of the monastery's past.

> *St Cecilia's Feast*
>
> My arrangements were splendidly sung by the monks at the church service.
>
> Adolphus Glaum was present along with his two daughters – it is the first time I have seen any of them. Glaum is a jowly person, thick-necked, with skin the colour and consistency of raw dough. There are deep furrows on each side of his mouth, suggesting he is more inclined to turn his mouth down, rather than to smile. It's curious how mouths can be far more an indication of character than eyes.
>
> Glaum's two daughters accompanied him. They are Miss Gertrude, tall and acidulated in black bombazine and feathered bonnet, and Miss Margaretta, who is as thick-set and coarse-featured as her sire, and who was wearing gabardine trimmed with plush. (For anyone reading that and wondering, I shall admit that I am perfectly familiar with the styles and fabrics of ladies' garments, from the choosing of them, and the donning of them, and also – at times – the discarding of them. I have only been at St Benedict's for six months, after all.)
>
> 'No Madam Glaum?' I said softly to Ranulf as we left the church.
>
> 'She died many years ago.'
>
> 'A happy release for the lady, I dare say.'
>
> 'Uncharitable thoughts, Brother.'
>
> 'I'll do penance later.'

Andrew had certainly delivered a few surprises about religious life. Nell, leaning back for a moment to assimilate what she had read so far, glanced at the time and saw it was not yet four o'clock. Gerald Orchard was still absorbed in tutting over his sheaf of papers and unlikely to interrupt.

The temptation to go on reading Andrew's journal was irresistible.

NINE

Before I entered the Order, I did not know that there are warning signs that precede many of the significant events in life. I know it now, though. It's as if a signpost juts out of the landscape. You don't always recognize it for what it is at the time – it's only when you look back that you realize – that you think, 'Ah yes, that should have warned me.'

The first of my signposts came on the morning that Father Abbot asked if I would arrange for the choir to sing one, perhaps two, suitable chants at a local funeral.

'It's the woman at Cliff House,' he said. 'All very sad – a widow, so I believe, and she died three or four days ago, quite suddenly, leaving a young daughter. The funeral is tomorrow and I understand they've already taken the coffin into the church. I've only just heard about it, though. The daughter is completely alone, no family whatsoever; it seems a charitable thing for us to contribute what we can to the service. I know it's very short notice, but—'

'Of course I'll arrange something,' I said at once.

I thought we could sing the seventeenth-century setting of the Psalm, 'O Bless the Lord, My Soul', and also Wesley's 'Come, O Thou Traveller Unknown' for the service. Apart from anything else, the choir already knew them, so no rehearsal was necessary. But I needed to look over the music that evening, to remind myself of the phrasing.

It was annoying to realize, later, that I had left the score for the Psalm in the church – we had sung it at a St Luke's Day service for the village, and I remembered putting the music in the organ loft cupboard. But it was only half past eight – not so late that I could not go along to the church there and then and collect it.

I murmured an explanation to Brother Ranulf, received a nod of permission from him, and set off.

The church was only about fifteen minutes' walk from the monastery, but it was an unfriendly night, dark and rainy. Several times my oil lamp flickered and was almost quenched. The wind tossed the trees from side to side so that they looked like giant hands flexing and unflexing, and I could hear the sea below the cliffs as I walked. There are times when it sounds benign and gentle, but tonight it was angry and restless – almost as if something deep inside it was sobbing and struggling for life.

As I neared the church I heard a different sound – a steady, inexorable sound, but so faint and faraway I could not be sure I was actually hearing it. It was like a pulse beating on the air – a sound felt rather than heard. I stood still for a moment, vaguely puzzled, but the wind was too strong for me to identify the noise or where it came from. Then it stopped and I went on towards the church, but I had only gone a few paces when it began afresh. And now, the sounds were slow and measured, and I knew what I was hearing. The chime of a bell. At first I wanted to believe it was from the small local church to which I was heading, but that bell was small and sweet and quite high-pitched. This was a massive sound, ugly and somehow warped.

The only other bell within miles was the ancient Glaum bell in the old cliffside tower. The dead bell that had been silenced more than three hundred years ago. But it could not be that, or, if it was, it would be due to a freak of the storm disturbing the disused mechanism. An animal might even have got in and found its way up to the bell chamber. Whatever it was, it was eerie to hear those flawed chimes sounding through the storm.

There's an old legend about the bell tower – I daresay there are old legends about all the ancient towers the length and breadth of England, and probably of most other countries as well. But the Rede Abbas tower is said by the superstitious and the credulous to be a tomb. They tell that, on occasions, whatever is buried in there wakes and tries to get out. At those times it activates the bell to call for help.

I had never believed the tale, of course, and I had never met anyone who had heard the bell actually sound. But walking through the dark storm, I had the sinister impression of a sentience – an awareness – within the chimes.

Then two things happened. The chiming stopped, as suddenly as if someone had slammed a door.

And, ahead of me, I saw a light burning inside the church.

There was no reason why someone should not be in there tonight, perhaps spending time in prayer or in remembrance of a loved one. Most likely it was someone connected to the Widow Eynon – I remembered Father Abbot telling me her coffin was to lie in the church overnight, ahead of tomorrow's funeral. It seemed strange for anyone to hold a vigil in such weather, but grief is unpredictable.

The storm was increasing. Clouds scudded across the moon and rain dashed into my face. The oil lamp flickered, then went out, and I gasped, repressed a curse, and went towards the church, thinking that if nothing else I could probably re-light the lamp in there.

I reached the church, pushed open the door and stepped inside. The interior was partly lit by candles burning near the altar. They washed over the old stones and archways, leaving deep pools of shadow between. Their light fell across the coffin resting on its bier before the altar, and upon the girl bending over it.

I stood looking at her. The bereaved daughter. There was no one else it could be. I wanted to believe she had come out here to pray at her mother's coffin – I wanted to believe that very much – but I could not. When I entered the church she had been bending over the coffin, and I saw with cold horror that she was intent on levering up the lid.

She gasped when she saw me and backed away, putting out her hands in the classic gesture of defence. The candle-light flared up, turning the tumble of pale hair into melted honey, briefly making her into something fey and wild and strange.

I said, as gently as I could, 'Don't be frightened. I don't

mean you any harm. I'm Brother Andrew from the monastery – I'm arranging some music for the funeral tomorrow.'

She absorbed this, then said, 'Andrew,' slowly, as if trying out the name. 'Yes, I know who you are.' There was a faint lilt to her voice, not quite foreign, but not entirely English, either. 'You're the Precentor.'

It's not often that rather ancient title is used nowadays, and at such a moment it was absurd and irrelevant of me to feel pleased that she knew it and that she had used it.

'I am. And I think you must be Miss Eynon,' I said.

'Yes. Theodora.'

Theodora. The strange, fey creature who was the second of the dreadful bloodied signposts along that grim road. The one who was to change my world for ever, and tumble both of us into chaos and tragedy. And if she had said her name was Mab or Rusalka or Faye, I should not have been surprised.

But I said, 'You were doing something to the coffin? Theodora, I know it's tragic and terrible that you've lost your mother, but you must hold on to the knowledge that she's at peace. Tomorrow we shall commit her body to the ground and send her to God. You will get over this grief in time, I promise you will.'

'It's not that,' she said, with a touch of impatience, but her eyes were wide and fearful.

'Then what? Tell me.' As she hesitated, I went closer to her. 'You can trust me,' I said.

Theodora said, 'I don't think my mother's dead. That's why I'm trying to open the coffin. To stop her being buried alive.'

I had no idea what to do or say. I don't think anyone would have had any idea what to do or say in the face of such a statement. I'd better set down here that I did not believe her. She was disturbed – grief-stricken, refusing to believe her mother was dead. I think it's not an uncommon reaction.

Eventually, I said, 'I understand your fears, Theodora, but they're groundless.'

'Are they?'

'I'm certain they are.' She stared at me, then shrugged, turning away, indicating as clearly as if she had spoken aloud that she had not expected me to understand anyway.

The small gesture sliced into me, and I said, 'I really am certain, Theodora. But let's make assurance doubly sure.' Even as I said the words, I wished I had not chosen to quote from *Macbeth*, so dark and so laced with macabre superstitions.

'You'll help me?' She looked at the coffin, then put her hands out to me. Instinctively I took them and held them firmly and, as her fingers closed around mine, I was aware of a startlingly strong response. You forget, after even a short time inside a monastery, how soft and gentle – but also how strong – a woman's hands can be. Velvet over steel. Thin fur over hard bone.

I hesitated, then I heard my voice say, 'Yes. I'll help you.'

I was deeply reluctant – of course I was! – but it would have been a cruelty to walk out of that church and leave her alone. I could not do it. Nor could I see any other course of action. So I hunted in the vestry for a suitable implement, and found a couple of screwdrivers and a chisel, which I brought back to the altar. She had managed to loosen several of the screws fastening down the lid, but clearly she had only just begun the task, because most were still tightly in place. I am not a very practical man, but I could see it was going to take some time to work them free.

'You sit on that pew,' I said to her. 'I'll do this.'

'I must see – I must know . . .'

We looked at one another. 'I understand,' I said. 'And you will see, Theodora. But let me do this part.' In truth, of course, I wanted to prevent her seeing her dead mother's body in its coffin if I could. The other truth was that I was simply intending to reassure her that her mother was dead and peaceful.

Theodora sat where I had indicated, and as I worked the candles burned lower and the shadows edged closer. It was more difficult than I had expected. Several times I had to pause and, each time I did so, Theodora leaned forward, her hands tightly clasped as if willing me to go on. Once, when the chisel slipped and fell clanging to the ground, she gasped, but she did not say anything.

Did I realize I was probably breaking several laws? I don't know. I think Theodora and I had entered a dark half-world, where normal rules no longer had any meaning.

> The sound of the wood scraping protestingly as I lifted off the coffin lid is, I think, one that will walk through my nightmares for many years to come. And there, wrapped in a thin muslin shroud, was Theodora's mother. Clearly dead.
>
> 'It's perfectly all right,' I said. 'She's quite peaceful.'
>
> But before Theodora came to stand by my side, I reached into the coffin, doing so as quickly but as unobtrusively as I could. The body's eyes were wide open – they were staring up at me. But it was probably not unusual – who knows what physical changes take place after death?
>
> There was, though, something else, something I shall always be grateful I managed to conceal – something I know I will never tell Theodora. One of the hands was clenched and raised. As if she had tried to push open the lid of her coffin after it was screwed down.
>
> But it only took two seconds to slide the eyes shut and push Thaisa Eynon's clenched hand down by her side.

Thaisa, thought Nell, abruptly jolted out of Andrew's nineteenth-century world. Thaisa Eynon. Thaisa and Theodora. The names that were written on the wall at Quire Court.

Theodora. October 1850 . . . If anyone finds this, please pray for me, for it will mean the dead bell has sounded and I have suffered Thaisa's fate . . .

It can't be coincidence, she thought. How many Theodoras do you encounter in the space of a few days? And even more so – how many Thaisas?

The ink of the last few pages was in a slightly different colour. This might indicate that pages had become detached or that Andrew had not written anything for a few days. Or these pages had been left in sunlight and the ink had faded. With this thought Nell had a sudden vivid image of stone mullioned windows with sunshine streaming through them, lying across a sheaf of pages covered with slanting writing . . . Of a blurred distant view of an ancient bell tower. And the dark head of a young monk bent over the pages as he wrote.

She began to read again, doing so slowly because she did not want to leave Andrew's world.

It was bitterly cold for Thaisa Eynon's funeral next day, and the service and burial took place against iron-grey skies with flurries of stinging sleet.

I led the choir through the music, but I have no idea how it sounded, because I was aware of little other than Theodora sitting quietly in her place. She wore black and her pale hair was tied back, throwing into prominence the slanting cheekbones that gave her such a fey, other-worldly look. There were marks of tears on her face, and there was pain and almost bewilderment in her eyes, and I wanted to grab her to me and smooth away all the grief and loneliness. I did not, of course. I fell into step with Brother Ranulf and Father Abbot and together we walked to the cemetery for the burial service.

It's an old graveyard, the Rede Abbas one. Ranulf says it is becoming impossibly full, and new land will have to be found before much longer. Someone else murmured that the ground had been so hard and unyielding that the sexton's men had been unable to break through it, and the coffin would be lowered into a shallower grave than was customary. Hearing that, a terrible thought slid unbidden into my mind. *If the grave is shallow, it will be easier for her to get out if she is not dead . . .*

Adolphus Glaum was among the mourners – I had to repress the suspicion that he was there to show how kindly a person he was, and how concerned he was for local people. He wore a solemn expression, and I disliked him all over again. Once I caught him watching Theodora with . . . with what I can only describe as a lascivious glint. After that I did not just dislike him, I hated him, and that's a terrible admission for a man of God to make. He suddenly seemed to become aware of my regard and the pious expression reappeared as swiftly as if he had clapped a mask over his features and his feelings. I wanted to hit him. I wanted to put my hands round his thick neck, and say, *How dare you look at her in that way?*

I did penance later for those violent thoughts about Glaum, but I did not do penance for the scalding thoughts and longings coursing through my mind and my body for Theodora Eynon.

TEN

It's strange to realize that massive events can be set in motion by the smallest, most ordinary of details. That night – the night of Thaisa Eynon's funeral – if a pan of stew had not boiled over in the monastery's kitchens, sending the kitcheners running distractedly around with damp cloths and jugs of water to quench it, our supper would not have been twenty minutes later than normal.

If Brother Wilfrid, Reader for the week, had not chosen a particularly wordy passage from St Thomas Aquinas to accompany our meal, supper would not have been even more delayed. And I should have reached Theodora in time.

It was almost nine o'clock when I finally slipped out by the garden door and walked out to Cliff House. The night was moonless, but as I drew near to Cliff House I could see the light burning in a downstairs room. It drew me, that light, like the magnetic north. 'Thither is my north and there my needle points.' And, oh, yes, I do know there's a very earthy and deeper meaning in that line, and it's not a meaning any monk with respect for his vows should know. Also, Cliff House lies to the west of the monastery.

There was a rickety gate in front of the house that almost fell off its hinges when I pushed it. It screeched like a soul in torment, but I stepped through on to a broken and uneven path beyond. I think I hoped she would hear my step on the broken path and open the door to me – that she would stretch out her hands as she had done last night. But there was no answer to my knock, although a light burned in one of the windows. After a moment I tried the door. I did not expect it to open, but it did, and I pushed it wide and stepped inside. Beyond was a dim corridor with three or four doors leading off. Everywhere was dark and dingy, and somewhere nearby was the maddening dripping of a tap. Through two of the half-open doors I could see threadbare curtains and chair coverings, and although I know that such things do not matter or count in the greater scheme of things, and that Theodora's mother might not have had very much money, I wanted nothing more than to pick Theodora up in my arms and take her somewhere safe and warm and comfortable. How I thought that could fit with the Benedictine vow of poverty, I have no idea.

There was no sign of her, but as I looked into a long, gloomy drawing room – it did not look as if anyone had used it for years – I heard sounds from above. From the bedrooms.

You don't, if you're a gentleman, go scurrying up to a lady's bedroom without at least hesitating or calling out. If you're a Benedictine monk (even not fully professed and received into the Order), you do more than hesitate.

I did hesitate for several moments, then I went towards the stairs. The shadows of Cliff House came out to meet me, and as I went up the stairs they creaked, as if old, juiceless bones were struggling into life. At the top were several windows along a short corridor. They rattled uneasily in their ill-fitting frames, and the tattered remnants of curtains moved like beckoning eldritch fingers.

Then Theodora screamed, and I forgot about being a gentleman and I certainly forgot about being a monk, and ran like a mad thing towards the sounds.

She was in a bedroom at the far end – the door was open, and for the space of six heartbeats I stood there, staring in horrified disgust.

You forget – probably most people never have cause to think about it – how grotesque the act of love can look when viewed by a third person, especially if one of the people involved in it is ugly, thick-set and mean-eyed.

There was no love in what was happening on the bed, though. Adolphus Glaum was straddled over Theodora, one hand imprisoning her two wrists, the other fumbling greedily at the fastenings of his breeches. He pulled open the flap, and fell heavily forward on to the bed, on to Theodora, thrusting her skirts up to her waist, and pushing himself between her legs.

'You let me do it, you bitch,' he said, his words thick with horrid greed. 'Let me do it now, hard and strong, or they'll all know about your ungodly goings-on in the church last night.'

She was sobbing and trying to fight him off, but Glaum only gripped her more tightly. 'Struggle away, you hellcat, it only makes it more exciting. Because I saw you in the church – I saw your precious monk as well; the one that pretends to be so saintly and pious and all the time he's standing like an autumn crocus for you, under his robes. A fine tale all that would make for the monastery, wouldn't it? Breaking open a coffin – and what did you do with him afterwards? But you'll find me as vigorous as any cowled monk, my dear.'

'Vigorous?' shouted Theodora, her voice full of hatred. 'You're not vigorous, you weakling. Didn't you know they tell in the village that you're no better than a three-inch fool.'

Even from where I stood, I saw Glaum's face flood with crimson. He said, 'Prick teaser,' almost spitting the words into her face. 'Submit and you'll find me generous. But refuse me, Theodora, and it'll be the worse for you – and for your precious Brother Andrew.'

I bounded forward then, snatching up a candlestick from the dressing table, and bringing it smashing down on Glaum's head. He gave a grunt of anger and surprise, and then, only momentarily stunned by the blow, rounded on me with a snarl. He was ridiculous – half undressed; the jutting manhood that had been so insistent a moment ago flopping out of his breeches. But he was still threatening, and he was a heavy, muscular man. Seething with such fury he would not find it difficult to overpower me.

Before I could deliver a second blow, which I was certainly prepared to do, Glaum knocked the candlestick from my hand, and lunged towards me, his hands reaching for my neck. I stood my ground, but before he reached me Theodora leapt up from the bed, seized the candlestick and lifted it above her head. I think I called out to her to stop – to leave Glaum to me – but it was already too late.

For a second time the heavy brass crashed against Glaum's skull, and this time the blow was more telling. His eyes bulged, and his body sagged, as if the bones had been pulled from it. Then he fell heavily on to the floor and lay there motionless.

I went to him at once and bent over him – of course I did. I had no notion of leaving the man to lie untended – as appalling as he was, as deeply as I hated him.

Theodora shrank back against the wall, one hand going to her throat. In a thread of a voice, she said, 'Have I killed him? Oh God, I didn't mean to kill him.'

I was feeling for a heartbeat, in the way I had seen Brother Wilfrid, the infirmarian, do with seriously sick patients in the infirmary. There was no trace of any pulse. I said, 'I don't know. Have you a small mirror – a looking glass?'

'Here.' She handed it to me from the dressing table by the bed, and I held it against Glaum's lips, praying – genuinely praying – that the surface would become misted, showing that the man still breathed. But again there was nothing.

At last I sat back, my eyes still on Glaum's prone figure. Theodora waited, and finally I said, 'I'm not sure, but I'm dreadfully afraid he's dead.'

'Oh, Andrew, no . . . No . . .'

'We'll manage,' I said, at once. 'Help me fasten his breeches – we can't let him be seen like that – then we'll carry him downstairs. He mustn't be found in your bedroom.'

'All right. Yes.'

'When we've got him downstairs,' I said, 'I'll fetch Brother Wilfrid – the infirmarian. Also Brother Ranulf. They'll know what to do.'

'Can they be trusted?'

'I hope so.'

We – that is Ranulf, Wilfrid and I – tried to keep the truth of Glaum's death a secret. We told his daughters – Miss Gertrude and Miss Margaretta – that their father had been on a mission of comfort to the young, bereaved girl at Cliff House. While there, he had tripped and fallen, hitting his head against a brass fender, we said. Brother Wilfrid, imperilling his soul's salvation, as he later told me, stated firmly that it was perfectly clear what had happened, and that in his view death would have been instantaneous. The local doctor, given a carefully arranged version of the facts, confirmed this. A shocking accident, he said, firmly. Father Abbot, accepting all he was told, said it was a tragedy and Adolphus Glaum would be a great loss to our little community.

My own presence in Cliff House that night was also kept secret, although Ranulf delivered a severe reproof to me in private, suggested a series of stringent penances I should perform, and advised that at the earliest opportunity I should confess any sins that might be dragging down my soul, and receive full absolution.

I carried out the penances, but I did not confess any of it. God forgive me, I could feel no remorse for the death of the man who had been about to rape Theodora. All I could feel was an increasing wish to protect her.

Despite the subterfuge and the lies and half-lies, there was talk almost immediately – virtually within hours, because Rede Abbas was that kind of tight, enclosed community.

The talk was the corrosive poisonous kind that spins its own false cloth, and winds that cloth stiflingly around people's minds. As early as the next evening, Theodora was being looked at askance. She and her mother, alone and apart in their dark old house, had ever been strange figures to the local community, and the gossips seized on Glaum's death at Cliff House, and picked it over, fashioning it to their own beliefs.

And the irony of it all was that they had stripped away the pretence, and peeled back the lies and got down to the truth. Theodora had indeed killed Adolphus Glaum.

Glaum's funeral took place three days after his death.

I did not want to attend, but Brother Ranulf and Father Abbot were insistent.

'Andrew,' said Ranulf, 'I have lied for you and for that poor child, and I shall go on lying. If you cannot support that lie by being present at the funeral, I wash my hands of you.'

So I went to the service, of which I do not remember a single prayer, and afterwards joined the solemn procession to the graveyard. Prayers were chanted as the coffin was placed on its designated shelf inside the family's mausoleum; someone had brought candles and a tinderbox, and someone else spent a few moments in lighting the candles and setting them out in the dark interior. The acrid tang of the smoke mingled strangely with the odours of dank stones and of old, dry wood, and the flames flickered across the older coffins with their tarnished brass plates. It was a macabre sight – generations of Glaums, stretching back to the sixteenth century, all of them lying in the sour dimness.

One of the mourners, presumably trying to infuse a note of metaphysical romance to the grim proceedings, commented that the candle flames gave light in the dark of the charnel house, but the two Glaum daughters were not of a metaphysical or a romantic turn of mind, because Miss Gertrude dissolved in a fit of noisy sobbing and Miss Margaretta let out a wail and clutched at the wall to prevent herself from swooning. Both were helped out to the waiting carriage and driven back to Glaum House.

That same night, ignoring Brother Ranulf's strictures and Father Abbot's probable apoplexy if ever he found out, I again took the narrow cliff path to Theodora's house.

I would like to record that I was heedless of the cold night, or of the rain and wind, but of course I heeded it. But what lover ever cared for a drenching or a chill . . .

Lover. That's the first time I've used that word. *Lover.* But I was not Theodora's lover on those nights. She was alone and grief-stricken and the community had turned against her because of Glaum's death. It was possible that she was in danger from the law because of his death. I wanted only to comfort her. So I obeyed the precepts of a gentleman, and I kept the vows I had made.

They were vows I should never have taken in the first place, of course, and certainly I should never have flung myself into St Benedict's on that wave of resentful bitterness against the world in general and a lady in particular. (A lady whose name I now have to think hard to recollect in full. Not that I was ever especially fickle, you understand. Well, not much. And not often.)

But I did not break any of my vows, except perhaps the vow of obedience, for the Rule of St Benedict does not permit a monk to go out into the world alone and by night. It certainly does not permit him to walk up to a house in which there is a lady for whom he has the deepest feelings.

Lights burned in the rooms of Cliff House that night, but as I reached for the brass door knocker, I became aware that someone inside the house – presumably Theodora – was playing a piano. This should have been an ordinary thing – a good thing to hear – but it was not, for the music was the strangest I had ever heard. I was partly repulsed, but also fascinated by it, but as the cadences reached silkily into my mind, I wanted to grasp them and write them down so they should never be lost.

I plied the knocker again, but the music continued, so, for the second time, I pushed open the door and entered Cliff House without being invited.

The music was coming from a room at the back of the house. It was a small room, and if it had been warm and if lights had burned there it might even have been cosy. A fire had been laid in the hearth, but it had not been lit, and the only light came from outside – through tall windows open to the night. Pale curtains billowed wildly in and out of them, twisting into reaching, snatching arms, and into pallid, impossibly elongated wraith-creatures, with open mouths stretched in silent cries.

Theodora was seated at the piano, and she was so lost in the music and in the song she was singing that at first she did not realize I was there. The words of her song reached me in fragments, but even those fragments informed me that this was a language I did not know.

Then she turned and stopped playing, and said, 'Andrew,' and there was pleasure and welcome in her voice, although there were shadows in her eyes.

'I came to see how you are,' I said. 'You didn't hear my knock, so I came in anyway. Is that all right?'

'Of course. Let me light the fire – I hadn't noticed how cold and dark it had got.'

'I'll do it,' I said, and as I knelt before the grate, I said, 'What was that you were playing?'

At first I thought she was not going to answer, then she said, 'It's a Death Song.'

'A death song? Do you mean a lament?'

'No, not a lament. My mother said it came into our family

more than three hundred years ago. It was brought by someone they say was a *plentyn cael*.'

'You'll have to translate that' I said, after a moment.

'A changeling. The human child is exchanged – the real child stolen away and something else left in its place. Something that isn't human at all. That's when the music came to us. Real changelings can never resist music, you see. I don't believe the story, of course,' she said, but her eyes were dark and inward looking. 'The music becomes lost at times – sometimes for a century or more – but it's always found again. My mother thought it had been destroyed for ever – burned, perhaps. Or perhaps it was drowned, buried fathoms deep . . . But I found it. Someone always does find it. Two weeks ago I played it. And then my mother died.'

The fire was burning up now. It sent little tongues of warmth and light into the room. I sat down in a deep old chair and looked at her. 'You made a connection between playing the music and your mother's death?'

'The music brings tragedy in its trail,' she said, evasively.

I suppose most people would find the concept of music holding a power utterly absurd, and of course it is. But there are uneasy tales that cling to some pieces of music. Whoever you are, reading this, have you ever heard of the 'Lost Lament of the Dewin'? Or of Tartini's infamous 'Devil's Trill', said to have been given to him in a dream by Satan? And there are the even stranger tales of Niccolò Paganini, whispered by some of his contemporaries to be the son of the devil, and refused burial by the Church for five years after his death.

'Tragedy?' I said. 'Is that what you believe the music causes? Is it why you were afraid your mother might not be dead?'

She dodged the question again. 'I needed to be sure,' she said. 'I'm glad you were there that night, Andrew. I'm glad I know she was all right.'

I thought: but there's something you don't know, my poor trusting love. You don't know that her hand was raised as if she had tried to beat her way out of the coffin before they buried her. You don't know that I've had sleepless nights wondering when she really died – whether she died when the doctors said, or whether she died later, alone and terrified, trapped inside her coffin in the church. And all those other nights when I've wondered whether she beat on the lid of her coffin from within the grave – whether she might still do so, even now . . .

Absurd and fanciful, all of it. I said, 'Tell me about the music, Theodora.'

'It's called "Thaisa's Song". I don't know if that was its original name. It was my mother's name, though – I think it's a family name. I played it for her before she died. She asked me not to – she was afraid of it – but I played it anyway.'

She appeared to wait for a response, and with the idea of dispelling her own nightmares, I said, 'It's a piece of music, that's all. It can't do any actual harm. Prove it tonight, Theodora. Play it for me.'

'No. I shan't play it for you,' said Theodora. 'Not ever, Andrew. I don't dare.'

There was a silence – a silence that I am not sure I can ever forget. The firelight fell across her face, creating little pinpoints of red in her eyes. In that moment it was as if a different person was looking out of her eyes – and it was a person I did not recognize and whom I was not sure I trusted.

Then a log broke apart in the hearth and the light changed back to the comfortable warm glow. The moment passed; Theodora was Theodora again.

She said, very softly, 'I won't play it for you, but I'll play it for Adolphus Glaum.' Then she turned back to the piano, and began to play and to sing. As she did so, the same repulsion and fascination I had felt earlier stole over me. And then . . . I am not sure how this came about and I am not sure how far my memory can be trusted, but incredibly and chillingly a second voice joined in. It was blurred, as if the singer was a very long way off, and the sounds were not absolutely in time – they were like an echo, a half-note behind. The distortion was unnerving; I began to feel slightly sick, as if, deep within my mind, something had been wrenched out of its socket.

But after the first few bars I began to discern some of the meanings of the strange language of the lyrics. I have no idea how I was able to do that – perhaps Theodora and I had forged some sort of link – but it's what happened. There was something about an unknown person asking for admittance to a tomb – something about the tomb's occupant, blind and deaf, trying to call out to know who was there.

As she played, I wanted to watch her and listen to her and be as close as this to her for the rest of my life. I tried to think it was weak of me to be unable to fight my feelings, and then I thought it was an irony to use the word *weakness*, because my feelings were not weak – they were making me strong in that very part of a monk's body where he is not supposed to be strong at all . . .

When she finally took her hands from the keys and turned to smile at me, I knew, once and for all, that I must either do something about my feelings, or find a way to walk away from them.

Except I knew I could never walk away from Theodora. Whatever she was.

ELEVEN

I copied out the music and the words that night from the battered, foxed score that had been propped on Theodora's music stand. I still do not know why, unless I wanted to preserve them in case 'Thaisa's Song' became lost again.

As I walked back to the monastery, I was uneasily aware of the carefully folded copy tucked into the sleeve of my robe. The deep sleeves of the Benedictine robe make a good pocket for papers and even small books, so the three sheets of music notation ought not to have felt strange. But they did. They felt as if they were scraping my skin, as if there was a burr in there, or as if the song was tugging at my mind, wanting attention.

The soft light chimes of the church clock came faintly to me. Ten o'clock. Not a late hour when applied to my old life, but very late indeed for a monk. I went quickly past the graveyard – graveyards are eerie places at night; through the iron gates I saw that the graves were wreathed in swirling grey and indigo shadows. Beyond them the Glaum mausoleum stood out blackly. I paused to look across at it, remembering how Adolphus Glaum's coffin had been carried in there only that morning. It was a squat, ugly place, and by night it was downright sinister. There was a sliver of half-window near the door, like a single slitted eye. The moon cast a thin radiance over it, and I was just thinking it was a bit unusual to have a window of any kind in such a building, when a jab of fear thrust itself into my ribs.

There was a light inside the mausoleum.

All the half-remembered, never-believed legends rushed into my mind. Ghost candles and tomb lights. The will o' the wisp, the ghost-child bearing the *ignis fatuus*, the 'foolish light' of the legends, kindled to trap unwary travellers . . .

Then I remembered that candles had been lit in the mausoleum that morning, and logic returned, because quite clearly one of them had not been properly snuffed. Or perhaps the two Glaum daughters had left one burning, intending to return and hold a candlelit vigil at their father's coffin. I thought that improbable, though. It was more likely that several people had simply assumed someone else would snuff the candles upon leaving.

A single candle flame could not do any harm; it would simply burn itself down and die. And if anyone was going to commit the supreme madness of entering an old charnel house in pitch darkness, it was not going to be me. In any case, the place would be locked and I had no idea who kept the key. (I'm slightly ashamed to admit I seized on this fact with considerable alacrity.)

There was also the point that if I raised an alarm, everyone – by which I mean Father Abbot in particular – would discover I had been out of the monastery at a forbidden time of the night. And Theodora's reputation, already in tatters, would be even further shredded. So I continued on my way, slipped back in through the garden door, and made a stealthy way to my own cell. But once there, I found it impossible to sleep. I suppose sleep did come in snatches, but as the hours slid by, the conviction that there was something wrong increased. I cannot supply any real logic for that feeling, unless my mind was linking two things: Theodora's mother might have been alive in her coffin. And earlier tonight, there had been a light inside the mausoleum, where no light should have burned.

The monastery chimes had not yet sounded for Lauds, our Dawn Prayer, when the memory of the mausoleum being locked after the service came more clearly to me. The key had been placed in a small stone niche on the left-hand side of the door. You see, said my mind. You could get in there without anyone knowing.

There were faint streaks of grey across the sky when I finally got up. I sluiced my face with cold water, wrapped a thick cloak around my shoulders, and went quietly out.

The graveyard, when I reached it, was grey and somehow insubstantial. I thought: if ever ghosts do walk here, they'll do so in this blurred half-world, not at dead of night, not at the traditional witching hour when churchyards yawn and hell breathes out its contagion . . .

And *why* is it that such lines are so readily to hand! I would much prefer not to have remembered that particular one at that moment!

Beyond the graves I could see Cliff House. In my mind I touched the thought of Theodora, and at once I felt as if something had laid a warm and comforting hand over my heart.

The candle flame was still burning beyond the small window – it was pallid in the thin morning light, but it was visible. I walked up to the door, which was laced with lead strips and edged with ornate iron scrollwork. And there, on the left-hand side, was the niche in the stones, worn away by time or scooped out by the hand of man, I could not tell which. But when I slid my hand into it, my fingers closed around the key.

I suppose most people would feel a qualm at entering a charnel house alone, although probably very few people have actually been called to do so. I was not being called to do so now, but I did not want to ignore that tiny flame any longer, and risk hearing later that the entire charnel house had burned to a cinder, along with the score or so mummified bodies inside it.

I hesitated, though. How far was this a desecration? And

yet they were all dead, those Glaums, and all forgotten. All entombed in the urns and the sepulchres of mortality. Who was it who had said that? Someone mourning the lost noble Houses of England centuries earlier, I thought. Well, the Glaums, as far as I knew, had not been especially noble, and remembering Adolphus Glaum's attack on Theodora, I should not have shed any tears if the family had been lost. And yet, and yet . . .

When I slid the key into the door and turned it, the lock gave way unprotestingly. I pushed the door inwards, but it resisted – not as if the frame was warped or the door swollen from damp or age, but as if something was blocking it from within. My heart gave a bump of apprehension, but I tried again. This time something on the other side slithered as if it had been jammed there, and as if the door's weight was now forcing it back. There could not be anything there, though. I tried once more, and at the third attempt the door opened properly. I pushed it all the way back against the wall and stood in the doorway, looking in. The remembered stench of age and dust came at me.

There was not just one candle burning, there were several – all of them set close to the window. Near to them was the tinderbox used during the service to light the candles. The small flames flickered uneasily across the stacked coffins and the cobwebbed stones, and I knew my earlier instinct had been right. Something was wrong. Something I was seeing was dreadfully wrong. But what? I waited for my brain to understand what my eyes had already seen, and then I understood. I wish to God I had not. I wish I had locked the place up, and left it to its nightmares.

Adolphus Glaum's coffin had fallen from its shelf, and lay on the ground. The lid was splintered and the narrow section at the foot had broken away. Smashed outwards from inside, said something in my mind. The music brings tragedy, remember, and Theodora played it last night, and she played it for *him*.

I pushed the thought away, and on legs that felt like cotton threads I went forward. I think I prayed aloud at that point, wanting to see Glaum in his coffin, wanting him to be lying as peacefully as when he was placed in it, wanting reassurance that the coffin had simply slid off the shelf through some natural cause.

With shaking hands I picked up one of the candles and shone its glow on to the coffin's interior. It was empty. Oh, God, the man interred here yesterday was no longer in there. I forced myself to kneel down to examine the coffin's interior more closely. What I saw will stay with me for ever, I think. The satin and silk lining of the coffin was torn to tatters, and when I tipped the lid back, there were long scratches on the underside – deep gouges in the wood. A cold sickness began to creep over me, and the shadowy charnel house tilted and spun.

Behind me the heavy old door creaked, then began to swing inwards. I spun round, seeing the light from outside starting to vanish. If it closed completely, I would be trapped in here. *The music brings tragedy . . .*

I bounded forward, seizing the door by its edge; as I did so, a white-clad figure that had been pressed back against the wall behind the door toppled forward.

He fell straight on to me. His heavy cold arms dropped on to my shoulders and his head fell forward, the forehead thudding sickeningly against mine. A dry, foetid stench gusted into my face as the dead eyes of Adolphus Glaum – fixed and terror-filled – stared into my face.

After I had stopped yelling and fighting to get free of the nightmare embrace, I managed to make sure that he really was dead.

It was clear what had happened. He had been behind the door when I pushed it – he must have been standing there, beating his fists against it until his heart gave out, then fallen against the door and remained there, still in a standing position. When I opened the door and pushed it back, it had pushed Glaum's body back too, trapping it between the door and the wall.

But although he was dead now, terribly and obviously he had not been dead when he was put in his coffin. After the mourners left, he must have come out of whatever stupor or catalepsy that had held him, and broken his way out of

> the coffin. How long had that taken him? I glanced with pity at his hands, seeing that the fingernails were broken and the fingertips crusted with blood.
>
> Once out of the coffin, Glaum must have felt huge relief, but then had come the second and perhaps even deadlier realization. He was trapped inside the mausoleum – inside a place that was remote and seldom visited. His lips were stretched wide in a final silent scream, blood-specked froth staining the corners, but he could have screamed until his throat burst and no one would have heard him. Then what had he done? The lighted candles, of course. Lighted candles might be seen from outside, causing someone to investigate. I visualized him fumbling his way through the darkness, striking the tinder, firing the candles, and setting them as close to the tiny window as possible.
>
> And someone had seen those lights. I had seen them on my way back to the monastery. Had Glaum been dead by then? If I had got in here last night would I have saved him? It was a torturous thought, but I should never know the answer.
>
> And whatever the medical cause – heart attack? apoplexy? – the real cause of death was terror: terror that had initially been induced at being inside the coffin. Terror that must then have spiralled into stark, blazing panic as he realized he could not break out of the mausoleum.
>
> To all intents and purposes, Adolphus Glaum had been buried alive.
>
> Buried alive. Theodora's nightmare for her mother.
>
> But even though Glaum had been buried alive, there was no proof to indicate that the same thing had happened to Thaisa Eynon.

Nell saw there were only a few more pages remaining of Andrew's journal, and although the writing was unquestionably still his, it had altered. It was hurried, the letters badly or hastily formed, as if this final section had been written under extreme stress.

'I think this will be my last entry in this journal,' Andrew wrote.

> It has helped me through such difficult times, so I want to set down as much of what is happening as I can – as I have time to set down. Then I shall leave it in my room here at St Benedict's,

perhaps concealed behind a loose stone or under a cupboard floor. Knowing it's there will help me believe I shall return. Perhaps, too, it will calm my mind and even clarify my thoughts to set everything down.

Theodora is with us here in the monastery – she is in the common room as I write this.

After I found Glaum's body, the two Glaum ladies gathered together almost the entire village and whipped up the already-existing suspicion and dislike for Theodora and her mother. Feelings ran so high that Father Abbot, appealed to by Brother Ranulf, Brother Wilfrid and myself, agreed that Theodora must be brought to the monastery for her safety.

'At least until the inquest is over and a proper official verdict is pronounced,' he said, and reminded us all, very solemnly, that it was not so long since all religious houses had been regarded as places of sanctuary.

'By then the Misses Glaum will see that their feelings are the result of their own grief and shock,' he said. 'And until that time, the village people will not dare come to our doors to get to Miss Eynon.'

He was wrong. Gertrude and Margaretta Glaum did not recover from their hatred of Theodora. The inquest is tomorrow, and an hour earlier, just as we were finishing supper, there were angry shouts from outside, and torchlight flares showed through the darkness.

Brother Ranulf and I went warily to one of the upper windows, and below us we saw at least a dozen local people – people whose faces we knew, but whose expressions, tonight, we did not recognize. At the head were Gertrude and Margaretta Glaum, their faces twisted and ugly with hatred, their voices raised above the shouting people.

'Theodora Eynon! Bring her out to justice! She killed our father!'

The cries of the villagers, whipped up to a dreadful exultant anger by those two, joined in.

'Bring her out to justice! Bring her *out!*'

And now I am writing this in the common room. We are all here, and even through the thick walls, we can hear the shouting still going on. Some of the terms they are using about Theodora are ugly and gross, and several have caused Brother Egbert to clap shocked hands over his ears.

I suppose it was not to be expected that the discovery of Glaum's body, alive inside the tomb, could be kept secret. The news crackled through this village and the outlying communities like a forest fire, sparking a vicious torrent of hatred against Theodora – and against the monks for harbouring her. So fierce is the emotion that I could almost believe it to be strong enough to burn through the walls and reach us.

Father Abbot says – and Brother Egbert agrees – that the people cannot maintain this anger. We have only to wait, he says, and they will go back to their homes. In the meantime, he is leading us in a series of prayers. I am joining in, but it is difficult to summon any degree of humility and devotion. I keep remembering other angry crowds throughout history, when people have taken the law into their own hands. The Black Death persecution of Jews in the 1300s. The ransacking of Rome in the 1500s. The storming of the Bastille in 1789. The Gordon Riots in this century, described so eloquently by Charles Dickens in *Barnaby Rudge*, and the rebellions of the Luddites.

All set in motion by ordinary people, ordinary citizens made furious by injustices. They seized the law into their own hands and meted out justice so rough it is engraved on history. And tonight it seems as if the people of this community are about to attempt the same thing.

The invasion of our small remote monastery would be a minuscule affair in comparison with any of those events, but if Theodora were to die it would not be minuscule to us. The thought of her death is like a spade turning in my stomach.

We have huddled together in the common room, but whether it is for safety or comfort I do not know. Theodora is hunched in a corner, not speaking. I do not dare to talk to her or even to sit next to her, because I am afraid my feelings would betray me.

A few moments ago, Father Abbot said that he would go out to reason with the people.

'They will listen to me,' he said, but his words rang false.

None of us has ever encountered violence before, and I do not think any of us knows how to deal with it on this level.

I said, 'Father, they're beyond reason. They won't listen to anyone.' I tried to keep the impatience from my voice, but when I looked across at Ranulf, I saw we were both thinking the same thing: even if those people were in a mood to be reasoned with, Father Abbot – thin, elderly, accustomed to a quiet and ordered monastic life since he was in his twenties – would be useless.

'They've listened to the Glaum ladies,' said Wilfrid. 'They might listen to Father Abbot.'

'The Glaum family has been ordering the people of these villages around for centuries,' said Ranulf. 'And tonight the villagers will listen to Gertrude and Margaretta, just as they listened to the old man, and they'll do whatever those two want of them.'

None of us voiced the thought that what those two ladies wanted was punishment for the woman they believed had murdered their father. They wanted her dead. Hanged.

'The practical thing,' said Wilfrid, 'and the immediate solution is surely to get Miss Eynon away from here.'

'How?' I said. 'And where would she go?'

For a moment no one spoke. Then Ranulf said, 'Father, doesn't the Order own some property in Oxford?'

'Quire Court,' said Father Abbot, nodding. 'It's curious you should mention that, though, Brother Ranulf, because—'

'Yes?'

'Because that piece of land in Oxford, and whatever buildings are on it now, once belonged to the Glaum family. Oh, centuries ago,' said Father Abbot, as several of us looked up in surprise. 'I believe one of my predecessors acquired it from the Squire Glaum of the day.'

Ranulf said, 'Was that the infamous Abbot Seamus Flannery, by any chance?'

'It was Father Seamus, as it happens. I have no idea how he acquired it. I don't think anyone at the time dared ask him.'

'But,' said Ranulf dryly, 'however the land came into our possession, it has to be said that our Church has always had an eye to acquiring valuable possessions, whether it's gold, silver, or, indeed, parcels of land.'

'Well, yes. I am not a venal man and I do not really understand such things,' said Father Abbot, humbly. 'But it's possible that Quire Court might be a place of safety for Miss Eynon.' He looked across to Theodora, still huddled in her chair. 'It's a long journey, though. And she would have to be got away from here at once. Tonight.'

'We can't send her out into the night on her own,' said Wilfrid at once. 'Apart from her state of health, which is fragile, she's never been outside Rede Abbas in her life.'

'We can't risk keeping her here.' As Father Abbot spoke, there was the sound of glass breaking somewhere.

'They're smashing windows,' said one of the older monks, in alarm, and several of them started up, clearly much frightened.

'We're safe in here,' said Egbert. 'We've locked the doors.'

'That won't keep them out indefinitely. It's Miss Eynon they want,' said Ranulf. 'And if they do break in here . . .' He looked at me very directly.

That was when I said, 'I'll get her away. I'll take her to Oxford.'

And now I am preparing for our journey with as much haste as possible, and in a little while Theodora and I will slip out of the monastery by way of the cloisters. Brother Ranulf will let us out through the garden door, and once he is sure we are safely beyond the grounds, he will lock the door after us. It's a door that we believe is unknown to the village people and the two Glaum ladies, who will not be familiar with the layout of our grounds. We think it will be safe to use it. Once Theodora and I are outside, we shall go across Musselwhite's Meadow, which will be dark and deserted. It's an odd feeling to remember we shall be treading in the footsteps of other travellers there, because Musselwhite's is the home of gypsies each summer, and we will be able to walk the track they made over the years.

From there we will be far enough inland to begin the journey to Oxford, and to this place, Quire Court. I have no idea what it will be like, but Father Abbot thinks it is a small conclave of quite modest buildings.

There is a task I would like to carry out before leaving, but I do not believe it will be possible. That is to find the two music scores for 'Thaisa's Song' and destroy them – burn them and tear the words to unreadable shreds. One copy – Theodora's copy – is at Cliff House. We dare not go out there, for we should certainly be seen by the Misses Glaum and the villagers. The other copy is the one I made that night, which is in the library, here at St Benedict's. But I dare not go there either, for it means crossing the inner courtyard, and I think I would be seen by the villagers. I am trying to believe no one will find it, though. I put it on a shelf bearing several books about early Ambrosian plainchant.

And perhaps somewhere in the future, I – by which I mean Theodora and I – will be able to return and I can find the music then, and tear it to unreadable shreds, then burn the shreds to cinders.

TWELVE

Incredibly and infuriatingly, Andrew's notes finished there.

But you did make it to Quire Court, thought Nell, staring at the pages, aware of a feeling of loss. You were there, Andrew, you and Theodora. You must have been, because I found Theodora's scribbled message:

Pray for me, for it will mean the dead bell has sounded and I have suffered Thaisa's fate . . .

Had Theodora known by then that her mother might have been alive inside her coffin? Had Thaisa indeed been alive, though? Andrew had not been sure. But Adolphus Glaum had certainly been sealed up in the mausoleum while still alive, and Nell thought Andrew's account of that could be trusted. There were enough accounts of old coffins being opened to reveal twisted, agonized bodies who had been consigned to the grave in some kind of death-like coma. Squire Glaum had sounded like a lascivious Victorian thug, but he had certainly not deserved the appalling fate he had suffered.

It was easy to imagine Andrew in that long-ago monastery, absorbed in his work and his prayers and his music. He had copied Theodora's music that night, but it did not sound as if he had taken the copy to Quire Court – he had left it in the monks' library. And Theodora's copy had been at Cliff House. So whose was the brittle, faded score Beth had found?

Thaisa's Song. Copied from the original.

The lyrics on that copy had not been in English, but having read Andrew's journal, Nell thought they might be a form of Celtic, perhaps an old version of the Welsh language. But whatever they were, she was glad she had stopped Beth playing more than a few bars.

She turned back to Andrew's account of hearing the song in Cliff House. He had not set down the actual lyrics, but he had referred to the start of an understanding of them.

'. . . an unknown person asking for admittance to a tomb – something about the tomb's occupant, blind and deaf, trying to call out to know who was there . . .'

This was a deeply disturbing line, however you looked at it. Taken in conjunction with those two macabre deaths – of Thaisa Eynon and Adolphus Glaum – it was chilling. There could not be any link though. Or could there?

Theodora had seemed to fear the music, but she had played it that night. To impress Andrew? To lure him to bed? If so, it was a wildly bizarre seduction technique. Or had she played and sung it from sheer bravado – a kind of, 'See how unafraid I am' gesture?

Nell replaced the pages carefully in the display cabinet, rather sadly aware of the door to Andrew's world closing against her. Or had it closed? The copy of the song was still at Quire Court. Might it provide a pathway back into Andrew's world? She could not, for the moment, think how that might be done, but she saw that it was six o'clock and time she was back at The Swan for her early supper.

She thanked Gerald Orchard for his help, returned the gloves, then found herself drawn into a discussion about Rede Abbas's past, which was unexpectedly enjoyable. Gerald was knowledgeable and interested in local history. 'I suppose because my family have lived here for . . . well, for generations and generations.'

Nell said, 'There's a reference to someone called Orchard in the document I've just been reading – it's part of a journal from the old monastery, but it quotes from a sixteenth-century paper. That mentions a Job Orchard. Would he have been an ancestor?'

'I should think he might. How interesting,' said Gerald, eagerly. 'I didn't realize we went quite that far back. I didn't really look at those documents, you know – I just picked out the best-preserved ones for the display. But I'll read that one without delay. Thank you very much. The third cabinet along, did you say?'

'Yes. Brother Andrew from St Benedict's. Mid-1800s. It makes fascinating reading.'

As Nell went out, Gerald was already heading towards the museum section, and there was the sound of the glass-topped display cabinet lid being lifted.

She was determined not to crowd Beth, who would want to be with her schoolfriends, and Nell was perfectly happy to have a quiet meal on her own, then wander along to the square to find a seat for the evening's entertainment. She did not in the least mind sitting by herself for that. But on her way back to The Swan, she met Beth's teacher, Chloe Carter, whom she knew fairly well.

'Are you on your own?' Chloe asked. 'Because, if so, I'm about to supervise that wild gang over a meal and then hand them over to the hostel manageress. She's very good and trustworthy, so I'm going to leave her in charge while I go along to the morality plays. Would you like to join me? It'd be much nicer to have company.'

'I'd enjoy that,' said Nell, who liked Chloe and was pleased to be asked.

'Your Beth and the rest of the unruly cherubs don't want to see the morality plays,' said Chloe. 'It'll probably be over most of their heads, anyway. And in fact the wicked little imps are planning a midnight feast. They think I don't know, but of course I do. Providing they don't stuff themselves sick or get too raucous, it won't hurt them, though, so I'm turning a blind eye and so are the hostel people.'

'Probably the best idea,' said Nell, not wanting to admit to the birthday cake Beth had so gleefully smuggled in. 'How about if we meet in the square at quarter past seven and take in the Seven Deadly Sins over a glass of wine?'

'What a good idea. Sinning is always better for a glug of vino.'

Nell enjoyed the performance of the morality plays depicting the Seven Deadly Sins of the early Christian teachings, and she enjoyed

Chloe's company and the wine, which they drank out of disposable plastic cups.

I can forget you for this evening, she said to Andrew in her mind. But I'll tell Michael about you tomorrow. There was great satisfaction at the prospect of relating everything to Michael and knowing he would find it deeply interesting. Nell might even take him into the library so he could read Andrew's journal for himself.

Each morality play was quite short and Nell thought they paid appropriate and enthusiastic tribute to the spirit of the occasion and the revived tradition of the Revels themselves. The plays capered their way through the sins, kicking off with Gluttony, portrayed by a well-upholstered gentleman who dined not too wisely but well, and brandished chicken legs in the manner of Charles Laughton in his famous Henry VIII role, before sliding into an overfed stupor. Sloth came next and featured an actor in a caterpillar-like costume, snoring on a mound covered with what looked like snooker-table baize. This was followed by rather indeterminate depictions of Pride, Wrath and Envy, with Envy suitably clad as the green-eyed monster of jealousy, to a slightly unexpected soundtrack of Queen's *Jealousy*.

At this point Nell had to smother a fit of giggles, which was probably as much due to the wine as to the portly lady, swathed in too-tight green satin, stomping majestically across the stage, beating her breast and tearing her hair. The discovery in the festival programme that the portly lady was none other than the authoritative Olive Orchard, and the further discovery that the wispy Gerald was in the front row wearing an expression of disgruntled embarrassment, discomposed her even further.

'I know it's hysterical,' said Chloe, in a muffled voice, 'but specifically . . .?'

'I'm sorry,' said Nell, struggling for composure. 'I was just imagining Michael's reactions.'

'Ah, the Byronic Dr Flint. Is he joining you here?'

'Yes, he's arriving tomorrow.'

'Half my sixth form swooned over him after he came with you to Beth's end-of-term concert,' said Chloe. 'They think he's half gothic, half romantic, or something. I think he might unknowingly have started a trend. I suspect Oriel College will see a hike in applications next spring. By the way, Beth says you're starting a series of workshops in the New Year. The head's quite interested in that – she thinks we might sign up a couple of batches of students. There's a section of funding we can call on.'

The antique workshop project seemed to be catching fire of its own accord. Nell, pleased, said, 'I'd love to have batches of your students. I'm intending to have some professionals to speak and demonstrate – lecturers in the history of furniture, but restorers and cabinetmakers as well. And I'm going to buy in pieces that need renovating, so it'll all be quite hands-on. I'll let the head have details as soon as they're printed.'

'Sounds good.'

The finale of the morality play series was Lust.

'Which,' murmured Chloe, 'is the one everyone is here to see, of course.'

The festival organizers' idea of Lust owed more to the *Carry On* films or a Henry Fielding *Tom Jones* romp than to the early Christian precepts of a mortal sin, but this did not matter in the least. Scantily clad girls were chased by grinning gentlemen, and a virginal and white-draped heroine was rescued by a knight in Bacofoil armour.

Nell and Chloe thoroughly enjoyed it, and the audience cheered and catcalled. People at the back stood up and shouted ribald comments. The actors took somewhat sheepish bows, the stately Olive Orchard kissed her hand and curtseyed, diva-fashion, the Bacofoil knight brandished his lance enthusiastically, and the audience finally dispersed.

'Great fun,' said Chloe as she and Nell walked back to their respective hotels. 'Thanks for your company.'

'I've enjoyed it. I hope the midnight feast isn't too disruptive,' said Nell.

'I'll only intervene if they start breaking up the furniture.'

Nell left Chloe at the hostel, and walked back to The Swan. It sounded as if the revels were still going on in various parts of the square – there was laughter and delighted squealing from one of the little side streets, and it sounded as if someone was still singing one of the pieces of music from the performance of Lust. Good thing it isn't 'Thaisa's Song', thought Nell with an inward smile. That really would spook me tonight.

She was just walking up to The Swan's oak-beamed front entrance when a new sound shivered on the air, and she paused, and turned her head to listen. What had Andrew written? 'A pulse beating on the air – a sound felt, rather than heard . . . The sounds struck the air dully, each one seeming to leave a bruise . . .'

It's a church clock chiming, thought Nell, determinedly. Ten o'clock. That's all it is. I've been reading too much Gothic prose at the hands of a nineteenth-century monk. And I've had a few glasses of wine into the bargain.

Once inside The Swan the sounds vanished. Nell made a thankful way to her own room. It was quite early, and she considered whether she should type a few notes about Andrew on to the laptop before going to bed. But it had been a long day, and an early night would be good. She would read for half an hour or so – she had brought a couple of books with her. She opened Dorothy L. Sayers' *Gaudy Night*, which was a good travelling companion and always made her think of Michael.

It was after eleven before she finally put down Sayers' and Harriet Vane's gentle scholarly world of academe. As she switched off the bedside light she wondered if Beth's midnight feast had started yet.

From: Olive Orchard
To: Daniel Goodbody

Daniel –

It's 11.30 p.m. – but I had to send you a quick email before going to bed. A pity you couldn't accept my invitation to come in for a nightcap after the evening's events, but of course you have a great deal to do at the moment, I understand that.

Didn't our Morality Plays go *well*! Such enthusiastic applause, and we were all positively smothered with compliments afterwards. I think Gerald is a real old nit-picking killjoy to say the first four rows laughed aloud when Pride forgot his lines halfway through and had to be prompted by Gluttony. It's a gross exaggeration as well, because Pride only stumbled a bit, and Gluttony was swigging down a pint of beer at the time anyway.

Now then, the big news is that Gerald thinks he's found a definite clue to 'Thaisa's Song'. Apparently there's an old nineteenth-century document from St Benedict's monastery which refers specifically to it. The writer was a Brother Andrew, if that means anything to you . . .? The monastery's choirmaster, I think. His memoirs or notes or something were actually in the current library display, only Gerald hadn't read it in full – he says he hasn't time to read every word, for goodness' sake, and he had simply set out some old documents as corroborative detail to give artistic verisimilitude to an otherwise unconvincing narrative. (W. S. Gilbert?). It seems someone came in to see the exhibits and asked if that particular display cabinet could be opened to allow her to read the entire document. They had quite an interesting discussion about it – Gerald says she's an antiques dealer from Oxford. Her name is Nell West, and 'twixt thee and me I think Gerald was rather smitten. I don't mind in the very least bit, of course; Gerald and I have our separate interests – have I told you that before? *Quite* separate.

Anyway, it seems there's a clear reference to a copy of the song being placed in the monks' library – specifically behind a shelf of books on church music. You'll know, of course, that the entire contents of that library were brought out for preservation when the building was steam-rollered in the mid-1970s. Such a pity that the area lost another piece of Rede Abbas's history, although I believe the building had become unsound (wretched English Channel creeping up on us and destroying our coast-lines!), and there was no alternative.

So Gerald is currently bustling around the house like a demented earwig, saying he won't be able to sleep a wink tonight, and he'll be off out to the library at crack of dawn to search the monastery papers and books stored in the cellars. (I swear Gerald spends more time in those cellars than he does anywhere else). But if he finds the song, he intends to distribute copies to the choir. If he can do that by nine a.m. tomorrow, he says they'll have a good three hours' rehearsal, and we can make an announcement at the start of the evening's concert, telling the audience it's about to hear music (and lyrics, I presume) that haven't been sung or performed in public for the best part of five hundred years. I pointed out that (a) 'Thaisa's Song' is generally supposed to be in quite ancient Welsh, which might faze even the most enthusiastic modern chorist, that (b) the programme is already arranged, not to mention printed, and that (c) we can't go shoe-horning in an extra item a few hours beforehand. But Gerald says phooey and pish, the whole thing won't take more than ten minutes to perform and will be a splendid finale.

If you happen to pick this up before going to bed, I'd be glad to hear from you. Do feel free to ring, and also I'll leave the laptop switched on for the next hour or so. I'm also wondering if somebody ought to warn Maeve Eynon that we could be on the verge of actually performing her private and particular bane. What do you think? She did seem really upset at the prospect.

What a long email! But I had to bring you properly up to date.

All best,

Olive

From: Daniel Goodbody
To: Olive Orchard

Olive – it's almost midnight, so I didn't like to ring you.

It's a slightly strange-feeling midnight, as well – I'd swear I heard the old bell chiming a short while earlier. Probably it was just a church clock from Puddleston or St Mary Abbas, though.

Please try to dissuade Gerald from disinterring 'Thaisa's Song' for tomorrow night! I definitely remember we all agreed to have a good rousing piece of music for the finale – something in which everybody could join, although at this hour of the night (and without looking out my notes), I can't remember if we decided on 'Land of Hope and Glory' like the last night of the Proms, or 'All You Need Is Love'.

I'm afraid he's also being a tad optimistic about the choir's abilities. They're good, but I shouldn't think they're so good they can learn and perform a 500-year-old song after only a couple of hours' rehearsal. Particularly not if it's in ancient Welsh and with dear old Mr Budd conducting them, because he's as likely to tumble off the rostrum as to draw an ancient Welsh lament out of a group of modern-day singers.

You'd better let me know if Gerald does find this wretched

song. As you say, in sheer humanity, somebody will have to let Maeve Eynon know if it really is going to be performed, and I suppose that somebody had better be me.
Daniel.

From: Olive Orchard
To: Daniel Goodbody

Daniel, I've just spent fifteen minutes trying to talk Gerald out of his proposed search for 'Thaisa's Song' (at this rate none of us will get any sleep tonight), and I've put all your points to him.

He won't be dissuaded, though. He says we should have flexible minds, and that Mozart (or perhaps it was Beethoven) often handed out final orchestral parts before a performance with the ink still wet on the pages, and Shakespeare and Ben Jonson thought nothing of penning the last scene of a play while the actors were on stage performing the first one to the audience. (I feel this could be something of an exaggeration, although I suppose much can be forgiven Elizabethan geniuses.)

To answer your question about the closing music, we went for 'All You Need Is Love', on the grounds that it can go on for as long (or as little) as the audience want. There were objections that it was too modern, but somebody pointed out that it's a universal message and everyone knows the chorus. The only suitably Elizabethan alternative anyone could think of was either 'Greensleeves' (beautiful but impossibly over-used), a composition by John Dowland (beautiful but very religious), or one of the bawdier sixteenth-century ballads (lively but extremely irreligious, and we have to remember there will be children present).

Curiously, I heard that chiming bell too. It'll certainly have been from St Mary Abbas, though. It can sometimes be heard if the wind is in a certain direction.

Olive

THIRTEEN

Michael Flint contemplated his Saturday with pleasure. He was looking forward to travelling to Rede Abbas and to being with Nell. He was even looking forward to the train journey.

First, though, he dealt with the newest Wilberforce instalment, emailing it to his editor at a quarter to eight, after which he logged off very firmly, because Saturdays meant nothing to his editor. Michael had once received a request on Easter Sunday to condense two chapters into one on the grounds of production costs and the shocking price of paper, along with a plea that the work be done by Tuesday evening so the typesetters could start work as soon as they returned from their long weekend.

Jack Hurst, rather surprisingly, rang him five minutes later.

'Dr Flint, I'm not calling too early, am I?'

'Not at all.' Michael remembered Nell saying something about shelving or flooring being fitted in the shop over the weekend. 'Is anything wrong?'

'Well, you might say it is. Only I don't want to trouble Nell – Mrs West – what with her being all the way in Dorset and not wanting to spoil her weekend—'

'What's wrong?'

There was a pause, then Jack Hurst said, 'I can't explain over the phone. Could you possibly come over to Quire Court?'

'Now?'

'Yes, now.'

Quire Court, when Michael reached it, was still wreathed in an early morning hush. He parked the car and went across to Nell's shop. Jack Hurst was waiting for him, his usually healthy, amiable face pallid and distressed.

'Jack, what on earth's happened?'

'You'd better come and see for yourself,' said Jack, leading Michael through Nell's part of the building and beyond the wide archway that now linked Nell's shop to Godfrey's. Michael had just time to register that Hurst was making a very nice job of the conversion.

'It'll come as a shock,' said Jack, pushing open the door to a small storeroom. 'I'm sorry, but I can't find the words to explain – I did try on the phone, but it's upset me so much—'

'My God, you haven't found a body, have you?' said Michael, trying for a lighter note.

Jack Hurst said, 'That's just what I have found.' He pushed the door wide.

The storeroom was windowless, but a thin light came in from the main shop and Michael saw clearly what lay in a hollow in the partly broken-up floor.

Small. Impossibly and heartbreakingly small and vulnerable. The skeleton of a tiny child – a baby surely? It was lying on its back, the head turned slightly to one side. As if it was looking towards the door, thought Michael, through a scalding tumble of emotions. As if it wanted to watch the light for as long as it could. And its hand – oh God, one of its hands is lifted, and the finger bones are splayed out like a tiny starfish. Exactly as if . . .

Exactly as if the tiny creature had tried to push away the earth covering it.

He became aware that Jack was saying something about digging up the floor. 'I started on it first thing, see, smashing up the stone flags, because that Darren's bringing the oak strips to lay down, before we get on with the shelves. Only then—'

'You uncovered this.'

'Like a grave, isn't it?' said Hurst. 'That poor little soul laid there, wrapped in a cloth – although it's no more than strings of fabric by now, as you see – and a crucifix with it, and a small book. Prayer book, I should think.'

Michael had already seen the book. He said, 'Jack, we need to phone the police. This has obviously been under the floor for years – centuries, I should think – but I'm sure the police have to be called in for any kind of body.'

'Would you phone them, Dr Flint? I'll only start filling up again – you'd think I'd have more self-control, wouldn't you, but I look at that little heap of bones, and I start thinking of my own kids – there's a granddaughter now, did you know?'

'I didn't know. That's a very happy thing to hear, though—'

'And I've been thinking about when they were this tiny and helpless,' said Jack. 'And I keep looking at the way that hand's lifted – you can see it, can't you? Almost as if when it was laid in there it wasn't—'

'Yes.' Don't say it, thought Michael. Because if you say the words, that might make it real. He said, 'It'll be the way the earth fell when it was shovelled in. It would have heaped up and displaced the arm.'

'It would be that, wouldn't it?' said Jack, eagerly. 'And there could have been subsidence in a building this old. That'd cause a bit of movement.'

'I'm sure it would,' said Michael, who had only the haziest idea of what subsidence was, and an even hazier idea of what it might do.

'But,' said Jack, 'I keep thinking how I nearly put the hammer straight through the poor little thing's skull— I couldn't know it was there, though, could I?'

'Of course you couldn't. Don't think about it,' said Michael, but his own mind had already seen, and shuddered from, the image of the hammer smashing down on the fragile skull.

'And if I have to say all that to the police, I'll get that upset, and they'll think, Well, what a soft prat Jack Hurst is, silly old fool.'

'They won't think that; they'll be used to people being upset over – over bodies,' said Michael. 'In any case, it's much nicer to have feelings and emotions. Jack, if the power's on in Nell's shop, go through and put the kettle on and we'll have a cup of tea while we wait for the police. I'll call them now while you do that.'

Because there's the book, said his mind. I need to see the book before anyone else.

He made the phone call first, though, explaining as well as he could what had been found, having to break off once because, as Jack had described it, he too was filling up with emotion. Who were you? he said to the small shape lying patiently there.

The police were helpful and reassuring. Dr Flint would be surprised how often this kind of thing happened in old properties, they said.

'We often say there's a whole library of books you could write about the mysteries that get found in old houses,' said the sympathetic sergeant who answered the phone. 'Except that mostly they never get solved. But we'll need to send out a forensic team – no, it doesn't make any difference that it's an old skeleton, we still have to try to identify it. Or to put a date to it at the very least. It's a long procedure, and of course it's not something that gets priority. But everything'll be done respectfully, Dr Flint, you can be sure of that.'

'Thank you very much,' said Michael, gratefully. 'Do you want me to wait here? I'm supposed to be catching a train later this morning, but I can probably delay that a bit.'

'Well, we'll send someone out right away to get the initial details and photographs. Could you wait there for that? If we can make the site secure until Monday—'

'I should think you can,' said Michael. 'The shop's got a security system and so on.'

'Sounds good. In that case, forensics can most likely come out on Monday and you can catch your train this morning.'

The small bones of the arm and hand had fallen back and were lying alongside the fragile little ribs. Michael was deeply grateful for this. Probably he had hit the right explanation when he had told Jack the piled-up earth had pushed the arm into that reaching-out position. This would be a case of a child who had died a few hours after its birth, or even been stillborn, with parents who could not afford a conventional funeral and burial. The fact that the crucifix and prayer book had been laid with the little body indicated care and love, and the absence of malice or violence.

Even so, it felt like a desecration to reach down to the small, faded book. It would almost certainly prove to be what Jack Hurst had thought – a prayer book, laid with the child when the makeshift grave was created, and Michael would show it to the police when they arrived. But if a king's ransom had been at stake, he could not have left it there without looking at it.

The book left behind its imprint and it also disturbed a faint flurry of something sweet and sad. Lavender, thought Michael, seeing the tiny grey flowers lying beneath. Whoever had put the book and the crucifix there had placed some sprigs of lavender there as well.

Lavender. One of the holy herbs used in the temple in Biblical times. Called *nardus* by the ancients, mentioned in the Song of Solomon. The lines, imperfectly remembered, brushed against his mind. Something about, 'Nard and saffron, calamus and cinnamon . . . And every kind of incense tree . . .'

Whoever had laid this tiny scrap of humanity here had cared enough to lay not only the crucifix alongside it, but also to sprinkle the holy herbs of the ancients over the little body. And then had added the book.

The book was very old indeed. The cover was thin and soft, and the pages were so severely foxed they had assumed the shade of tanned leather. When he opened the book, using extreme care, the writing leapt up at him, faded, spidery, the crammed, crabbed script of at least three centuries earlier.

What had Nell said? That she and Beth weren't expecting to find a first-folio Shakespeare or an undiscovered Chaucer in the baked-bean carton. This would not be either, of course, and yet . . . Michael carried it out to the main part of the shop and sat down on a windowsill to study it. He could no longer hear the usual street noises, nor could he hear Jack Hurst rattling cups and saucers. The shop seemed to have fallen into a deep silence, and there was the impression of something fragile and cobwebbed being drawn aside. Other scents were overlaying the aura of newly sawn timber and freshly applied plaster – the scents of ancient furniture, which had stood in the sun for so many decades it had soaked up the warmth . . . And the lavender, he thought. Don't forget the lavender, the holy herb of the temple.

Above all of that, though, was the scent of forgotten vellum-bound books, crusted with age and scholarship; of long-ago memories confided to lost diaries . . .

With extreme care he opened the first page, and was instantly aware of sharp disappointment. He could read the date at the top, which he saw with a leap of excitement was 1538, but he also saw that he would not be able to read much more. The writing was too spidery, too elaborate – too sixteenth century, thought Michael, torn between frustration and annoyance. Damn and blast, if I sit here for the next week, I won't be able to decipher more than a few fragments of this.

Odd words and phrases stood out, though. The name Seamus at the foot of the first page. The same name was on the next page, but this time it was written as Brother Seamus. On the same line was the word *monastery*. On the next page, clear as a curse, was the unmistakable name of Cromwell.

Cromwell. 1538. And a monastery. The three things came together in Michael's mind, because surely that was the era when the greedy, ambitious Thomas Cromwell had rampaged across the English countryside, ransacking the monasteries, his men looting the great treasure-houses of the religious fraternities. And it had all been in the name and in the service of a king of England – an England already poised on the brink of reform – but a king who gave that reform a hard push, because he intended to have Anne Boleyn in his bed, even if it meant slaughtering monks wholesale and burning alive any who dared say him nay. Henry ap Tudor: extravagant, wayward, arrogant sprig of a line that some whispered were usurpers. Henry VIII, King of England, Defender of the Faith.

As he turned a couple of the pages with extreme care, Michael shivered slightly. It was all very well to make light-hearted jokes about Quire Court being haunted, and paint cartoon word-pictures for Beth about amiable ghosts, but what he was feeling now was on a different level. It was deep and chilling. He set the book down with as much care as if it really might be an undiscovered Shakespearean manuscript, and was grateful when the present came back into focus in the shape of a car pulling up outside, and then a voice calling to know if it could come in, and announcing itself as DS Cherry.

Michael had thought the shop would have to be smothered in police paraphernalia and girdled with official tape saying things like, Crime Scene, Do Not Cross, with men stomping around in plastic suits and paper boots. He was more than half expecting that he would have put his departure to Rede Abbas even further back, but the police were surprisingly quick to appear, and dealt with the initial examinations very promptly. There was a team of three: DS Cherry, to whom Michael had spoken on the phone, a young forensic technician who looked as if he might be on work experience, but turned out to be extremely knowledgeable, and a uniformed constable who made careful notes. The forensic technician took photographs and measurements and soil scrapings, and Michael found himself willing the man not to say it looked as if there could have been movement after the soil and the stone slab were laid over the body.

To avoid this possibility, he said to DS Cherry, 'And there's this. We found it next to the child.' He held out the book.

'What . . .?'

'I'm not sure what it is,' said Michael. 'It's handwritten, but all I can make out is the date: 1538. And an odd word here and there. I'm inclined to suggest to you that I contact a colleague from Oriel who's very knowledgeable about this era.' He said this firmly, but he had had to remind himself that he was a senior member of an Oxford University, and that his advice about an early Tudor document would be respected.

'That'd be very helpful, Dr Flint,' said DS Cherry at once. 'We're not used to handling such valuable items, and we'd never hear the last of it if it got damaged. But we'll get photos if you don't mind, and make a few notes. And if I could have the name of the colleague—'

'Dr Owen Bracegirdle,' said Michael, reaching for his phone.

After phoning Owen, he called Nell. Her phone went straight to voicemail, so Michael left a message, explaining as well as he could what had happened, and that the ten o'clock train was now nothing but a fond memory.

'But there's one shortly after eleven that I should be able to get – it'll be a bit of a scramble, but I think I can make it. I'll phone once I'm actually on it, and let you know when it gets in. Hope you can still pick me up at Axminster.'

After this, he drove back to College, with the book on the passenger seat. Every few moments he stretched out his left hand to touch it, as reverently as if it were an update of the Rosetta Stone, or the codex that would decipher the universe's secrets.

For the first time it occurred to him that the ownership might have to be debated in the weeks ahead. Michael had no idea whether the book rightfully belonged to Godfrey, as the former owner of that part of the premises, or whether Nell, as the new leaseholder of both units, could be considered the owner, or even whether Christ Church College, as the freeholders, would weigh in with their own claim. Christ Church would undoubtedly find the idea of owning a sixteenth-century journal very seductive indeed.

Owen was waiting for Michael in his own rooms, and demanded to know what was happening. 'Because you were as cagy on the phone as if you thought the whole of MI6 was listening in. I thought you were going into darkest Dorset this morning. And this had better be good, Michael, because I've got a pile of second-year essays to read this morning, never mind a lunchtime meeting of . . . Good God, what's that you're brandishing?'

'I don't know yet.' Michael set down the book on a relatively clear space of Owen's desk. 'It seems to be sixteenth century – there's even a date on the first page – and to me it looks genuine. But for all I know it could be a William Ireland-type forgery or a manuscript version of Piltdown Man. But whatever it is,' he said, 'it was found in the shallow, unhallowed grave of a child who probably died over four hundred years ago.'

Owen stared at him. 'As a hook to reel in an unprepared listener, that probably rates as one of the best I've ever heard.'

'I can't help it, it's the truth. The date written on the first page is 1538, and,' said Michael, 'the writing doesn't look as if it's all in English. So between that and the medieval script, I can't read more than an occasional word.'

'It certainly looks sixteenth century.' Owen spoke with the scepticism proper to any historian, but as he sat down at the desk and turned a few pages, his eyes were bright with excitement.

'Can you decipher it?'

'Well, not right off. I can make out a few phrases . . .' Owen bent over the pages, frowning, pushing his glasses more firmly on to his nose. 'Whoever wrote it was frightened – on this page at any rate. There's something about, "Terror is filling up the room, and this must be done before anyone finds us." I'm paraphrasing that, and I might not have hit the exact phrasing—'

'Any more?' said Michael, as Owen pored over the page.

'I think this line says, "I never thought to be in a place like Glaum's Acre, or to be performing the task we are about to perform . . ." Glaum's Acre? Wasn't that on the deeds for Quire Court? The original name?'

'Yes.'

'And there's a reference here to Cromwell – my God, Michael, with that date of 1538 this would mean Thomas Cromwell.' He looked up. 'This is from the era of the suppression of the monasteries.'

'And,' said Michael, 'the word monastery leaps out on the first page. I did make that out, if nothing else.' He indicated the line.

'You're right. If this is genuine,' said Owen, sitting back, 'it could be worth . . . Well, it'd be priceless.'

'I know. I've squared it with the police, and they're happy with me having it and keeping it here. I've given them your name as well. I've left a message with Nell, and I'll phone Godfrey later. I don't know who can be classed as the owner, but I shouldn't think either of them will mind you taking a preliminary look at it. So keep reading.'

'I'll have to spend time on it,' said Owen. 'Compare the lettering with accredited contemporary examples, and so on.' He was still poring over the faded, crabbed writing, and Michael knew he would not want to move away from the book for a very long time. 'Wait, though, there's something here about the monastery being a hospital order, and the monks hoping to be safe from the Commissioners. That strikes an authentic note, because a few of the religious infirmaries were spared during dissolution. Still, any forger worth his salt would know that and throw it into the mix, so we won't get carried away. There are a fair few Latin phrases as well, so it'd be a case of disentangling them and translating them. And if it's Ecclesiastical Latin, which I think it is, it'll take a bit of time. In fact it almost looks like medieval Latin – maybe even from what's called the Silver Age.'

'Would Latin be unusual for the era? In a document like this, I mean?'

'It looks like what I'd term a domestic document as opposed to an official or a legal one,' said Owen. 'So Latin would be unusual, but not out of the question. That date was a kind of crossover period for the country. Catholicism was being ground under foot, and Latin – Ecclesiastical Latin especially – was the language of the Church. People of any learning tended to use it in documents. Silver Age Latin is rarer, though. But again, it'd be a good forger's ploy.'

'The grave and the body didn't look forged,' said Michael, and Owen glanced at him.

'Upsetting, I should think.'

'Very.'

Owen merely nodded, and bent over the page again. 'If we can trust the surface evidence, I'd say the writer was used to employing a mixture of English and Latin when writing anything. Or came from a background where both were used. But language changes, as you know; it's a live thing. I can probably get most of this, but it might need a real expert. And don't quote the hoary old line about an expert merely being someone who lives more than fifty miles away – you know what I mean. The paper would have to be subjected to the usual tests,' said Owen. 'Carbon-dating and x-rays and so on. Ink's difficult to date, of course, although there's something called chromatography–mass spectroscopy – I don't know a great deal about it, because it's a *very* highly specialist field.'

'I can leave it with you though, can't I? I mean – you can lock it safely away somewhere? I didn't want the police to take it and just shovel it into an evidence bag, and I don't want to leave it in my rooms while I'm away. I certainly don't want to take it to Dorset.'

'Of course you can leave it here,' said Owen. 'I'll guard it with my life and my virtue; in fact I'm likely to be sitting up all night working on it. And if it turns out that we do need an expert, I'd suggest contacting Brant. It's very much his field and he's very good. He helped with the *Carmina Cantabrigiensia* – the Cambridge Song Cycle – when they discovered several new ones, and he'd fall on this and devour it.'

'Sounds good. Can you really not get any more from it?'

'I don't think so. Although there is just one corner here—'

'Yes?'

'At the bottom of this page, the writer says, "To drive out the fear and the pain, I have been singing my family's song – it is familiar and comforting . . . No one here will understand the words, just as no one at Rede Abbas did . . ." Rede Abbas,' said Owen, staring at Michael. 'That's where Nell is now. That's where you're going.'

'Yes.' Michael stared down at the corner of the page.

'Underneath that is another line, crammed in quite tightly,' said Owen.

'As if the writer was in a hurry, or not wanting someone to see?'

'More likely trying to save paper,' said Owen, caustically. 'It's quite difficult to read it and probably I'm getting it wrong, because—'

'What?'

'Well,' said Owen, 'it's a curious statement, and it doesn't make complete sense to me. But I think that what it says is this. "If they find me, I shall die as well. The dead bell was sounding even as we left, and it is never left hungry, that bell".'

FOURTEEN

Nell slept deeply and dreamlessly in the soft wide bed, woke up to soft early sunlight, and contemplated with pleasure the prospect that she would be waking up in this bed tomorrow morning with Michael next to her.

The dining room provided a delicious, disgracefully unhealthy breakfast, which Nell thoroughly enjoyed. She wondered if Beth and her friends had managed their midnight feast, and hoped that if they had, it had not been too indigestible. But when she checked her phone, there was an exuberant text from Beth, shamelessly timed at one a.m., reporting a double-brilliant feast; they had eaten absolutely everything, somebody had dropped a piece of birthday cake and trodden in it, so they had had to sneak out to find cloths and soapy water to clean it up.

Nell grinned, sent a suitable reply, and having finished her breakfast collected her jacket and shoulder bag. She considered taking the car, but she wanted to investigate the narrow side streets, and perhaps even walk towards the cliffs to see if she could identify the places Andrew had written about, so the car might not be practical. She would enjoy a brisk walk, anyway. The helpful receptionist at the desk provided directions to the cliff paths, and gave Nell a tide table.

'It's hotel policy to make sure guests have them when they walk along that path,' she said. 'But it's low tide at the moment, and it won't turn for several hours, so you aren't likely to be in any danger.'

It was still quite early, and the next Revels event was not until midday, when there was some kind of dancing display. Nell did not particularly want to see that; she would rather try to peel back a little more of Rede Abbas's past. Cliff House should be easy enough to identify – it was almost certainly the gloomy building she and Beth had seen on the way here. It sounded as if Andrew's monastery had been quite close to it, along with the old graveyard and the Glaum mausoleum.

She followed the hotel's directions, and after about ten minutes' walking found herself beyond the little cluster of shops and the straggle of houses, with a narrow road ahead, signposted, 'To The Coast'. It was uneven and rutted, just about wide enough for a car, but probably primarily a walkers' path. It was quite steep, and twice Nell had to pause to catch her breath. Good exercise, though, said to elevate the heart-rate and send the blood scudding around the system. She would bring Michael up here tomorrow. He would probably pause several times, pretending to be searching for an apt quotation while he got his breath back. Dear Michael.

The path snaked around tortuously, and Nell began to lose her bearings slightly, although there was no danger of getting lost, because it was a single track. Then a final corkscrew turn brought her into sight of the clifftop house.

Theodora's house, thought Nell, standing still and looking towards it. Thaisa's house as well, presumably. She could see the old graveyard, as well, now. Even from this distance it looked sad and abandoned, the headstones mostly askew with age or subsidence of the ground, a thin mist clinging to the sparse trees.

It looked as if people still lived in the clifftop house – even from here Nell could make out curtains at the windows, and the gardens looked neat and well tended. There was no reason why she could not walk past the house, giving it a cursory glance, then go on to the graveyard. She would see if the Glaum mausoleum still existed.

She set off again, but as she did so she heard someone coming down the path towards her. Whoever it was, was hidden from view by the bend, but Nell was suddenly uncomfortably aware of the path's loneliness. She glanced behind her, prepared to retreat as fast as was possible on the rutted slope, then a woman came into view, and she relaxed, because this was such a very ordinary, unthreatening figure. The woman was thin and wore a flapping raincoat, with wellingtons and a sou'wester. Her face was weatherbeaten and her shoulders were bowed, as if she was accustomed to hunching them against the strong sea winds. Nondescript hair straggled out from beneath the sou'wester's brim.

The path was sufficiently narrow to make it impossible to pass by without some cursory acknowledgement, so Nell smiled and said, 'Good morning.'

The woman hesitated, then said, 'Good morning. You startled me. It's not often I meet anyone on this path.'

'I'm exploring,' said Nell. 'I'm here for the Revels, but I'm interested in local history.' She was slightly annoyed with herself for appearing to provide an explanation of her presence, but the woman seemed friendly and, if she was local, she might know a bit about the surroundings, so Nell said, 'I'm quite intrigued by that place,' and indicated the clifftop house.

'That's Cliff House,' said the woman. 'Actually, I live there.'

Nell looked at her with more attention. Theodora's house, she thought. The place where she played 'Thaisa's Song', and where Andrew listened to it and fell in love with her – or at the very least, in lust with her.

'Really?' she said. 'I've already found a couple of references to it, so it's interesting to be actually seeing it in the flesh – and to meet someone who lives in it.' She was careful not to say any more – this stranger might not know about Theodora, and it would be unkind to tell her a murder had happened in her house. And she had said, '*I* live there,' not, '*We* live there,' as if she might live alone.

But the words seemed to have struck an unwelcome chord anyway, because the woman was looking at Nell so intensely that Nell felt a shiver of apprehension.

Then she said, 'References to it do crop up now and again in old documents, I believe. It's very old, you see – a good deal older than it looks from the outside. Bits have been added on, and things have been patched up.' In a rather offhand voice, she said, 'Did you say you'd found some reference to it?'

'I think it was part of a kind of journal,' said Nell. 'Written by a monk who was at the old monastery here in the mid-nineteenth century. Brother Andrew, he was called.'

The woman had been staring down the track, but she looked sharply back at Nell. Her eyes, partly shaded by the sou'wester, were a curious light shade, as if something had washed all the vitality from them. It was probably Nell's imagination to think there was sudden enmity in the expression.

'That would be St Benedict's Monastery,' said the woman, after a moment. 'It was demolished – oh, a good forty years ago. I didn't know any documents were brought out.'

'It was only a few pages,' said Nell. 'Part of a display in the library. I got the impression the librarian had only recently found it. Andrew seems to have been the monastery's music master.'

'Precentor,' said the woman, at once. 'That's what they'd have called it. Look here, if you're interested in Cliff House, why don't you walk back up with me? I'm Miss Eynon, by the way. Maeve Eynon.'

Nell had been about to make a polite refusal, but at these words she felt as if hands had reached out to pull her forward. It had not occurred to her that Theodora's family might still be in the area, even less that they might still live in the same house. This woman, this Maeve, had to be Theodora's descendant. The name was too unusual for it to be anything other than the same family.

She said, eagerly, 'I'm Nell West. But Eynon – spelled EYNON? That's a name that's mentioned in Brother Andrew's journal. Would it be the same family?'

'I should think so. The family's lived here for centuries. Rather unadventurous of my ancestors never to move away, really.'

'But marvellous if you want to trace their history,' said Nell.

'I suppose so. I've never thought about it much. The journal you found sounds interesting, though. I'm intrigued to find the family gets a mention. Did he – Brother Andrew, did you say? – did he write anything about his work as Precentor?' There was the tiniest pause. 'I'm rather fond of music, you see,' said Maeve Eynon.

For a moment Nell was not sure how much to say, but the journal had been on public display, and the woman could go down to the library and read it for herself if she wanted. So she said, 'He mentioned some of the music he arranged for various religious festival. Choral stuff, mostly. And there was something—'

'Yes?'

'Something about a very old song,' said Nell, choosing her words with care. 'It sounded as if it was something local.'

There was no doubt about the reaction this time. The light eyes flinched as if suddenly faced with a blinding light, then Maeve Eynon said, 'That all sounds a bit gothic. Diaries found in a monastery library and an old piece of music.'

'I shouldn't think the music survived. Andrew just says he left it in the monks' library, although the librarian – Mr Orchard, isn't it? – said he was going to see if it was in some old papers that were brought out of the monastery when it was pulled down.'

'He would,' said Maeve Eynon, and she seemed to take a deep

breath, and stand a little straighter, almost as if preparing to take a great weight.

'I should think it's more likely that the music didn't survive demolition,' said Nell.

'Yes,' said Maeve Eynon. 'I should think so, too.'

She began to walk back up the cliff path, and Nell found herself falling into step with her. She was slightly wary, but in the forefront of her mind was that she was talking to Theodora's descendant, and that Maeve might know more about Theodora.

The track widened out slightly and Nell glanced towards the cliff edge, wondering how close they were to the bell tower. As if noticing, Maeve Eynon said, 'We could cut across that bit of hillside on the right to reach the house. There's a footpath somebody created about thirty years ago. Something to do with the gypsies who camp on Musselwhite's Meadow every summer.' She pointed. 'Or we could keep on this path which would take us past the old bell tower. It's very much a local landmark and legend, and if you're interested in local history . . .?'

'I'd like to see the bell tower,' said Nell, after a moment. She had already decided to remember an appointment that would take her back down to the village and preclude her from actually going inside Cliff House with this unknown woman, but she was curious about the bell tower. And there could be no harm in walking a little further.

They went down the narrow path to the cliff ledge, and Maeve pointed. 'There,' she said. 'Just below us.'

Nell stared down at the tower, and Maeve Eynon said, softly, 'It's impressive, isn't it? A good half of it's submerged at every high tide, you know. We can get just a bit nearer if you like.'

'Is it safe?'

'Oh yes, if you know the area and the tides,' said Maeve. 'The tide's out at the moment, and the tower isn't dangerous, providing you don't get trapped in there. It's very eerie, though. Children egg each other on to go up to it, and teenagers have ghost-hunts. You know the kind of thing.'

'Yes,' said Nell, remembering Beth's teasing threat to come out here at midnight. A vampire tower, she had called it. A *Twilight* tower.

'The local council keep putting up signs and fences, but they never last very long,' said Maeve. She made a vague gesture at the cliff's edge, and Nell saw for the first time that iron railings enclosed part of the ledge. 'What vandals don't destroy, the sea does. And if fences fall down, the council are always too busy or haven't got the funds to replace them.' She began to walk down the path towards the tower and, after a moment, Nell followed.

The tower walls were stone; they were black and worn, and there were huge discoloured patches which was probably the sea's constant lashing, but which made it look as if some inner disease had leaked its poison. As they reached the ledge itself, the tower loomed higher above them than Nell had expected. She looked up at the bell chamber. The thought of the massive silent bell – the dead bell Andrew had believed he heard that night – was chilling.

'No one can get to the upper levels,' said Maeve, following Nell's gaze. 'Part of the stairs have crumbled away, but nobody's ever bothered to repair them – I don't think anyone knows who the place belongs to any longer. The National Trust came to look at it years ago, but they said they couldn't take it on because it's on such a dangerous part of the cliff and it probably wouldn't last much longer anyway. But no one wants to tear it down, because it's a kind of landmark. A bit of Rede Abbas's history.'

'I can understand that,' said Nell. She stared up at the tower, then rather unwillingly walked a few paces closer. It brought her into line with the side of the tower that faced the sea, and this time when she looked up, horror swept over her. Mist clung to the tower's sides, but through the mists a face stared down from the ancient stones – a face that was ancient and blind, and terrible in its implacable stare . . .

Nell gasped and took an involuntary step back, because the stone face was monstrous, menacing – a giantess's face, forever gazing out to sea, blind and remote, and terrible.

'What's wrong?'

'What on earth is that?' said Nell, pointing a bit shakily.

'It's the stone figure,' said Maeve Eynon. 'It's carved into the side of the tower. It's not really visible from the landside, so most people don't see it unless they walk all round.'

'It's malevolent,' said Nell, staring at the figure with repulsion, seeing through the sea mists that there was, indeed, a complete figure. 'What – who – does it represent?'

'No one knows. It is malevolent though, I agree with you. At high tide – the really high one, I mean – the figure is completely submerged. I've always found it a bit uncanny to imagine it staring into the under-sea world for hours every day.'

Nell said, 'It's more than uncanny.' She walked determinedly back to the tower's inland side, and saw that Maeve had gone up to the tower's door. It was small and black with age, and there were what looked like iron staves around the edges. Maeve reached out to the iron ring handle, and Nell said quickly, 'Oh, please don't open it.'

'It's stuck anyway. Oh no, wait, it's yielding,' she said, and Nell saw the handle turn around and door give way.

She said, 'I really have to be getting back.'

'So do I. Although now we're here— I haven't been inside the bell tower since I was a child. I once did a school project about it – I wonder if it's as spooky as I remember.' She pushed the door wider and Nell winced at the screech of the old hinges. Maeve peered inside. 'Oh, my goodness—'

'What is it?'

'Do come and look at this. Someone must have left it. How extraordinary.'

'What have you found?' Nell wanted nothing more than to get back to the village and The Swan, but common politeness forced her to walk up to the partly open door and look inside. A dank stench gusted into her face – dead fish and the dregs of the sea. She shuddered, and made to step back, but without warning small, hard hands thrust into her shoulders and pushed her forwards. She stumbled against the hard edge of the door, and let out a cry, at the same time trying to regain her balance. But a second push came, harder and more vicious this time, and Nell fell forward on the damp stone floor of the tower.

There was a scrabble of sound, and the dreadful wizened creak of ancient hinges. The door of the tower was slammed and there was the sound of the handle being turned on the other side.

The sunlight shut off and the dreadful rancid stench of the sea closed sickeningly around Nell.

FIFTEEN

At first Nell thought it was a mistake. She thought Maeve Eynon had tripped and grabbed at the door to stop herself falling, sending Nell tumbling forward, and then accidentally slamming the door.

She scrambled up from the ground at once, but falling had made her slightly dizzy and the sudden shutting off of the light had disoriented her. She stood for a moment, waiting for her eyes to adjust to the dimness, and gradually the door's outline became visible. It was not so very dark after all; light trickled in from the stairs. Treading warily Nell went thankfully to the door. It had opened inwards – she remembered that clearly – but there would be a handle or a latch to turn the ring handle from this side and pull it inward.

But there was not. Nell frowned, then thought it was too dark to see properly, and reached out to feel all round the door's edge. The old wood was faintly damp and it felt repellent, but she forced herself to explore all round the edges. There was no handle. Nell tried again, examining the whole door, and this time her hands found an oblong plate on the left-hand side, with four – no, six – screws or nails. It was about the right place for a handle or a latch; the trouble was that there was no handle or latch there now. She felt for a spring within the plate that might release the handle, but there was nothing and she stepped back from the door, quelling panic. Maeve Eynon would open the door at any minute, of course, and in an hour – probably less – Nell would be in her bedroom at The Swan, showering and shampooing away the disgusting smell of this place.

But there was no sound from the door or from beyond it. Nell stood as close to it as she could, and shouted.

'Miss Eynon? Maeve? I can't get the door open. Let me out!'

Nothing. She banged hard on the door, bruising her fists, and shouted again. 'If this is a joke, it's a very bad one. Open the door, for goodness' sake!'

Her words echoed dully in the enclosed space, but still there were no sounds from outside – no shouts of apology or reassurance from Maeve Eynon. It was almost starting to look as if this had not been an accident. Had the woman known the door could not be opened from inside? When she said, 'Come and look at this', had she been luring Nell into the tower so she could imprison her? There was certainly nothing of any interest to see in here – only the small stone room with the marks left by the sea. Scatterings of salt glistened faintly, and there were slimy ribbons of sea plants in places, and scatterings of shells that might once have enclosed tiny creatures.

Maeve Eynon could not have shut Nell in here deliberately. They had only met that morning, and they had had the briefest, most casual conversation. Unless, of course, Maeve Eynon was mad. But this was so wild a theory that Nell discarded it immediately.

There was no real need to panic. If Maeve did not open the door soon, all Nell had to do was phone for help. She delved into her shoulder bag for her phone, then paused. It seemed a bit extreme to call 999 for a stuck door, but she could not think who else to call, and she was beyond caring if she brought out the entire Dorset constabulary and the complete range of emergency services, providing she escaped from this noisome place. The phone's screen lit, and she tapped out the number. It was slightly disconcerting to encounter silence, and Nell tapped the number again. This time the screen flashed a message, greenish in the uncertain light, but dreadfully legible. Nell stared at it in horrified disbelief. *No signal.*

She walked all the way round the small chamber, holding the phone up in the hope of picking up a signal, trying the number over and over. Nothing. Only the infuriating impotency of those two words. *No signal.*

It would be all right, though. She would get a signal eventually; she just had to keep trying. But she looked about her at the thick walls of the bell tower which might well block a mobile signal permanently – and remembered that this was the very edge of England's south coast, and that it was entirely possible that there was no mobile signal out here at all.

All right, so what now? There would be a way out of this. She would laugh about it later – tonight, with Michael, certainly. She would make a good story of it for him. She looked across the small room to the worn stone steps that would lead up to the bell chamber.

Even if she had to climb up those steps, all the way up to the tower's top and yell for help through the openings, or throw stones at cliff walkers, she would get out. That would make an even better story to recount. I was up there with the bats in the belfry, she would say. There was also the point that she might get a signal up there.

She crossed the room to the steps. Light was filtering down, and it was easier to see her way than she had expected. She tried to remember if there had been any windows nearer to the ground than the bell chamber, and could not. The stairs were steep and worn, and although bits of rotting rope hung from iron staves, she did not trust either the rope or the staves to be secure. But the light reminded her that it was broad daylight outside and the real world was not far away.

She rounded another curve in the stair; above her was a slit-like window. Light slanted in and lay across the steps, but in that light Nell saw there was a massive chasm in front of her – a gaping well where the rest of the stairs had been. Maeve Eynon's words came back to her with sickening clarity. 'No one can get to the upper levels,' she had said. 'Part of the stairs have crumbled away.'

The stairs finished just before the narrow window, but the phone signal might be accessible there. Nell went as high as she could and tried the phone again. Still nothing. She swore, and looked across at the window, and her heart leapt, because beyond the window was the massive stone figure. She had not realized she had climbed to that level, or that the stairs had spiralled her round to the seaward side of the tower. She stood for a moment, staring at the stone face, seeing how it gazed out to sea. It was submerged at high tide, Maeve had said. Then the sea must come up to this level. Nell looked at the stairs again, and this time saw the stains of salt and damp on the walls a little way above her.

Maeve Eynon had said the tower was safe when the tide was out. But then she had added, 'Providing you don't get trapped in there, of course.'

Nell was trapped. The tide was out at the moment – she could remember seeing the expanse of beach as she walked up the cliff path, with the thin glistening line of the sea, far away. But the sea would turn its course at some point, and storm across the beach. The tower's ground-floor room and most of these stairs would be submerged. And Nell would not be able to get high enough to be above the water level.

She remembered the tide table and unfolded it. There was just enough light to see the small print and, after poring over it for several minutes, she understood that the tide had been at its lowest point at around half past ten that morning. It was now coming up to eleven, which fitted with what Maeve Eynon had said about low tide. The next high tide was listed as five o'clock. That meant she had a good six hours, which made her feel better because she would certainly have got out before then. She would regard half past three as the deadline before she needed to actually panic.

She switched off the phone to save the battery, and wondered whether to go back up the stairs and to see whether it was possible to get across the collapsed stairs and up to the bell chamber. It was then that a shudder of something reached her. At first she thought it was a sound, and then she thought it was a movement, and she looked eagerly towards the door, hoping it was the vibration of it being pushed inwards.

But it was not. The sound – the sensation of sound – was coming from above her. From inside the tower. Nell stood very still. At first there was only silence and she thought she had imagined it; then it came again – a faint thrumming as if something had banged against a giant mass of bronze. The sound shivered through the tower, and Nell felt icy prickles of fear, because she knew instinctively what she was hearing. It was the ancient bell – the dead bell, silenced many years ago. Its bronze tongue had been taken out – the library's exhibition had referred to it, and there had been several illustrations depicting the process. It had looked as if most of Rede Abbas had turned out to enjoy the excitement.

But disabled the bell had been, and it was now regarded as a dead bell.

Pray for me, for it will mean the dead bell has sounded, Theodora had written . . . The words formed in Nell's mind, and she shuddered again with fear. The bell would not chime – it could not – because its tongue had been torn out. But something was happening to it. It was as if a faint echo of what it had been lay on the air – as if ghost chimes were sounding from some lost, dead fragment of the past . . .

This was so wildly fantastical a notion that Nell swore aloud to drive the fantasies and the phantoms away, then found a relatively unscathed, moderately dry bit of stair to sit on, and began to think how she could get out of his place if Maeve Eynon did not come back.

It would be academic, of course. Maeve would let her out.

Once Maeve had slammed the door on this prying, meddling woman, this Nell West, she had no intention of letting her out.

She stood outside the bell tower for a good ten minutes, to make sure Nell could not get the door open. It was unlikely in the extreme, because Maeve had twisted the ring handle all the way round, but she waited anyway. Aunt Eifa had brought her up to be thorough in everything she did. But she was sure it would be all right. Some years ago a couple of children had shut themselves in there, and had only been discovered an hour before the sea had started to lap over the ledge. There had been a massive outcry, and the council had fitted a handle inside the door so that nothing of the kind could happen in the future.

Maeve had seen Nell from her window. She often sat at one of the downstairs windows, looking out to make sure no one was creeping around and spying on her. When she saw the unknown woman she had been instantly alert, and she had put on her coat and boots and gone out. It would look like one of her frequent walks, and if she took the cliff path she would pass the woman and they could exchange a polite good morning. If she seemed harmless, Maeve would walk on.

But within minutes it transpired that Nell West was not harmless at all. She was prying into the past – she knew about the song, even though she had not used its actual name, and she knew about Andrew. She had read things about him that Maeve had not – she had read part of a journal Maeve had not even known existed. It was an indication of the danger Aunt Eifa had feared all her life and had brought Maeve up to fear – the danger that had been edging closer since the reviving of the Revels. The Revels had revived the past – Rede Abbas's history. Old records, old documents, were looked out and arranged into exhibitions. People talked about the past, about the monastery – both monasteries, in fact: Andrew's and Sean Flannery's.

From all of that it would be only a step to the Eynon history – to the history of Cliff House and the history of the bell tower. Maeve could guard Cliff House from prying eyes, but she needed to guard the bell tower, too.

When it began to be apparent that the Revels were catching fire and gaining momentum – that the past was waking and surfacing – Maeve knew she had to plan ahead. She thought for a while, then, on one of her walks, she took screwdrivers and a hammer with her. Years of dealing with the general maintenance of Cliff House meant she was quite capable of unscrewing the inside handle of the tower door – the handle so trustingly fitted by the council. She removed the handle from the steel plate, withdrawing its spline and leaving the steel plate in place. It was a simple enough job and no one saw her. But, once done, anyone exploring the tower might find themselves shut in. Better still, if Maeve kept a careful watch on the cliff path from her own windows, she could even follow any snoopers and slam the door on them herself. It would just be one more drowning tragedy, and there would be a new round of warning signs and fences. People would avoid the bell tower, and the past would stay sealed in its secrecy.

Walking back to Cliff House, Nell West trapped, Maeve was aware of a deep satisfaction. It had been an extreme measure to take, but she had not been able to see any other way. She could not allow the woman to delve into the past and the tower's history, and she could not allow her to know about Andrew.

Andrew.

Over the years, Maeve had rationed herself to the times she read Andrew's journal, because she was afraid of his words becoming too familiar and starting to become meaningless or even boring. She could not have borne that. But today, with the sea creeping towards the bell tower, she would enter his world for a couple of hours.

She let herself into the house, locking the door behind her as she always did. She had never once forgotten to lock doors and windows, not in all those years she had lived here.

All the years. It was more than forty-five years since she had found the recording of 'Thaisa's Song'. Forty-five years since she had found Andrew's journal. It was nearly as long as that since she had finally read the whole of it, and had found out why he was facing death.

She remembered it, because it had been the day that two men came to see Aunt Eifa. That in itself had been remarkable, because no one ever came to Cliff House. Aunt Eifa did not allow it. 'What do they want, poking and prying?' she would say if someone knocked on the door. Or, if Maeve asked whether she could have schoolfriends to tea, Aunt Eifa would reply that they did not want strangers snooping into their lives. Better to keep the house to themselves, she always said, and a look so strange and so almost-frightening came into her eyes when she said this that after a while Maeve stopped asking.

But on this day two men were in the house when she got home from school. They smiled at Maeve, and Aunt Eifa told her to go up to her room to do her homework. But she did not close the sitting-room door, and Maeve sat down on the stairs where she could hear almost everything that was said. She knew you should not listen to other people's conversations, but this might be important.

The two men were here because Cliff House – the house that had belonged to Aunt Eifa all her life – was becoming unsafe. They said so several times.

'It's coastal erosion,' said one of them, and papers were rustled at this point. 'You can see for yourself,' said the same man. 'Here on the map, and again here.'

'And in these photographs,' said the other man, and there was more rustling.

'And we have analyses of material taken from the cliff face – soil and chalk and lime.'

They wanted Aunt Eifa – they called her Miss Eynon, of course – to sell Cliff House and move out. The council or something would buy it, and a fair price would be paid – Maeve did not follow this part very clearly. But, said the men, Miss Eynon would not be out of pocket, and she and her niece could buy a cottage or a bungalow further inland. A nice, neat little place with a small garden, and all of it much easier to manage than this sprawling old house.

Aunt Eifa said, very sharply indeed, that she did not want a nice little bungalow or a neat cottage, no matter how convenient or easy.

'And now please leave,' she said. 'Don't bother me again or I shall call the police.'

She would not, of course, Maeve knew that, but it sounded quite threatening, and the men must have thought so, too, because they got up immediately.

But as they were going along the hall, the older one said, 'It will have to happen in the end, Miss Eynon. Parts of this stretch of the cliff are becoming very unsafe. The sea will take this house – it's taken several buildings already. Did you ever hear of a place called Glaum Manor?'

'I remember Glaum Manor very well,' said Aunt Eifa. 'They tore it down when I was a girl. They said the foundations had been eroded.'

'They did indeed tear it down. And now St Benedict's Monastery is going, as well. Did you know that?'

'The monastery's an historic building,' said Aunt Eifa, at once. 'Nobody tears down historic buildings. And where are the monks to go, I should like to know?'

'It might be historic, but it's gone far beyond restoration,' said the man, 'and it certainly doesn't qualify to be a listed building or a candidate for the National Trust, not the state it's in and the position it's in. It'll slide into the sea if it's left there.'

'The bulldozers are going in next month,' said the other man. 'As for the monks, there are only two left, and one's nearly a hundred and the other's ninety-seven. They're going into a St Benedict's nursing home, and perfectly happy to do so. Sign of the times, Miss Eynon. We'll wish you good-day, but you have our phone number if you want to talk to us again.'

Aunt Eifa gave what sounded like a snort of annoyance, and saw the men to the front door.

She told Maeve what had happened over supper that evening. Maeve listened carefully, pretending not to know any of it. She asked if they would have to move from Cliff House.

'No, we won't. Not ever. No one can make us.'

'Don't you want a smaller house with less work?' asked Maeve a bit timidly, because Aunt Eifa was always bemoaning the amount of work that had to be done and what a drudge it all was, and grumbling about crumbling brickwork and leaking lead pipes.

'It's nothing to do with work,' said Aunt Eifa. 'Family property brings other things as well as bricks and mortar. Things are handed down.'

For a moment her eyes had the sudden fixed look that Maeve always found scary, and her face seemed to freeze, like the surface of a stone. Then she frowned and made an impatient gesture with one hand, as if pushing something away, and told Maeve, quite sharply, to fetch the pudding unless it was to be burned to a crisp in the oven.

'As for that tale about the monastery being demolished, I daresay those men were simply spinning a story.'

The men had not been spinning a story at all. The demolishing of St Benedict's Monastery took place that summer and caused quite a flurry of excitement in Rede Abbas. People declared they had been saying for years that the place was unsafe – you would have thought, wouldn't you, that the Church could have done something about it before it started to tumble into the sea. Still, the English Channel had a good deal to answer for – at least this part of it did. And never mind demolishing the monastery, wasn't it high time the old bell tower on the cliff edge was demolished? That really was something that would topple into the sea one night, and a good riddance as well, nasty ugly old place.

Maeve's school had lessons and a slide show about the monastery's history. The teachers, pleased at the opportunity to teach the children a little local history mingled with the wider history of England's complicated religious reformation, set essays on it. The children were all to write something about the monastery's history, they said. Details about the Order that had lived there for hundreds of years, and even about the much earlier monastery that had long since vanished. They could include illustrations if they wanted. Modern photographs of how the monastery looked today and older ones of its past, or even sketches or lithographs if they could find any. It would be a good exercise in research, and an interesting project.

Maeve, sitting at her desk, thought: I could write about Andrew. Things about the monastery in his time, things about the monks who he knew. She thought that would be interesting; the teachers would say she had done well. Aunt Eifa might even say so, too.

But to do so meant she would have to read the rest of Andrew's journal.

It was frightening but it was also exciting to steal out of bed late that night and take the box from the bottom of the wardrobe. As she reached into the box for the journal, her hand brushed against the tape of 'Thaisa's Song'.

One day I'll play that recording again, thought Maeve, and with this in her mind, she opened Andrew's journal.

SIXTEEN

'I do not think there is more than an hour of life left to me,' Andrew had written. 'It's growing darker by the minute, and it's difficult to see the page to write this.'

His writing had become untidy and sprawling, the letters badly formed and hard to read. Maeve hated this – she did not want Andrew to be untidy or dishevelled; she wanted him to be serene and clever and brave, right up to his death.

'The sea is rushing in fast,' he wrote. 'I can hear it lashing against the rocks and soon – oh God, very soon – it will reach these cliffs, and the tower will become submerged. I can still hear the voices singing "Thaisa's Song", but I have no idea if it's real or part of my madness.

'It's a madness that began before I was imprisoned here, though.'

The page stopped there, and at first Maeve thought it was the final entry. But, no, it was all right – he had started another page. Was he about to write why he had been imprisoned in the ancient tower and left there to drown? Left with something nailed beneath the floor, said her mind, and she turned back to that entry.

'If I start to think about what's underneath those lengths of timber nailed over the floor, I shall surely succumb to real madness,' Andrew had written. Immediately after that, he had put, 'The thought of what lies beneath the floor is enough to send the sanest man into madness.'

Maeve hesitated. She did not want to find out that Andrew had done something terrible that had caused him to be shut inside the tower – that he had killed somebody, even. Apart from anything else, she could not put that in an essay.

'We got safely away from Rede Abbas that night, and somehow we followed Father Abbot's hasty directions,' wrote Andrew, and Maeve frowned, because this, surely, was the first time he had referred to leaving Rede Abbas, or making any kind of journey. She pulled the bedclothes more warmly around her, and read on.

A small sum of money had been given to me for the journey.

'We cannot give you much,' Father Abbot said, 'because we do not have much. But it should suffice.'

It did suffice, but only just. We were able to pay for a night's modest lodging, and we bought food, which we ate as we went along. Most of the journey was by the public stage, which was uncomfortable and crowded, but cost only a few pence and took us across vast stretches of roads. Twice we were taken up by amiable farmers on their way to market, most of them in dogcarts or drays.

And after three days – or was it longer? – we reached the outskirts of the City of Oxford.

My companion was bewildered – never having seen such a large place, the noise and the crowded streets and squares were frightening. Carriages spun past us, and groups of people walked to and from their homes, or to shops or places of work or study. They were laughing and talking, sometimes arguing – all of them absorbed in their lives.

The city drew me at once – the golden stones, the glinting river, the scholars and poets and rebels who thronged the streets and the coffee houses and taverns. I stood on the outskirts looking at it all, and I thought: surely this is where I belong. This is the place to which I should have fled all those months ago. Because there are places in the world – soul places, I have heard them called – which the mind recognizes and to which the body and the spirit are irresistibly drawn. They beckon. For me, Oxford was one of those beckoning places.

Quire Court was the heart and the core of that beckoning.

I don't know what I had expected to find in Quire Court. The streets around it were lamplit and narrow – there were enticing doors into shops and taverns and coffee houses, but we walked past them and went determinedly to our destination. People gave us barely a second glance, for which I was grateful. We were travel-stained and weary, but Oxford has seen far worse and far stranger. I was wearing plain, ordinary clothes – 'Not precisely a disguise,' Brother Ranulf had said when we left, 'and I do not think anyone will follow you. But it would be as well not to draw people's attention to either of you.'

None of the monks had seen Quire Court, and Father Abbot

had only been able to tell me that it was a straggle of buildings near the city's centre.

'But whatever it is, I hope it will provide sanctuary for you, Andrew.'

At first it did indeed do so.

Sanctuary. It conjures up timeless images. Safe, bastioned places. Churches and ancient religious houses, where the beleaguered or hunted – or even the merely mad – might find a haven.

Even this place where I lie now, this cold dank tower with the sea creeping towards it – even that might once have been a place of safety. Not now, though. The light is fading and I can smell the strong salty tang of the sea. And the crashing of the waves is much louder. Not long now. Oh God, let me face it bravely. But who will know if I don't? Who would know if I scream and fight at the end?

I'm having difficulty in writing this, but I shall continue to do so, for it feels like a last link to the world I will soon leave.

The first sight of Quire Court was by the light of flaring lanterns in the early evening. Warm shadows lay across the stones, multi-coloured and harlequin-patterned, and we stood under an old stone archway at the entrance. I think neither of us wanted to be the first to step through that archway. I have no idea what my companion was thinking, but I had the strong feeling that we were about to enter a different world and that, if we walked forward now, we should be in a place that might be safe and good.

How wrong I was! How naïf and trusting.

The buildings were arranged in what was almost an oblong – there were six or eight of them, mostly with jutting bow windows and small squares of garden. Two houses had signs proclaiming one to be a printing business, the other a jeweller's and silversmith's. The rest appeared to be private houses, with lights burning in the windows. Through the uncurtained ones were homely scenes – people reading or writing. In two of the windows an evening meal was being set out. You forget, when you enter a religious house, about the ordinary family things. Knives and forks being set out on a table, a man reading a newspaper, a woman setting down a dish of food.

> There was a moment when I – when both of us – felt excluded from those scenes of normality and warmth; then it was as if something held out welcoming hands, and we walked through the arch.'

The writing broke off, but Maeve, turning to the next page with care, saw that it resumed, but that it was different – stronger – and that the ink was a different colour.

'I have with me,' wrote Andrew, 'the diary I kept during those few nights in Quire Court. It seemed to me vital to preserve the notes of what I found there, and the pages have remained with me. I cannot transcribe them here in this appalling place – the light is too poor and I do not think there is much time left, for the sea is lashing in loudly and relentlessly. So I am putting my Quire Court diary here in these pages. I would like to think this account will be found and read – that some day my story and Theodora's will be known.

'The pages tell part of Thaisa's story as well, of course, and her story is woven with ours. I cannot know, though, what Thaisa's fate eventually was. I wish I did know.'

This was the point at which the ink and the writing changed so strongly. Maeve turned over carefully and continued to read.

> Father Abbot had said that one of the buildings in the Court was not occupied, and it was to this building we were going.
>
> 'The gentleman who owns the printer's business – a Mr Ernest Thread – has the keys and will direct you to the right house,' he had told us.
>
> Mr Thread – who resembled an anxious but friendly caterpillar – did indeed have the keys, and on my producing Father Abbot's letter of authority, handed them over. If there was anything we required, we were please to let him know, and in the meantime he would let us have a jug of milk and some bread and cheese along with half of a cold pie that his wife had left out, for he could see we were travel-stained and weary, and likely hungry, too.
>
> At first I found that house quiet and welcoming. The rooms had a few pieces of furniture, which made it unexpectedly comfortable, and there were curtains at the windows, and rugs

on the floor. There were even bookshelves, with books which someone had forgotten, or had not bothered, to take away. When I foraged at the back of the building, I found a small supply of chopped logs, with which I made a fire in the largest downstairs room.

'We have warmth and light and a roof over our heads,' I said, smiling across the room. 'What more do we need?'

'Are we safe?'

Her words struck a harsh note, but I said, 'Yes, we're safe, Theodora. I won't let anything happen to you.'

It's a vicious irony to remember I said that to her, and yet tonight I'm here, and she . . .

I can't write it.

Instead I'll go on describing that first night. How we ate Mrs Thread's kindly given food, then washed the supper dishes in a small scullery, how we banked down the fire for safety, then made our way to the two makeshift beds we had set out upstairs.

Two beds, you'll note. And two rooms.

But I lay wakeful for a long time, and panic crept up on me – not suddenly, but slowly and insidiously. I had brought my fey, strange girl all this way to keep her safe, and I had no idea whether we could be safe. Not then, not ever.

That was when I heard the scrabbling sounds.

At first I thought Theodora had woken and was exploring the house, making sure no one lurked in the court below. But when I lit a candle and went into her room, she was deeply asleep. Her hair was tumbled over the cushion she had for a pillow, and there was a faint sheen of moisture on her eyelids, and I wanted to lie down next to her so much that I had to go out of the room. (I did go out. I'd like that to be known.)

The sounds came again. I'd hope I've always been as courageous as most men, but I was in a dark, unfamiliar house, with no help at hand save a fragile girl. If there was an intruder . . .

But I took the candle and went down the stairs. There was a faint glow from the fire we had lit earlier in the evening; its dying radiance mingled with the light from the candle. Shadows danced and gibbered, and once I flinched and threw up a hand because I thought a man had stepped out of the shadows and was coming towards me.

As I peered into the room where we had eaten supper earlier, the scrabbling came again. It was a curious sound, almost rhythmic, although I do know how odd that must sound – I know how odd it looks written down.

I closed the door on the room and went through to the back of the house. As I did so, another sound reached me, and if I had been apprehensive before, now it was as if icy hands closed around my heart. In one of these downstairs rooms, someone was singing 'Thaisa's Song'. It was soft and low, and it was slightly different to the way Theodora had sung it, but it was unmistakable and recognizable. I know that is a somewhat contradictory statement, but 'Thaisa's Song' is so extraordinary and so very individual – it's as if it possesses an essence, a core, that can't change or be changed, no matter what.

It took several minutes before I could summon up courage to go closer to the sounds, but eventually I did. The shadows came with me, sometimes stalking me, sometimes going ahead of me, all of them distorted to grotesque proportions. In the first room nothing stirred and everywhere was still. But when I went on to the next, the singing came closer.

On the other side of that room was an archway into a kind of inner hall with two more doors. One was closed, but the other was ajar. And standing in that partly open doorway was a figure. It was bowed over, as if examining something on the ground. It gave no indication of having heard me or having seen the candlelight.

The small flame burned up in a faint gust of air, and the indistinct outline was gone. I walked towards the open door. It gave on to what looked like a storeroom. It was dark and cool and there was a stone floor and stone walls, and a thick marble slab, clearly used for keeping meat and perhaps milk cool.

But that small room reeked of sadness and pain – so much so it was like stepping into a deep dark well where light had never penetrated, and never could penetrate. There was such dreadful loneliness in there that my stomach lifted with the force of it, and for a moment I was afraid I might be sick.

And then came another sound, and this was the most terrible of all.

The thin, desperate crying of a child.

It mingled with the music, like blood running into water, and at first I thought the crying was coming from outside the building – that it was some ordinary child crying for some ordinary reason. But I knew it was inside the house, and I knew, as well, that it was in this small stone room with its smothering despair. The early Christian monks feared despair, which they called *accidie*. St Thomas Aquinas referred to it as the 'sorrow of the world'.

Whatever name it's given, despair is a very terrible thing. It's the abandonment of all hope. It's the giving up in God – the belief that He can't help the suffering human soul – that He's no longer even there.

I have no idea how long I stood in that room, listening to those sounds, hoping something would happen to explain them. I was prepared to believe that the scrabblings had been mice or rats. I was also prepared to accept that my mind, tired and anxious, could have mistaken ordinary noises. Oh God, I would have seized with both hands on a sane, unthreatening explanation. But there was nothing to explain the sounds, and in the end I went up to my own bed.

We bought food in the town the following morning, although we did not dare use too much of Father Abbot's money.

After we had eaten our midday meal, Theodora took a book into the tiny garden behind the house and curled up in the shadow of an apple tree. I stood looking at her through the window for a moment, seeing how the dappled sunlight fell across her hair, then I went back to that small room.

Even in the middle of the day no light reached it, and I had to fetch an oil lamp. I held its flickering radiance close to every inch of the stone walls. I am not sure what I was looking for – I thought I should know when I saw it, but at first there was nothing.

Then I knelt down and tilted the lamp's light on to the floor. Several of the stones were out of true with the rest. They made for an unmistakable rectangle in the floor – roughly three feet in length and almost two feet in width. I sat back on my heels, frowning. There could be any number of reasons why the stones of this floor had been taken up then re-laid, but surely anyone laying down stones for a floor would ensure they were even? The more I stared at that oblong, the more unpleasantly suggestive it seemed.

I'd like to think it was scholarly inquisitiveness that drove me in what I did next, but it was not. It was a deep-seated need for reassurance.

In the hour that followed, I entered a world of flickering lamplight and drifting shadows and of mingled singing and sobbing that came and went in distorted fragments. A world where my hands, unused to any labour other than the playing of a musical instrument or the writing down of musical notation, became blistered and sore.

I made use of the implements to hand – a triangle-shaped trowel, a thin-edged chisel, a small clawed tool whose purpose might have been anything at all, but which could be used to dig into stone and, later, earth.

The stones came up with difficulty, but when they did move, they did so with a kind of dry sigh, as if grateful to be torn from their place. Beneath them was hard-packed earth, ordinary and apparently undisturbed, with nothing to suggest why this oblong piece of floor should be so strongly and so symmetrically out of true with the rest.

I scooped the soil away then knelt down, using my hands on clearing the soil, working with care to uncover what lay beneath.

What lay beneath.

It was, as I had known it would be, a tiny, heartbreakingly fragile, heap of bones. A child – no, it was less than a child, it was a babe. It was impossible to know if it had been girl or boy, for the flesh had long since fallen from the bones. It lay on its back, the head straight, as if the eyes had been staring upwards. But there was something I had not expected.

The hands and also the feet were raised in grotesque supplication.

The child had not been dead when it was put into the grave.

The dim small room whirled around me, and my stomach

lifted with such nausea and horror that I backed away from the room, and half fell against the door in my desperation to get outside before I was messily sick into the actual grave.

I did get out in time, but it was some moments before I finally stopped retching and gasping, holding on to the small garden wall with one hand, to stop from falling over. Theodora had not noticed or heard; she was still beneath the apple tree, still immersed in her book, smiling occasionally as some pleasing phrase caught her eye.

I went back inside and washed my face and hands at the scullery tap (one of the real amenities of the little house), then forced myself to return to the stone room.

This time I saw more details than I had been able to absorb the first time. I saw that the small hands and feet had fallen back alongside the body, and did not look quite so terrible – so much so that I wondered whether I had imagined that first, shocking sight. But I knew I had not, and that was partly because there were other images jostling for remembrance.

Theodora's mother in the coffin, one hand raised as if trying to push open the lid.

Adolphus Glaum, fighting his way out of the tomb after it was sealed, falling on to my neck in that dreadful macabre embrace.

And Theodora herself, seated quietly at the piano in Cliff House, and singing the death song of her family. The song I had heard accompanying a child's crying in this house last night.

The shadows were thickening in Quire Court, and Theodora would soon come looking for me, but I stayed where I was. It will sound absurd and overly sentimental, but I did not want to leave that small body on its own. There was nothing I could do for the child, not now, but the thought of consigning it back to the silent darkness – of covering it with earth and stone slabs again – twisted a knife in my vitals.

It had to be done, though. I could not let Theodora see or know about it. I would restore the makeshift grave, then tomorrow I would find some way of getting a proper burial for the child. It was something that could make no difference to the child – or could it? Prayer is a strange thing. But it would make a difference to me.

I could not lock the door of the storeroom, but I thought I could wedge it sufficiently firmly so that Theodora would not get in. I would tell her some tale about mice or even rats to keep her out as well. In the meantime, I could at least say a prayer over the makeshift grave. I did so, then bent over to lay my own crucifix on the child's breast before covering it with the soil once more. It was then I saw the small book lying next to the body.

SEVENTEEN

I assumed the book would be a Bible or a prayer book, but it was neither.

The leather binding was soft and smooth with age and, when I opened it, using extreme care, the glow from the lamp fell across handwritten pages. At the top of the first one was a date – 1538. The writing was spiked and elaborate – a far cry from the script we use nowadays. I am no scholar, but I am not entirely unacquainted with ancient script – I had transposed the work of the Elizabethan music-makers and adapted their lyrics so that nineteenth-century ears could understand them and nineteenth-century voices could sing them. If I concentrated hard I should be able to read this without too much difficulty.

The first pages were blurred, either from age or because something had been spilled on them, I could not tell which. But I found I could make out phrases – occasionally whole sentences – on the later pages.

'Tonight I wanted to sing my family's song for company and for reassurance,' the diarist had written. 'I did not dare do so, but once I reach Glaum's Acre I shall do so. No one there will understand the words, just as no one at Rede Abbas does.'

Reading those words, something snapped to attention in my mind.

'That piece of land in Oxford, and whatever buildings are

on it now, once belonged to the Glaum family centuries ago,' Father Abbot had said, before Theodora and I left St Benedict's.

It is hardly the act of a gentleman to read the diary of another person, but after that opening sentence I defy anyone not to have read more. And it was over three hundred years old – older than the famous chronicles left by Samuel Pepys.

Also, whoever had written this was long since dead. With the thought, something seemed to brush thin, light fingertips across my face, the sketched-on-air figure I had seen last night shivered on the edge of my vision, and I thought the faint sobbing came again. Then it faded, and I read on.

'I have always thought Seamus understands about the song. Not all of it, but enough. But then Seamus Flannery has eyes that see into your heart and that read what lies buried there – eyes that would melt your soul . . . And he has a soft voice that would turn your bones to water so that you would do anything he asked, even though you know – you KNOW – it to be the worst sin ever to lie with a man of God . . .

'Seamus could sing my family's song if he bothered to try. No one else could, though. Dear Brother Cuthwin once tried, but he could not twist his tongue round the words . . .'

Cuthwin, I thought, coming briefly back to the present. Could that be the same Cuthwin whose lively but fragmented records Brother Egbert had been transcribing with such diligence? In the next line, the diarist wrote, 'The monks and the people here noted Cuthwin's failure and it made them uneasy. They whispered to one another of the warning in the Bible – the warning about those who spake with unknown tongues . . .'

Theodora and I have just finished our supper, and we have talked about something – everything, anything – but I cannot remember any of it, and now I am alone in the room overlooking the Court. I have adjusted the candles and the lamps so that their mingled light falls across the dim pages of the diary buried with the child. There is no longer any question as to whether I should or will read it. It is calling to me with all the seductive insistence of a siren. I intend to transcribe as much of the contents as possible, and copy it into my own journal, which I have to hand, and which I have kept in a rather sporadic fashion since entering St Benedict's. It may take all night to do so. It may take much longer than that. I do not care how long it takes.

As I write this now, midnight has just chimed from a nearby church. That is a very late hour by the standard of a monk accustomed to early retiring and even earlier rising, but not at all late for someone whose life before entering a monastery had often included drinking and talking with friends into the small hours.

All is quiet and still beyond Quire Court – or is it? A few moments ago I heard faint sounds, and when I looked through the window I thought a dark-clad figure was standing in one of the corners. The head seemed to be turned towards this house, and I experienced a lurch of apprehension. I even went so far as to make sure the doors were both bolted and the windows firmly latched. It was all right, of course. No one could get in. There is no reason for anyone to stand out there watching the house and, in any case, no one knows we are here.

Having read the first few pages of the diary, writing them – which is to say my translation of them – into my own journal becomes easier. I find I can even fill in some of the parts where pages are badly faded or shredded by mice or rats or simply by sheer age.

An immense compulsion is driving me. Perhaps I am afraid that if I do not write it all down in modern parlance, the diary's contents may vanish like the fairy-dust they probably are.

Quire Court has sunk into a gentle shadowy world of its own. I cannot see the figure that I thought was watching earlier, and the only sounds are the occasional chime of a distant church clock, the soft splutter of the lamp as the oil burns down, and the scratching of my pen.

And within the first few sentences the writer's name has jumped out at me, and fastened sinuous fingers around my mind and my heart.

Thaisa. Not Theodora's mother, but another Thaisa. A Thaisa from long ago. From the year 1538. This is her diary.

As this is the first page of my new journal, I am writing carefully and neatly. The journal was given to me by Seamus

– one of the few gifts he has ever given me, and I treasure it for that reason. Also, of course, books of any kind are immensely precious and valuable.

So I shall write that I live in the grounds of St Benedict's Monastery, and that I occupy a strange position here. At least, I imagine it's strange, but I don't really know, because I don't know how other people live.

'We found you on our doorstep one night, Thaisa,' Seamus once told me in an emotional moment, as I lay in his bed. He did not have many emotional moments, but there were some, and I treasured them all, storing them carefully in my memory in the way I would lay a precious piece of silk in a drawer with lavender.

'A tiny scrap of a child you were, huge-eyed and solemn, and rain-drenched from the storm,' Seamus said. 'You only knew a word of two of English – I think you only knew a word or two of speech of any kind – and none of us knew where you came from. Myself, though, I would never be surprised to learn you're from non-human stock – that you're a changeling left by a race of sea nymphs or water naiads.' He tilted my head so that he was looking straight into my face. His eyes change colour with the light and his own emotions. 'Your eyes are narrow and long, and your ears are set a little too high on your head to look entirely human. And your hair—'

'Has no colour.' I dislike my hair very much.

'It's the colour of the primroses in Musselwhite's Meadow in the spring.' He wound a strand of it between his fingers. 'You were a little ragged elf-child, clutching a silk shawl around your shoulders.' His voice had slid down into the velvety caressing note that felt like a cat's fur across my skin. He could always spin poetry, Seamus. And I always listened, and I was always lured by it. I expect he knew that and made use of it. I expect he made use of it with a lot of people. I have no idea how many of those people might have been ladies, but I should think quite a number were. I try not to think about it.

'And the only possession you had was a sheet of music folded inside the shawl with your name written on it,' he said. 'I was an impressionable young novice of seventeen on that day, and you did not seem quite human to me.'

I said nothing, wanting him to go on, wanting him to unpeel a little more information about that time, of which I have only the haziest of memories.

'We gave you into the care of the Widow Eynon who lives on the clifftops,' Seamus said. 'But, as you grew up, you kept finding your way back here.'

'I hated it there.'

'Wasn't she kind to you?'

'Yes, but the clifftop house smelled stale and the Widow Eynon smelled worse than the house. I was afraid I might start to smell the same.'

'You never would,' he said. 'You're the scent of buttercup meadows and bluebell woods, and warm honey and wine on midsummer's eve.'

That's what I mean about him spinning poetry. I used to believe he read, and committed to memory, the writings of the great poets and scholars, so that he could present their words as his own. I know now that he does not. He does not need to.

'I came back here because the house smelt,' I said firmly.

'You came back to learn how to read and write,' said Seamus, at once. 'And how to speak and write Silver Age Latin – we're one of the few monasteries who still have that knowledge. And how to love beauty – literature and paintings and the illuminated tracts and manuscripts of the early Christian fathers.'

'I came back because I wanted to be with you,' I said. 'If that meant learning Latin and literature and all those other things, I was prepared to learn them. For you. Because I adored you from the very first.'

'You should only use that word "adore" about God.'

This was Seamus remembering he was a monk and reminding me of the fact. He forgot sometimes, and on the nights he forgot the most thoroughly, he came to my cottage in the monastery grounds.

'But,' I said, 'it wasn't until I was grown up that you fell in love with me, I do know that.'

'Thaisa, we shouldn't talk about love between us,' he said, in a suddenly ragged voice. 'I'm nearly twenty years ahead of you and a monk. I'm the Abbot of this monastery, may God help me. And you're a pagan child of eighteen.'

'How can I be a pagan after spending my life with monks?'

'You're a pagan when you're here in my bed, Thaisa. And this – what we're doing now – what we're about to do—'

'Again,' I said, and saw amusement darken his eyes. 'Is this pagan, too?'

'This,' he said, 'is a mortal sin. And so is this – and, oh God, Thaisa, this also . . .'

He was pulling me against him again and his mouth tasted sweet and sinless, and I would have killed for him and I would have died for him.

He did not say he loved me. He never did. But afterwards his arms stayed tightly around me and I wanted to remain like that for ever.

Today Seamus has told the monks he will address the community before supper in the refectory, and that everyone must be present.

Brother Cuthwin thinks it will be about the Bishop's Visitation, which followed the monks' celebration of St Benedict's Revels, but I have a premonition that it is something far worse.

I shall be in the refectory with them. No one will find it unusual, because I have always been free to go in and out of the monastery as I wish. I shall wear my green gown. Seamus once said I looked like a wood nymph in that gown. I do not look in the least like a wood nymph in – or out of – any gown at all, but I stored the remark away to unfold when I am alone.

I know it is foolish and vain to be thinking of what I shall wear and how I shall look, but if something is going to happen to me tonight, no matter what it is, I want to meet it looking my best.

My world is in ruins and lies at my feet in painful, splintered shards.

Two nights ago Seamus addressed the monks as he had announced. It was not my lover of all those enchanted, forbidden nights who stood before them, though; that man had gone and in his place was the Abbot of St Benedict's, implacable and ruthless.

The monks would have thought it was chance that had made their Father Abbot stand in front of the newly fitted coloured-glass window, so that the setting sun irradiated him and the light showered over him like a rose and gold cloak. It was not chance at all, of course. In fact Seamus had probably marked the floor earlier so that he knew the exact spot where the dying sun's glow would fall.

'As most of you know,' said Seamus, 'Master Thomas Cromwell is compiling a survey of the country's monasteries and their wealth for the King.'

The monks nodded. This was the *Valor Ecclesiasticus*, regarded with much suspicion.

'Cromwell's men,' said Seamus, 'are visiting a great many of the religious houses.' He paused. 'This morning,' he said, 'a message came to say the Commissioners are to visit us.'

There was a murmur of consternation. The monks all knew how Master Cromwell was closing religious houses across the land, scattering the monks and nuns as he went. Most of us knew, as well, of the brutality that was often employed in the scattering.

'Might they close this house?' asked Brother John, worriedly.

'If they find a reason, they will not hesitate.'

A reason. It might have been my imagination that Seamus's eyes flickered to me. But he only said, 'They will search for evidence of misbehaviour. So, during the visit, you will all behave with dignity and modesty. You will be pious and devout, and you will show complete obedience. There will be no rebellious mutterings or plans for deception. If you are asked about the monastery's possessions, you will not lie.'

'Of course not,' said several voices, shocked.

'There is another matter,' said Seamus, and I felt a twist of nervousness because a coldness had entered his voice. A sudden silence fell; then, into that waiting silence, Seamus said, 'Thaisa is to leave us for a time.'

A kind of murmur of understanding went through the refectory, as if the monks were saying – or perhaps only thinking – ah, yes, of course, Cromwell's men must not find Thaisa here. We do not say any more and we do not ask questions, but certainly Thaisa must not be found. I think several of them looked at me with pity, but I was in no case to know, because the room, with its mellow evening sunlight and the familiar scents of beeswax and old leather books and serenity, had splintered and was spinning around me. For a dreadful moment I thought I was going to faint, there in front of them all. It might have been minutes or hours later that I was able to listen again.

Brother Cuthwin was asking, somewhat hesitantly, where I was to go.

'To a house owned by the Order.'

'Another monastery? Surely that would not be—'

'Not another monastery,' said Seamus. 'She will go to a small house in the town of Oxford.'

'Oxford?' said Brother John. 'I didn't know we had property in Oxford.' John is the monastery's Prior and responsible for finances.

'There are a few small houses there,' said Seamus. 'Four in all, I believe.' His brows had slanted in the familiar, daunting way, but Brother John, a conscientious soul, pressed on.

'I'm sorry, Father Abbot, but how long have we owned these houses? I've never seen mention of them in our inventories. When were they purchased? From whom?'

'They have been bequeathed to us,' said Seamus, staring at his Prior coldly. 'By Squire Glaum.'

'Why would Squire Glaum bequeath something as valuable as property?' asked John.

'Perhaps he wishes to acquire merit in the eyes of God.'

'Father Abbot, if this has been the selling of indulgences or absolution—'

'I sold nothing,' said Seamus, so sharply that John flinched. 'I gave no pardon or absolution for any sins in return for the properties. No payment was made of any kind.'

'I am sorry if I seemed to suggest otherwise,' said John, after a moment.

'Whatever sins Edward Glaum has committed are between him, his maker, and his confessor,' said Seamus.

There were several murmurs of understanding. Edward Glaum's fondness for the ladies was well known, but he was generally thought of as kindly.

'I suppose,' said John thoughtfully, 'that the houses will yield some income for us?'

'I have no idea. The rents are a peppercorn,' said Seamus, sounding uninterested.

'Oxford is a long way from here, Father Abbot.'

'Four days' journey. Not beyond our reach,' said Seamus. 'And one day we may need to hide something, and to do so a long way from Rede Abbas. That is one reason why I accepted the bequest.'

'Hide something?' asked Cuthwin, anxiously. 'What kind of something, Father?'

'Cuthwin, you must be aware of the religious turmoil taking place in the land,' said Seamus, impatiently.

'Of course I am,' said Cuthwin, who always shut his eyes and his mind to anything unpleasant.

'The shape of religion is changing,' said Seamus. 'There may come a time when we need to hide our beliefs and even our very selves.' With that – and without so much as a glance at me – he turned on his heel and went out of the refectory.

So there is my world, rent asunder and the pieces tossed to the carrion crows. I am to be sent away, to this place, this Oxford. *Oxford*. I already hate it. I hate even the name. It sounds slow and heavy and mindlessly plodding. An ox is a creature of burden, used to pull ploughs and farm carts. Fords are crossings over rivers or streams – thick cold stones or massive slabs of timber that echo dully when you step on them.

Seamus touched lightly on the changing times and on how religion is being forced into different shapes, but all of us at St Benedict's know the stories. We know of the brutal punishments inflicted on the Carthusian monks who would not take an Oath of Supremacy to the King. Some of those monks were beheaded. Some of them were hanged. None of us believe the whispers that some of the monks were burned alive.

This morning the monks are preparing for the visit of Master Cromwell's men, scurrying back and forth, tidying everywhere, cleaning everything, and, I should think, in some cases, concealing items they think are better hidden.

I have been putting a few things into a carpet-bag which Brother John has found for my journey to Oxford, although I have no idea what I should put in, because I have never been away from Rede Abbas. I do not know what people take with them on journeys.

Most of the monks have found time to come to my cottage to wish me goodbye, Godspeed, safe travels. They will all remember me in their prayers.

Brother John has given me a Book of Hours, created in the scriptorium, with beautiful illuminations. The scriptorium is actually a rather cramped recess in a corner of the library, where Brother Angus illuminates religious texts, often grumbling about the lack of space and light. But his work is truly exquisite, and I am touched to have the book.

'We shall miss your light burning in this window,' John said sadly, standing in my cottage. 'It was like a small beacon in the dark night.'

The light had usually been left there for Seamus to find his way from the monastery's side gate, down the moss-covered steps and through the rose garden. It always seemed to me very right that Seamus should come to me through those flowers of ancient romance – scented fragments of Persia and Isfahan, their perfume heady and drowsy, lying on the air like mandragora, the sleep-juice, the love-syrup of the poets . . .

I could not say any of that to Brother John, of course.

Cuthwin has brought me a flagon of the monastery's mead, and some honey cakes for sustenance on the journey. He says the monks are hatching plans for concealing the monastery's most valuable possessions. They will bury the ciborium and the patens in the gardens, and somebody has suggested hiding several things beneath the floor of the privy.

'Father Abbot is pacing the monastery looking like Lucifer newly come from the dark kingdom of hell,' he said. 'We're afraid the Bishop might have talked about the last Revels festivities, and that Cromwell's men will seize on that as a reason to close down our house. Lewdness and debauchery, you see, Thaisa, that's what they'd call it. Lewdness and debauchery,' he repeated, examining the words with the curiosity of the innocent.

Oh, Cuthwin, if only you knew of the real debauchery that has been going on in these buildings. I do not believe that Master Cromwell's men will class the singing of a colourful song on St Benedict's Feast, and the quaffing of a few tankards of mead as sufficiently debauched or lewd to close the monastery.

But if they were to find other evidence?

If they were to find that Seamus Flannery had been in the bed of a young girl in his care, not once, but on many nights . . . If they knew that girl was to have a child as a result . . . They would seize on that hungrily. And then what would happen to Seamus?

Seamus has not spoken to me since I told him I am to have a child. I dare not seek him out, because I am afraid he may tell me that my banishment is to be for ever.

Tonight I hate him. I hate him deeply and strongly. But I have put the light in the window and I am sitting in the rocking chair that was made for me in the monks' workshop. I do not want to go to bed, because it will be the last time I shall do so here. I feel sadder and more alone than I have ever felt in my whole life.'

When Thaisa wrote about the child and about leaving Rede Abbas, I was so deeply affected I had to set her book down for a moment.

The little clock over the hearth has just chimed three o'clock. The sound startled me; I had not realized so many hours had passed since I sat down with Thaisa's diaries.

A few moments ago I went softly up the stairs. Theodora was deep in sleep, curled up on the narrow bed. I looked down at her, and I thought, She's a descendant of Thaisa. She bears the same surname – Eynon. And she has the music, she has 'Thaisa's Song'.

I stooped down to pull the cover more warmly over her shoulders. She smiled, as if something of the gesture had reached her, and her hand curled as if to take hold of something invisible and keep it safely. But she did not wake.

And now I've returned to my candlelit corner and the

window overlooking the court, and I'm reaching for Thaisa's diaries again.

It had not occurred to me that Seamus would accompany me to Oxford, but he simply appeared outside my cottage as the cart jolted up, and got into it with me. He made some remark about seeing the houses bestowed on us by Squire Glaum so the monastery could properly manage them, but he spoke in a tone which precluded – indeed, forbade – any questions. Other than that he said nothing, and I said nothing either, because before we had gone more than a short way out of Rede Abbas I started to feel dreadfully sick.

I do not remember much about the journey – only the jolting of the carts we travelled in, and the fact that I spent the hours curled into a tight huddle of misery. I am convinced my malaise was due to the unborn child protesting, but Seamus says sickness is a frequent occurrence with travellers.

I do recall that we ate in inns that I found noisy and bewildering, and twice we stopped at other religious houses. I remember Cranbourne Priory and Sherborne – both Benedictine houses. They, too, awaited visits from Cromwell's men, and they were clearly apprehensive.

Seamus was courteous and completely at ease in all these places. Once I said, 'You have travelled a good deal, I think?'

'Yes,' he said, and the shuttered look came down, so that I did not dare probe further.

Seamus had said that Oxford was quite a small place – 'Although there's talk of it being made a city.'

But to me it was huge and filled with people. The sounds and the crowds of people bemused me.

'Most of the people who live here depend on the university,' said Seamus. 'The students provide a large market for most goods. Ale, food, clothes. Oxford is full of craftsmen who supply all those items.'

When he talks like this, I am strongly aware that I have never been outside the small village of Rede Abbas until now.

I never imagined a place like Glaum's Acre. It's a huddle of stone buildings, set in a square around a small courtyard, and it's near a busy thoroughfare. The house is larger than my cottage at Rede Abbas, and there is furniture, although I have no idea whose it is.

It is strange to think that this all belongs to Squire Glaum. It is even stranger that he gave the houses to the monastery.

There is a deep wide bed in one of the upper rooms, and Seamus lay with me in that bed last night.

This morning he told me he has found a woman who will help me through the birth, when it comes. I suppose he is paying her for this, but I have not asked him.

The woman's name is Madge and she is a homely soul to look at, but full of common sense and helpful advice and a warm kindness. She has come to the house several times since Seamus returned to Rede Abbas. I never had a friend of this sort before, and I am glad to have her.'

There is a break in Thaisa's journal at this page, and it looks as if some sections have been torn out – or perhaps they have only crumbled away with the centuries. There are also a number of pages where the writing is all but obliterated by having something spilled on them. It is difficult to estimate the time that elapses between the entries, but in some cases it could be many weeks – even months.

However, the next part of Thaisa's story I could decipher, began with her referring to a 'terrible event' that had occurred.

EIGHTEEN

Today a terrible event occurred.

Seamus has returned to Rede Abbas, but Madge is with me, and she and I had walked to a nearby street market to buy food and provisions. This is something that is new to me, and I have had to learn how to hand over money for the goods and demand a cheaper price. I like the market; I like seeing the people and listening to them exchanging talk.

Beyond the market is a square, enclosed by tall buildings. It is usually a quiet place, but today people were massing there, talking furtively in little groups.

'It's a burning,' said Madge, her voice suddenly fearful. 'They're going to burn someone. For heresy, probably.'

I remembered the whispers we had heard in Rede Abbas, and I said, 'But burnings don't really happen. They're just stories to frighten people.'

'Are they? Look there, Thaisa.'

At the centre of the square was a grim outline – a jutting spike, eight or nine feet tall. Bundles of wood were heaped around it, and there was a small brazier nearby, glowing and sending shivers of heat out.

'Someone will be chained to that,' said Madge, 'and the kindling around it fired.' I shuddered, and she said at once, 'So we'll walk past it and go straight home. No one should have to see this.'

But the square was becoming crowded, and we became hemmed in, backed against one of the buildings. A dreadful excitement lay on the air and I began to feel sick. The child stirred uneasily, sending a tremor of dull pain through my womb.

A man near to us pointed. 'They're bringing him out,' he said.

'Is he struggling?' asked another hopefully, standing on tiptoe the better to see.

'Of course he's struggling,' said the first man. 'Refused to take the Oath of Supremacy is what they're saying.'

'Daft, I call it. It's only a few words.'

'He says it'll risk his immortal soul to say them, though. More fool him.'

As the doomed man was dragged out, there was an uncertain cheer. A small wind blew across the square and the hot smell of the brazier gusted into my face. The sick feeling and the cleaving pain worsened.

Some of the people began to chant the Lord's Prayer. I did not join in. I could not see how the recital of words could dilute the agony of burning flesh and bone and eyes . . . And yet words can hold such power.

Two men chained the prisoner to the stake, then lit torches from the brazier and plunged them into the piled faggots. The wood caught at once, and scarlet and orange flames leapt upwards. The flames caught the man's garments, then burned higher, and he began to scream and to fight like a mad creature against the chains. The sounds tore through my brain, scraping at every nerve I possessed, and now the smell was not just hot iron and burning wool – it was the scent of roasting meats, of fat melting and crisping . . .

The child moved uneasily again, and I pulled my cloak around my shoulders. It was absurd to feel icily cold when within yards a man was burning alive. Madge's hand gripped my wrist and she pulled me through the crowds, and into a narrow street on the far side.

I did not see the moment when the man sagged, but I know the moment when he stopped screaming.

Seamus is with me again tonight. He has travelled between this house and Rede Abbas several times over the last months, each time bringing me news – of the Commissioners' visit to St Benedict's, and of how it was thought it would not fall victim to closure.

'But the Commissioners are still watching us,' he said. 'Two of them have remained in the village. They are everywhere – talking, listening, watching.'

I sensed his anxiety, and panic clutched at me, because Seamus was never anxious about anything in his life.

'Is it about the Oath of Supremacy? Do they want you to take it?'

'It's not about the Oath,' he said, and hesitated. 'Thaisa, they believe I've been selling pardons. They're going to accuse me of accepting these houses as payment for granting Edward Glaum absolution for his sins. They're gathering evidence – talking to the villagers, to Squire Glaum's servants.'

I had heard of this practice of selling absolution – it's called simony, and it's regarded as a very serious crime.

'Is it true?' I said after a moment.

'No.' His hand came out to me. 'But I can't tell the people of Rede Abbas – or Thomas Cromwell's Commissioners – the truth.'

'What is the truth?'

'That Edward Glaum gave the monastery these houses because I asked for his help in getting his daughter away from the prying eyes of the Commissioners – getting her to a place where she could give birth in secrecy and safety.'

'His daughter?'

'You, Thaisa.'

Seamus has left Oxford and tonight I shall sleep in the room under the eaves, which has a bolt on the door. There is a feeling of security in knowing that bolt might keep people out.

I suppose I knew that Edward Glaum was my father. I suppose I should be grateful that he cared enough to make it possible for me to leave Rede Abbas. But his kindness has brought Seamus under suspicion. Having seen those other religious houses on the journey here, I understand that St Benedict's is not a particularly large house. But Seamus is still an Abbot – a person of standing. If it's believed he accepted Glaum's Acre as payment for the granting of absolution – of committing simony – he would be dealt with harshly. Probably he would be deprived of his office and even deposed of his Order. If that were to happen, I would tell why Edward Glaum gave the houses. But could I do so without it becoming known that Seamus fathered a child? Because if that were to be discovered . . .

Writing that, I am back in that square with the flames licking around the chained prisoner. But it's Seamus's beloved body I'm seeing in the heart of the flames. It's Seamus who's burning, screaming as his blood boils and his bones start to melt, and his eyes, his sweet lovely eyes . . .

Reading this entry in Thaisa's journal, I knew she had been right to be fearful for Seamus on more than on level. Simony was, and still is, a serious offence, even in the enlightened nineteenth century. It's the sin and the crime of profiting from sacred things, including buying or selling ecclesiastical preferments and benefices – and absolving sinners. I don't think simony was ever punishable by death, even in the simmering cauldron of religious turmoil in Thaisa's time. But that other sin – the sin of fornication, the fathering of a child by an Abbot . . .

Yes, Thaisa had been right to be afraid for Seamus on that count.

The next entries I can make out seem to have been made after the birth of Thaisa's child – the child conceived in that candlelit, firelit cottage with the heady scent of the roses lying on the air like a drug.

They are fragmentary, though, and the writing is so wild I can only make out occasional phrases. But on one page Thaisa has written about, 'Such violent pain I thought I was being torn in half.'

Then they continue a little more clearly.

I have taken up this journal again in the hope that it will provide some comfort or companionship, even though I do not think there can ever be either of those things in the world.

I have tried not to cry, but I have cried, of course – for so many hours that my eyes feel as if they have been scraped from my head. My body is bruised with misery.

The little, lost creature who has engulfed me in the despairing darkness – the scrap of humanity that never drew breath – lies in a corner of the room. Seamus's son and mine. A boy who should have grown up with his father's charm and intelligence and impatience, and with light and life and love in his eyes.

'And with your music in his soul,' Seamus said, for he was with me all through the hours of pain.

But there will be no music, no life, nothing for the child. When we knew he was dead, when Madge told us, Seamus broke down and pulled me to him, and I felt his hot, difficult tears soak into my gown. It has made a new bond between us, but not all the bonds of the angels, nor all the chains of hell's devils can bring my son back to life.

Afterwards, he attempted to gather about him the mantle of his calling, and tried to pray. I reached for the Book of Hours given to me by John, but no prayers touched me or helped me. I do not think they helped Seamus, either.

I know when he really died, my poor lost little one. I know it happened as I stood in the square that afternoon, hearing the screams of a man burning to death.

Tomorrow Seamus will try to arrange a burial and a service. He says I need not be there and Madge says I am not well enough to leave the house. But I will be there to see my baby buried, even if I have to be carried into the church.

Midnight. Rain is beating down on the windows. Seamus is still here – he has lit candles and a fire in the downstairs room. I am lying as close to the hearth as I can get, but I am still cold with a deep, bone-coldness.

Midnight is usually an hour when everywhere is quiet in this part of the town, but tonight there is noise and disturbance. People are running and shouting in the street, and twice now the flares of torches have passed across the windows.

A few moments ago Seamus went out to see what was happening, while Madge and I remained inside. A hard, heavy weight is pressing down on my head, and I believe something dark and violent and terrible is coming. Then I look at the still small figure in the corner, and I think that nothing can ever be as dark or as terrible as that.

Seamus has returned. The disturbance is coming from a group of people from Rede Abbas. When I peered through a window, even though their features were distorted by the flaring torches and their own emotions, I recognized most of them. With them are two men Seamus says are from Thomas Cromwell's Commission.

They are shouting loudly. At first the shouts were, 'Witch! Bastard. Monk's whore!'

Then a new cry started up – this time Seamus's name, followed by accusations. Heretic. And hard on the heels of that: 'Pedlar of God's benefices. Seller of absolution.' And again, 'Heretic!'

Madge, the dear good soul, ran to the upstairs rooms, to see if we can get out through the little garden behind the house, but she has just returned, white-faced, to say there are more people there. If we try to escape that way, they will be on us in minutes.

We are trapped, but Seamus promises that somehow he will get us away. His eyes glow with the challenge, and I know the danger and the prospect of a fight stimulates him.

There is one other thing he has promised, though. Before we leave the house, we will give the dead baby as Christian – and as reverent – a funeral as we can manage.

We do not have much time, but a few moments ago we carried candles into a small room on the house's side. Seamus and Madge, working with furious speed, have levered up a section of the stone floor and scooped out a hollow beneath it. I am sitting near the door, watching them, writing this. The room is windowless – a storeroom – but I know the outer wall backs on to a lavender bush that grows immediately outside. I know it because I picked some lavender only a few days ago, so that I could dry it and let its scent infuse the rooms. I have some of the sprigs in my hand now, and I shall place them in the grave with my son to sweeten his rest. There is a lavender bush outside the window of my cottage at Rede Abbas – if ever I can return there, the scent of that lavender will feel like a link to the child who lies here on his own.

Seamus has his crucifix which he will put in the child's hands, and when I finish this last entry, I will leave my diary in the grave as well, so that our son will have my story and his.

As I write this, the windows are being smashed and there are great heavy thuds on the door. It can only be moments before they are in the house . . .

Seamus is beginning the prayers for the dead, and I am about to close this book for ever. The one last thing I shall do for our son, as his face is covered with earth and the stone slab, is to sing my family's song as we let him go home to God.

And then – I do not know. Despite Seamus's promises and his bravery, I do not think we can escape.

Thaisa's story ended there, but the strength of emotion that had driven her pen reached out to me. Her words about the scent of lavender creating a link to the child who would lie here on his own affected me very deeply. A hot, hard lump of misery formed in my throat, and for some moments I could not see the pages for the mist that obscured my eyes.

I put Thaisa's diary in a pocket, and made my way to the stairs, intending to go quietly up to my bed. Halfway up the stairs I heard shouts and running feet in the square outside, and so deeply was my mind in Thaisa and Seamus's story, that at first I thought I was hearing the lingering echoes from three hundred years earlier. From that night when Seamus Flannery and the woman, Madge, had dug that frantic, tragic grave.

But then Theodora came running into the room, her eyes wide and terrified, her face white, and the present snapped back into its place.

'People in the courtyard,' she said, clutching my hands. 'Oh, Andrew – it's the two Glaum women and other people from Rede Abbas. They're shouting for me to go out to them. If not, they'll break in. Can we get out without them knowing?'

It was as if the past – that segment of the past in which I had been so deeply immersed – had reached out and closed bloodied claws around us. Thaisa and Seamus Flannery with Madge had huddled in this house three centuries earlier, hearing the doors and windows being smashed, because the Rede Abbas villagers, led by Cromwell's Commissioners, believed Seamus had accepted these very houses in return for pardoning the sins of Edward Glaum – Thaisa's father.

And now Edward's descendants – Margaretta and Gertrude Glaum – were breaking into the house. Their motives were different; they believed Theodora had murdered their father and caused him to be entombed alive. For the murder, if nothing else, they intended to deliver her up to justice. But their intentions were the same as those of their forbears.

'We can't get out,' I said to Theodora. 'They'd be on us at once.'

'I'll go out to them,' she said. 'It's me they want anyway.'

She was halfway across the room when I caught her and pulled her back, because Thaisa's words had come back to me. 'Tonight I shall sleep in the room under the eaves which has a bolt on the door,' she had written. 'It gives me a feeling of security to know I could draw that bolt and it would keep people out.'

I had not been up to that room, but if the bolt was still there . . .

'There might be a way to evade them,' I said. 'We'll barricade ourselves into the attic room and bolt the door. Then we'll wait for someone to summon help. Mr Thread at the printer's shop – he'll hear. He'll help us. But the Glaum ladies and the rest will have given up long before then in any case. Go up there now, Theodora.'

'I'll fetch food to take as well,' she said, and made for the door, obviously meaning to go into the storeroom – the room where I had found the baby's grave; the grave that was still uncovered . . .

I said, 'No, I'll do that. You fetch the oil lamps.'

I waited until she had gone, then I ran to the storeroom. First, I tumbled a few things into a rush basket – bread, some cold meat and cheese. I added a jug of milk, careful to stand it upright.

And then I did something that may seem extraordinary to anyone reading this. I can only say, in mitigation or explanation, that in times of extreme fear the mind is a curious thing.

Thaisa's last recorded words about the child had lodged in my mind, and I did not think I could leave this house without trying to give him some form of rest.

It was a brief task to scoop up the disturbed earth and sprinkle it over the little body again. As I did so, I was aware of Thaisa's diary still in my pocket. I paused. Part of me wanted very much to take her with me in the form of her journal, but there was another part that was remembering how she had talked about the scent of lavender linking her to a child who lay here on his own. How she had left this diary with him, 'so that he will have my story and his,' she had said.

I had copied down her story in my own journal. It would not be entirely lost.

I bent over the grave, and pushed the diary as far down in the earth as I could. It was absurd to imagine a tiny hand came out and closed around the book, but for a moment the sensation and the image was very strong.

Then I was spreading the earth in place and replacing the stones.

'I'll keep hold of you in my mind,' I said, silently, to what lay beneath the floor. 'You'll be in my prayers and in my thoughts.'

As I picked up the food and the jug of milk, it occurred to me that I did not know the child's name. Had Thaisa and Seamus named him? Had Seamus baptized him? It was something I would never know. I would think of him as Anthony, though – after St Anthony of Padua, who is the patron saint of all things lost, and who is typically portrayed as holding a child in his arms. Using up minutes I could not afford, I paused for long enough to murmur the words of baptism over the grave.

How the two Glaum daughters found us, I do not know, but Quire Court – once Glaum's Acre – had belonged to their family, so they must have known of its existence, and thought it the likeliest hiding place. I have never believed that any of the monks told them where we were, and I never will believe it.

Once we had slammed and bolted the attic door, I felt safer – although not very much. In the courtyard outside, torchlight leapt across the old stones, turning the place into a devil's lair. I could see Margaretta and Gertrude Glaum, and with them were five men, three of whose faces I knew from Rede Abbas. How the long and difficult journey from Rede Abbas to Quire Court had been made, and how the men had been coerced into making it, I could not guess. Money had probably been involved, though, and the village people had long been accustomed to obeying the Glaum family. As well as that, Theodora had always been a strange, misunderstood figure in Rede Abbas. It would not have taken much persuasion to get a group of the villagers to Oxford, especially if the Glaum ladies had told them they believed Theodora had murdered their father.

If there had been just two men out there I might have tried to fight, but there were five, and I could not overcome five. Even in the torchlit darkness, I could see they were brandishing makeshift weapons – clubs and spikes. It was not out of the question that one of them had a gun.

Then they saw us, and a shout went up – triumphant, angry, greedy.

'Murderess,' screeched one of the Glaum females. 'Bring her out and we'll take her back to face justice.'

'My father was alive in the tomb,' shouted the other. 'He was buried alive. And it's that creature's fault!'

Theodora had been huddled in a corner – she was scratching at the bare plaster of the wall by the window, and I again had the sensation of the past overwhelming us.

'Your eyes are narrow and long', Seamus Flannery had said to Thaisa. 'Your ears are set a little too high on your head to look entirely human . . . Your hair is the colour of the primroses in Musselwhite's Meadow . . .'

He could have been describing Theodora, who was born three hundred years after Thaisa. I could almost believe it was Thaisa who crouched in the room now.

Then she stood up, and she was my Theodora again, and she was staring out of the larger of the windows, and saying we were on the corner of the house here. 'If we could get out through one of the windows, Andrew, and down to the gardens—'

'We couldn't do it,' I said. 'We can only wait and hope someone raises the alarm.' But even as I spoke, hope was dying, because most of the other residents of the Court went to their homes each evening, and the only other person who lived here was Mr Thread. He was as thin and timid as his name, and although earlier I had hoped he might summon help for us, now it was easier to visualize him cowering in his house, afraid to confront such an angry group.

I had barely finished speaking when a frantic crash came from below. The outer door smashed open and banged against a wall with a sound that reverberated through the whole house. Cold night air rushed into the house – I could feel it even in this attic room.

I pulled Theodora against me, and we backed away to the wall facing the door.

'They won't get in here,' I said. 'That door will hold.'

But of course it did not. And of course they did get in.

Theodora and I had no chance. We were dragged out of the house, and thrust into two waiting carriages. I recall Theodora

> screaming, and I remember casting agonized glances to Mr Thread's shop. But no one came to help us, and we were tied up and flung into the carriages. Then something hard and heavy crunched down on the back of my head, and my vision splintered into hundreds of jagged, hurting lights before blackness closed down.

Andrew's vigorous writing ended there, and the next page of his journal was in the faint, uncertain script again. Maeve felt the loss of the strong, courageous Andrew as sharply as if it was a blow.

'I think I must have been unconscious for most of the journey back to Rede Abbas,' Andrew wrote in the weak, straggling script. 'Because I remember very little of it. There were occasional interludes of awareness, but that awareness was filled with a dizzy confusion, and with the sensation of carriage wheels bumping sickeningly over uneven ground. I had no idea where Theodora was at that stage – I do not think she was in the carriage with me.'

> She's here with me now, though, in the bell tower. She's below the stone steps outside this room. Only a flight of steps separates us, but she might as well be several worlds away because I can't get to her. Forgive me, my dear, lost love, I tried to save you, but there were too many of them holding me back from you at the end.
>
> But I watched everything. I watched the Glaum women and the villagers thrust flaring torches into crevices in the old stones of this tower, and I saw how the flares leapt up, lighting the darkness to a dreadful and macabre life, horridly reminiscent of the medieval paintings depicting hell – of a Dante's *Inferno*, portrayed by Bosch or Botticelli . . .
>
> Dear God, I'm trapped in a dank old tower with my beloved Theodora, both of us helpless, with the sea washing inexorably in, and I'm writing about medieval art and thirteenth-century visionary poets!
>
> I promised myself I would set it all down, though.
>
> They tied Theodora's wrists and ankles, then laid her on the stone floor of the tower. Then two of the men carried in thick, solid-wood planks, which they placed over her, hammering them down. A coffin. That was what they fashioned

by the light of those greasy torches. A coffin that enclosed her, and a coffin in which she lay, living and breathing, just as Adolphus Glaum had lain living and breathing in his tomb. (And Theodora's mother? Did she live inside her coffin? Did Thaisa's son, Anthony, at Quire Court?)

'And now she's buried alive,' one of them – Margaretta, I think – cried. 'Both of them to be buried alive, just as our father was buried alive.'

'Murderess,' shouted the other, darting forward and thrusting her face close to Theodora's. 'Whore.'

They have the seeds of madness of course, those two. Perhaps it is something in their family – I have no idea and I do not care.

The hammer blows fell on the long nails driven into the wooden planks. I fought to get to Theodora for all I was worth, but they held me too tightly. Theodora was screaming by then, desperately and beseechingly, sobbing my name until it spun and echoed into every shadowy corner of this place, soaking into the stones. Will it echo back in the future, so that people will hear a faint stir of sound and wonder who 'Andrew' might have been?

The men finished their grim task, and straightened up. They looked at Margaretta and Gertrude, who nodded, clearly satisfied. Then the men seized me, dragging me up the stairs to this accursed room. They tied me up in a corner and hammered more of the thick oak planks across the door. They spent a long time over it, making sure the planks could not be torn down. I heard them go out through the door and slam it shut, then go off along the cliffside.

Leaving Theodora and me to drown.

I fought free of the ropes round my wrist and ankles fairly quickly. Then I tore my hands to bloodied ribbons trying to smash down the planks, but they are nailed too firmly and the oak is too thick. The sea is coming in – I hear it and I smell it.

I have called to Theodora repeatedly, but she won't be able to hear me, of course. I believe she will be dead by this time – from fear, from lack of air in that tiny space, I do not know which. My mind knows it for the truth, even though my heart cannot accept it yet. Down there, beneath those thick planks, next to the cold stone floor, she is dead. And even if a spark of life were still to be in her, the sea will snuff it out.

I would have given my life to save her. I'd like that understood by anyone who may one day read this. But there was nothing I could do.

The light is going now – I cannot write any more. I shall place this journal as high as possible. If I stand on tiptoe on one of the ledges I can reach just above the water marks, and there are several crevices in the stones. The journal may escape the sea's ingress, and it may one day be found. I will wrap it in the oilskin that Brother Wilfrid uses to keep his herbal mixtures fresh, and it's just possible that my words – or some part of them – may survive. I should like that. I should like to think that someone, some day, will read this.

As I write these final lines, I believe I can hear 'Thaisa's Song' somewhere close at hand. I would like to believe it is Theodora singing, but I know it is not.

So, thought Maeve, laying the journal down. Theodora. She did not know if she liked Theodora or if she hated her because Andrew had loved her.

She had not understood everything he had written, but she thought she had understood most of it. Andrew and Theodora had run away from Rede Abbas because Theodora had murdered the man called Adolphus Glaum – at least, people thought she had. But Andrew must have thought Theodora was innocent because he had taken her to a place in Oxford to hide. Quire Court. That was where he had found that little baby's body, and the journal of that long-ago woman – Thaisa. Maeve had found that part quite difficult to understand. She thought she might read it again when she was a bit older.

She would not use any of this for her school essay, of course. These were not things to put in an essay that everyone would read, and also—

Also, this was her own family. She realized it with a shock. Theodora and Thaisa had both had the name of Eynon. And Theodora might have been a murderer.

In the end she wrote her school essay on the monastery in the sixteenth century, finding some old cures and herb remedies that the monks had made and used. There was an old sketch in the library of how the infirmary might have looked in those days, and Maeve included this.

The teacher said it was a very good essay; Maeve came second in the competition and was given a book token as a prize.

NINETEEN

Michael had been so strongly affected by finding the little grave in Quire Court that he almost missed the later train to Rede Abbas. He grabbed his overnight case, hoped he had not forgotten to pack anything vital, and scrambled into a taxi, reaching the railway station with three minutes to spare.

He rang Nell from the train, but it went to voicemail again. Most likely she was watching some Revels performance and had switched off her phone. Michael left a message saying he was finally en route, and the train was scheduled to reach Axminster just after two o'clock. 'So if you could meet me there, that would be great.'

This dealt with, he attempted to complete the crossword in a newspaper somebody had left behind. After this, he checked his phone again. There was nothing from Nell, but there was an email from Owen. It was probably too much to hope that he had already deciphered some of the book, but Michael clicked on the email eagerly.

Even on the phone's small screen, Owen's enthusiasm came strongly across.

> Michael – I don't know when you'll pick this up, but as you'll imagine I started deciphering your discovery the minute you left. I haven't got very far yet, and I think we may still need Brant's eye on some of it, but even at this early stage, it's clearly a remarkable find. Your diarist appears to have been a female – rather a lively wench from the sound of things, because there's reference to certain romantic passages with the Father

> Abbot of a monastery – one Seamus Flannery. Well, I say *romantic*, but I think it was a rather earthier relationship.
>
> Without all the tests on paper, etc., I have no idea yet how far we can trust the actual contents, but so far I'm inclined to think they're genuine. And I shouldn't think the inhabitants of the sixteenth century were given to writing raunchy chick-lit, should you? I suppose what we must keep in mind, though, is the possibility of a very elaborate plot behind the whole thing. The famous old device of, 'Dear Mr Publisher, here's a manuscript I discovered in my grandfather's attic'.

Michael smiled, and scrolled down to read the rest of the email.

> I haven't found the diarist's name yet, but I'll let you know when I do. I'm hoping to find it – I'd like to allot her an actual identity. She mentions that dead bell again, by the way. I have no idea what – or where – it is, but if you happen to see any bells anywhere in Rede Abbas, I'd be interested to know about it. Sorry if that sounds like a cross between Victor Hugo and Henry Irving.
>
> This afternoon I'm going along to the Bodleian to have a better look at that sixteenth-century document written by Brother Cuthwin – you remember he was the lively sounding monk who chronicled the Revels at St Benedict's. I don't know how much of his scribings are extant, but I'll certainly ransack the august shelves and scour the cobwebbed archives. It would be good beyond all things if we could tie our diarist to Cuthwin – in printed and annalistic terms, that is. I'll keep you posted.
>
> Meanwhile, happy Revelling,
>
> Owen

Michael smiled again, closed the email, then collected sandwiches and coffee from the train's buffet section, and ate them staring out of the window. But he was scarcely noticing the countryside rushing past; he was still seeing the tiny body lying beneath the old stones of the floor, with the heart-rending hand reaching out . . .

He finished his sandwiches, rounded them off with an apple, and reached for the unfinished crossword. There was only another three-quarters of an hour before the train reached Axminster; it was unusual that Nell had not returned his call yet, but he would try her again when they got a bit nearer. Presumably he could hop into a taxi there if necessary – it was not much of a distance to Rede Abbas. It was possible that Nell had not got his message – the phone signal might be unreliable, or her phone might be out of charge. He found the number of The Swan, and tried that.

The Swan's receptionist was helpful. Mrs West had gone out just after breakfast, she said. She had been intending to explore the area a bit. No, she had not come back yet, but there were all kinds of events going on, so it was likely she had got caught up in something.

Michael said, 'Would you pass a message to her when she does come in. It's Dr Flint.'

'Oh yes, we've got you booked in for tonight, Dr Flint.'

'I've had to catch a later train, but I'm expecting to reach Axminster Station just after two,' said Michael. 'If I haven't reached Mrs West by then, I'll get a taxi out to you.'

'Yes, certainly,' said the receptionist. 'There's a taxi rank at Axminster, and it's only about twelve miles to Rede Abbas. If the train's on time you should be with us by three at the latest. You'll have a nice drive along the coast road as well.'

From: Olive Orchard
To: Daniel Goodbody

Daniel –
I've left several messages on your answerphone, but I suppose you're immersed in some part of the entertainments. Gerald says you've probably switched off your phone, or you're screening your calls or something, but of course I know you won't have done that – I know you're not answering because you're so busy.

I expect I shall see you at one of the events later. I'm going to the dancing display (the 'Bishop's Visitation' from the sixteenth century and an adaptation of 'Laudnum Bunches'), then the performance of that mumming play, *The Rede Abbas Tup*. That's the one people sniggered over, but actually it's an entirely seemly depiction of the slaughtering of a ram and the making of it into presents. Perfectly suitable for children, and it could be argued that it's very nearly ecologically friendly.

We adapted the famous 'The Derby Ram', and crossed fingers and toes that nobody from Derby would turn up and accuse us of snaffling their tradition.

I'd hoped to tell you my news in person, or at least by actually speaking to you – in fact I was going to suggest we might meet for a pub lunch somewhere between 'Laudnum Bunches' and *The Rede Abbas Tup*. But time's running out, so here's the news. Gerald has found 'Thaisa's Song'! (I'd put a fanfare of trumpets in there if I could.)

Needless to say he's as pleased as punch, and by half past nine he had rounded up the choir (well, most of them), and hauled dear old Mr Budd to rehearse them. Mr Budd is having to forgo his pie and pint at the Coach and Horses today, which is rather a pity, because he's gone along to the Coach and Horses every day at twelve on the dot, for the last fifty years. I should think he'd totter through their door even if Armageddon had just been announced, and the Four Horsemen of the Apocalypse were about to ride into town.

They're currently all closeted in the old schoolroom, trying to make sense of the score. Gerald unearthed it from a wodge of old monastery records – I'm surprised you didn't hear his shriek of triumph all the way to your house. The score is impossibly faded and foxed, and I wouldn't have thought it was readable, never mind capable of being sung, but Gerald brandished it at Mr Budd, and it was decided they would make the attempt.

I went along to the schoolroom at half past eleven with sandwiches and flasks of coffee – you'd think The Fox & Goose might have agreed to send in a few of their chicken legs and a bread roll or two by way of lunch, wouldn't you, but they're determined to be as unhelpful as possible. But there was the choir, singing away for all it was worth, Gerald dashing around making notes, and Mr Budd conducting like an over-wound clockwork toy. For all he's eighty-five he's still a commanding figure, dear old Bill Budd, and if anyone can get a reasonable rendition of this peculiar song out of the choir, he will. And peculiar it is, I can't stress that strongly enough. The bits I heard were in the strangest mixture of badly pronounced Welsh (at least, I suppose it was Welsh), and a few words of English that Mr Parry the milkman translated. Personally, I wouldn't trust

Mr Parry's Welsh from here to that door, because he's lived in Rede Abbas since he was three and the only bit of Welsh he knows is '*Sosban Fach*', which he sings every Christmas.

Anyway, do phone me when you get this.

Olive

'Hi Daniel – Olive again. I thought I'd try ringing again, but you're obviously still occupied. I was sorry not to have seen you at the dancing display. It went really well, and I honestly don't think anyone noticed that two of the dancers had been imbibing The Fox & Goose's specially brewed mead earlier.

'If you get this message in time, I'll keep a seat for you for the mumming thing.'

The Fox & Goose
Internal memo
To: All bar and restaurant staff

Please ensure that no more of the home-brewed mead is served, since there have been reports of unsocial and unstable behaviour by several people who have drunk it. This is most likely due to it having been left to ferment for too long.

If anyone does order, serve ordinary cider instead with a slice of apple and lemon. People won't know the difference and the home-brewed price can still be charged.

Michael arrived at Axminster on time, and was aware of a small nagging core of concern. Nell had not phoned back, and he had left two more messages. Alighting from the train he scanned the platform eagerly, hoping to see her with some tale of phone out of charge.

But she was not there. He waited outside the station for ten minutes, in case she might still appear, then reluctantly got into a taxi and gave the address of The Swan in Rede Abbas. The receptionist had been right about one thing: the drive along the coast road was spectacular. The tide was scudding in – huge foamy waves were lashing across the flat stretches of beach, towards the cliffs.

'Quite a sight,' said Michael, leaning forward to see better.

'We get used to it down here,' said the taxi driver. 'But it's still worth watching.'

'Is this high tide now?'

'No, there's a good couple of hours yet. High tide's about five. By half-past five three-quarters of the cliffs below this road will be submerged . . . Here for the Revels thing, are you?'

'Yes.'

'They say it's going really well – first time for more than a hundred years it's been done, so they tell. Here's The Swan now. Nice place, it is. They'll make you comfortable.'

Michael liked The Swan with its pleasing scents of old oak and its timeless air of gentility. He booked in, and asked about Nell.

'She's not appeared yet, Dr Flint, but I shouldn't worry. Most people are making a day of it. She'll be in soon, I expect. She went on foot – her car's still in the yard.'

'Is the Ramblers' Hostel nearby?' asked Michael, his concern switching to Beth.

'A few minutes' walk.'

'Michael put his things in the big double room overlooking the square, then walked along to the hostel. It appeared the children had all been taken into somewhere called Musselwhite's Meadow after lunch, to watch a display of dancing, followed by a mumming play. Oh yes, everyone had gone – a great time the children were having. They were due back at the hostel around five o'clock for a high tea before the evening's events.

At least it sounded as if Beth was all right, so Michael thought he would walk round the square. He was becoming increasingly worried by Nell's silence, but he did notice that the square was an attractive place; there were some nice old buildings, and shopkeepers had put tubs of flowers out and hanging baskets. At the centre were a number of street stalls, all with a medieval theme. It was quite busy; people seemed interested in the stalls' wares, and a number of them were consulting programmes, and discussing whether they would go along to see the medieval jousting and whether Musselwhite's Meadow would be muddy enough to require wellingtons, because you never knew with meadows.

He went back to The Swan and considered what to do next. It was just on four, and if the hotel receptionist's information could be relied on, Nell had been gone since nine o'clock. Seven hours. That was a long time, particularly on foot. At what point did you alert the police to the possibility of a missing person, and that person an adult? Michael thought he would make a search of as much of the village and the surrounding areas as he could, and if he had found no clues by, say, quarter past five, or had not reached Nell's phone by then, he would call the police. After that he would think what to do about Beth. He would not worry her yet, though.

It would obviously be quicker and more practical to search for Nell by car, and her car was here in the car park. What about the keys? She usually had one set with her, but she tended to leave a spare key in her luggage when she was away in case her handbag should be lost or stolen. It felt like the worst kind of intrusion to open her case, but Michael did so and was relieved to find the spare set. He checked his jacket to make sure he had his phone, then went out of the hotel, leaving a message of explanation at the desk.

'I think if I haven't tracked her down in the next hour, I'll have to contact the police,' he said, and the receptionist nodded sympathetically, and made a note of his mobile so they could call him if Nell returned in the meantime.

'I got the impression she was going out on the cliff road, Dr Flint.' She found a small local map of the area, and indicated. 'It'd be worth trying there first.'

'Thank you.' Michael took the map gratefully.

As he drove out of The Swan's car park the dashboard clock was showing twenty-past four.

TWENTY

After Nell West was safely imprisoned in the bell tower, Maeve went back to Cliff House.

It was long past what most people regarded as lunchtime. Maeve often did not bother about food and she was not hungry, but she made a cup of tea, which she drank sitting at the kitchen table. She and Aunt Eifa always had their meals at this table, to the measured tick of the old-fashioned kitchen clock on the mantelpiece. It had belonged to an ancestress of Aunt Eifa's – she had told Maeve that its original owner had vanished from this house one night. She must have taken some of her belongings with her, Aunt Eifa said, but she had left the clock.

Maeve was washing her cup and saucer – Aunt Eifa would have been very shocked to think of an unwashed cup and saucer lying on the table – when a car drew up outside the house, and a moment later there was the sound of the door knocker. This was deeply worrying, because no one ever came to this house and knocked on the door. But now a stranger – a man – was out there, and it was no good ignoring him because he might walk round to the back of the house and even look through windows, and realise there was someone inside. So she opened the door, but only part of the way, which should appear sufficiently discouraging.

The man was well-spoken and courteous, and at first Maeve thought he was only a tourist who had lost his way. But he introduced himself as Dr Flint – Maeve had no idea if he was a real doctor or not – and said he was looking for a lady called Nell West who seemed to be missing. She had not been seen since early that morning, and he wanted to know if Maeve had seen her walking along the cliff road. He provided a description, which Maeve listened to politely. But the name had already smacked against her mind like a blow. Nell West. This man, this Dr Flint, was concerned about her. He was looking for her.

'It isn't like her to simply go off without letting someone know,' Dr Flint was saying. 'The hotel think she was coming out here to look at the cliffs and an ancient bell tower, so I'm trying to retrace her steps before I call in the police.'

'I understand.' Maeve forced herself to speak in an ordinary, vaguely concerned tone, because he must not realise that hearing Nell West's name had thrown her into such panic. But he could not be allowed to investigate the tower – not until tomorrow's low tide at any rate – and he could not be allowed to call in the police either.

So, as he turned to go back to his car, Maeve said, 'Wait a moment, I believe I might have seen your friend. Shortly before lunch I think it was.' She tried to remember what Nell had been wearing, and said, 'Did she have on a brown jacket and a gold-coloured scarf?'

'Yes,' he said, eagerly.

'It sounds like her.' Maeve thought quickly. 'I have an idea she was going towards the bell tower.' She indicated the direction in a deliberately vague fashion. 'A remnant of the area's medieval past,' she said. 'But it's a bit lonely out there. The ground's very uneven – she could have tripped and sprained an ankle and not been able to get back.'

'Her phone doesn't respond.'

'Oh, the signal's dreadful out here. Everyone complains about it. But,' said Maeve, in a carefully worried voice, 'the tide will be coming in, and if she's fallen she could be in trouble.'

'I'll go out there at once.' He turned to go, and Maeve said, 'You won't get your car down there, not all the way to the tower. There's a footpath, though. I could come part of the way and point you towards it, if you want.'

'Thanks, but I'm sure I can find it. I won't trouble you.'

'It's no trouble. I often take a walk around this time of the afternoon anyway. And we haven't any too much time before high tide, and if you miss the path—' Before he could say any more, Maeve reached for her raincoat hanging on its usual peg, thrust her feet into the rubber boots that always stood beneath it, scooped up the door keys and came out of the house, slamming and locking the door. It was twenty minutes to five.

A plan that had worked once, should work twice.

Michael could not have said why he felt uneasy with this unknown woman. She had introduced herself quite pleasantly – she was Miss Eynon, she said, Miss Maeve Eynon – and she had lived in Cliff House since she was a child.

'Which is more years than I care to count,' she said. 'Are you in Rede Abbas for long?'

'Only a couple of days,' said Michael, trying to join in this polite small talk, but his mind taken up with finding Nell. 'Is this the path now?'

'Yes. It winds all the way along the cliff, but just along here there's a fork that goes down to a ledge. That's where the bell tower is.'

The path sloped steeply downwards and the ground was rutted. It would certainly be easy to slip or twist your ankle here. The sea was directly below them – a lashing, sullen sea storming in over the rocks, sending up showers of spray. As the tower came into view, Michael felt something flinch deep within his mind. Rede Abbas's medieval remnant of the past was like a decaying stump, blackened with age and covered here and there with crusted sections that might be from the constant lashing of the sea, or that might simply be the ravages of the centuries. Nell would have found it interesting, but it was doubtful if she would have walked out to it on her own. Still, Maeve Eynon had been definite about seeing her on this path, so it had to be checked.

'It's a strange-looking place,' he said.

'It's supposed to have been part of an ancient monastery – built by the original monks when they came here to spread Christianity,' said Maeve. 'In 700 or 800, I think. But most of that building was eroded by the sea – huge chunks of the cliff fell away, so the monks built a safer home further inland. The tower is the only bit that's left of the original.'

Michael said, 'How close does the sea come in?'

'At high tide it's a good halfway up the cliff face.' She pointed. 'It submerges the lower part of the bell tower. So you can see we haven't got much time to search.'

'Perhaps I'd better call the police after all.'

'We're almost there now. Let's check first, then you can call them. I can give you the local station's number. Calling them would be as quick as anything.'

They were near enough to the tower for Michael to see there was a small door set into one of the walls. He was about to ask if they could get right up to it, when Maeve said, 'Dr Flint – up there. Look.'

'What? Where?'

'The window halfway up. Can you see it? There's a figure up there – she's wearing an orange scarf. I'm sure it's your friend. Yes, look, she's waving.'

'I can't see anyone.'

'Can't you? No, I can't now, either. But I'm positive I saw her.'

Michael did not pause to think that he was on his own with a complete stranger in a remote and vaguely sinister place. He thought only that Nell might be in this grim old place and that she might be injured, and he went as quickly as possible across the few yards of scrubby, uneven ground towards the tower.

'She must be trapped,' said Maeve, at his side. 'The door might have jammed – there was some story years back about some children getting stuck; not able to get the door open from the inside or something.'

She was not exactly ahead of him, but somehow she reached the deep-set door first, and reached for the handle. She pulled on it, then frowned.

'You try,' she said. 'I think I was right – it seems to be jammed.'

Michael grasped the handle, prepared to tear it off with his own hands if necessary. But it turned at once and the door swung inwards. He stepped inside, calling Nell's name, and with overwhelming relief heard her say, 'Michael?' with disbelief and delight.

There was just enough light to see she had been sitting on a stone stairway and also to see that she appeared unharmed. She came towards him at once, but before Michael could say anything, the door swung back into place, and clanged shut.

'Oh God, no,' said Nell, in a voice that shook with tears and despair. 'She's shut us both in. She trapped me in here earlier – Michael . . .'

Michael was already at the door, searching for a handle, but Nell said, 'It's no use. There's no handle on this side – I've tried and tried.'

'But that woman—'

'She shut me in here this morning,' said Nell, and he heard the sob of panic in her voice. 'I have no idea why, unless she's mad. Michael, I've never been so glad to see you, but I wish you weren't here. I wish you were outside, calling out the rescue teams. Is Beth all right? Have you seen her?'

'I checked at the hostel,' said Michael, pleased that he could at least alleviate this concern for her. 'They were all about to scoff down a meal then set off for some entertainment or other. I haven't said you're missing.'

'Good. We'll probably get out before Beth even notices.'

'You've tried phoning, of course,' said Michael, nevertheless delving into his pocket for his phone.

'Yes, but there's no glimmer of a signal. And the tide's coming in fast, and it'll submerge this room, and we can't get up the stairs to where it's safe, because the sodding stairs have fallen away halfway up . . .' This time her voice broke properly. 'And I think we've only got about half an hour left.'

* * *

Maeve was extremely pleased with how well her plan had worked, particularly since there had been hardly any time to think about it. There was a pleasing symmetry about imprisoning Dr Flint and Nell West together. The tide was coming in, and they would not be able to open the door. They would not be able to use a mobile phone to call for help, either – those boys trapped there a few years ago had said there was no phone signal, and Maeve could remember people talking about how the thick stone walls would have blocked it.

Dr Flint's car was still on the track, of course, but, if questioned, Maeve did not need to know anything about it. At worst, she might say that yes, someone had knocked on her door asking about a missing friend, but she had not been able to help and she had not seen where he went.

As she reached the upper footpath, she looked down at the tower. If she stayed here she would be able to watch the sea come in – the waves were already scudding across the last strip of pebbly shore and the sharp tang of the wind, salt-laden, stung her face. Aunt Eifa had liked this part of the cliff. She used to come out here to watch the tide engulf the bell tower. It was where she had been on that last day – the last time she had ever gone out of the house.

The memories of that day closed around Maeve. She would never forget a single detail of it. It had been the day she had played 'Thaisa's Song' again.

It had been soon after the essay competition at school, marking the demolition of the monastery. She had found herself thinking about the song more and more – how her mother had found it in this house. The more she thought about her mother making that recording, the more she wanted to hear it again. It was strange and sad and she did not entirely understand it, but there was no reason not to listen to it again – to hear her mother laughing and her father teasing her.

She waited until a Saturday afternoon when Aunt Eifa set off on one of her long walks. A good brisk walk, she said, and Maeve should come with her. Maeve said she had homework to finish, and Aunt Eifa said homework was all very well, but if Maeve insisted on frowsting indoors, she could mop the kitchen floor and clean the mirrors. They were shockingly smeared with all the damp.

Maeve finished her tasks as quickly as possible, then went up to her bedroom and took the cassette player from its hiding place.

There was a plug in the corner of the bedroom, but Maeve carried it down to the music room. Theodora might have played the music to Andrew in that room – he had known about it, and he had written about copying it – and Maeve wanted to hear it in the place where Andrew had heard it.

She was nervous but she was also excited, although she would not be surprised if her parents' voices had been wiped from the tape as completely as if their lives had been wiped from existence. But the recording was still there, exactly as she remembered. The second voice – the odd, flawed echo that had spooked her so much last time – seemed to have vanished, though. It must have been a fault on the tape after all.

It was far easier now to understand the words her mother was singing.

Who is this, knocks on my tomb?
Asks where and what I am,
Who is this who calls to me?
I cannot see nor hear.

Maeve wound the tape back to the start, and sat down on the piano stool. When the tape began to play she sang with her mother, stumbling once or twice, but managing to keep up. It felt as if her mother had come back to be with her – it felt as if she had taken Maeve's hand and as if they were singing this together. But when she reached the line where the singer was asking who called from outside the tomb, a cold fear began to steal over her. The second voice was there again. It was soft, but it was unmistakably echoing her – a beat or a half-beat behind, almost as if correcting her, wanting her to get it right. She pressed Pause, then released it. The second verse began, and at first Maeve thought it was all right. Then the other voice came back, and this time it was so close she thought someone was standing behind her chair. She turned sharply, but there was no one else in the room. Or was there? Had the curtains moved just then, as if someone was standing behind them – someone who might at any moment draw them aside and look out at her . . .?

Maeve wound back to the start again, praying that this time the voice would have gone.

I cannot see, I cannot hear
Who knocks upon my tomb.
I cannot speak, I cannot reach
The one stands by my tomb.

The voice seemed to have gone and Maeve began to sing again, so deeply immersed in the music that she did not hear the door of the room open. It was only the loud gasp that made her spin round.

Aunt Eifa was standing in the doorway, her eyes on the cassette player. But there was a dreadful blankness in her face, as if something had reached behind the eyes and scraped out all trace of Aunt Eifa, leaving only emptiness. The stone look, thought Maeve.

She sprang up as if to shield the tape from her aunt, and the blank look vanished from her aunt's face. She reached out a hand as if to clutch at Maeve.

'"Thaisa's Song",' she said, and even her voice was different. It was hoarse and dry as if she had to fight to form the words. 'My grandmother said the last copy was destroyed. "Burned," she said, "and the words torn to unreadable shreds". But she said that, even though it disappeared at times, it was always found again. And she was right, because you've found it . . . A recording . . . I didn't think such a thing existed . . .'

Something was happening to Aunt Eifa's face – it was as if huge, invisible hands had seized it and were dragging it out of shape. She said, 'Maeve, you must never play that again. Never . . .'

Maeve was terrified. She had never seen her aunt like this – she had never seen anyone like this – but she went forward, and put an arm around her and led her to the nearest chair. Even this felt strange, because Aunt Eifa was not a person you touched; she had never given Maeve a hug or a goodnight kiss, even at Christmas or on her birthday.

But she said Aunt Eifa must go up to bed, and she would fill a hot-water bottle and make tea. The first-aid classes at school said you should give people hot sweet tea for shock.

Aunt Eifa seemed not to hear. She began tearing at her throat as if trying to fight off unseen hands. Maeve pulled her towards the stairs, to get her up to her bedroom, and it was then that the side of her aunt's body seemed to sag and become heavy and hard, as if it was a slab of stone. She slipped from Maeve's grasp, falling in an untidy sprawl on the hall floor, one hand still clutching at her throat, the other hand lifeless and flaccid.

'I'll get a doctor,' said Maeve, terrified, having no idea what had happened.

'Nooo . . .' It came out in a single streaming syllable, blurred but unmistakable. 'No – not doctor . . .' There was a clumsy, but unmistakable gesture towards the open door of the music room, and Maeve, not knowing what was wanted, closed the door. Then, because for the moment it was impossible to get Aunt Eifa up the stairs to her bedroom, Maeve did the next best thing, which was to half carry, half drag her to the sitting room, where there was a big sofa.

Once lying down, Aunt Eifa tried to speak again, but her words were so slurry it was difficult to understand her. In the end Maeve fetched pen and paper, not knowing if it would do any good, relieved when Aunt Eifa was able to hold the pen.

In shaky letters, her aunt wrote, '*No doctor – no one to know . . .*'

'But I must get a doctor,' said Maeve. 'You're ill – and you fell down.'

The pen scratched frantically again. '*No doctor. You do all I tell you. Might be safe then . . .*'

Maeve stared at her aunt, seeing the dreadful slipped-aside face, and the frightened eyes under the straggle of hair that had worked loose.

'I don't understand.'

The words were scribbled on to the page again. '*Feel as if I am encased in stone . . .*'

The pen fell from her hand, and she clutched at Maeve. Her face looked as if one half of her was dead. And yet even like this she was stern and insistent and Maeve did not dare disobey her.

She said, 'What do you want me to do?'

Years later, Maeve was to realize that in almost any other place, with almost any other people involved, what came afterwards would never have happened. In any other place, there would have been hospitals, doctors, visiting nurses. Maeve herself, barely thirteen years old, would have been placed in care – perhaps in a foster home. And in any other environment she would have rebelled.

But Rede Abbas was small and old-fashioned, and Maeve had

been under Aunt Eifa's domination for over three years. So what happened next, happened without anyone questioning or objecting – or even knowing.

Aunt Eifa was disabled by the stroke – which was what Maeve later supposed it to have been – but she continued to dominate.

She refused to be got up to her bedroom, although Maeve had no idea how she would have managed to move her there on her own anyway. Instead, writing with the furious anger that now drove her, Aunt Eifa stated that beds were where people died. She would not be shut away. A bed – more correctly a bedsitting room – must be set up for her downstairs.

It took almost three days for Maeve to arrange things so Aunt Eifa could live downstairs. She had to shunt a bed-frame – then a mattress and blankets – down the stairs, and make up a bed. The sofa that had always stood in the window of this room was banished to what had been the dining room. Aunt Eifa wrote that they did not need a dining room anyway. The dining table could be folded down and set against a wall and the room closed up.

The left half of her body and face were completely useless. At the start she had written that it felt as if it had been encased in stone, and Maeve thought this so dreadful that she did everything her aunt told her without demur.

Eifa Eynon could not walk a step unaided. On Saturday mornings, when Maeve had collected the shopping, her aunt had to be taken into the kitchen, a laborious step at a time, so she could sit at the scrubbed-top table and watch the week's groceries being stored in cupboards and fridge and larder. Maeve found it disconcerting to have Aunt Eifa's small, watchful eyes on her all the time, and to hear her aunt rapping on the table with her walking stick if things were put in the wrong cupboards. The clock on the mantel ticked malevolently as Maeve stored away tins of fruit and packs of rice and tea and flour.

She had to come home from school in the lunch hour each day to make lunch for Aunt Eifa, and at weekends she did the washing and cleaning. There was a small, very old-fashioned lavatory on the ground floor, but there were several steps down to it because of the uneven ground of Cliff House; even with Maeve's help, Aunt Eifa could not manage them. So a horrid wooden structure with a chamber pot inside had to be disinterred from the brick outhouse – Maeve had no idea who it had originally belonged to – and put at the side of the bed. It had to be emptied and scoured every day, but even with liberal use of disinfectant, a sick, sour odour gradually permeated the room. Maeve put dried lavender on the windowsill, but Aunt Eifa said the smell of lavender made her feel sick, so it had to be thrown out.

She insisted on seeing every scrap of paper that came into the house, and if she could not make herself understood through the blurred speech, which was most of the time, she wrote down what Maeve must do. Money had to be drawn out of the post office to pay all the bills, which must never be allowed to go over their due date by so much as an hour in case anyone came to the house to ask for payment. It was God's mercy that her right hand was still as good as ever, and that she could sign cheques, but she made Maeve spend an entire weekend practising her signature so she could sign cheques as well. Maeve thought this might be against the law.

Sometimes, during the evening, if Maeve was trying to watch a TV programme or read or listen to the radio in the small music room, Aunt Eifa rapped sharply on the wall with her stick, wanting something – a drink, a cushion, a book. Sometimes she rapped on the ceiling in the middle of the night, for Maeve to come down to her. Maeve did not dare ignore any of these summonses, but it was exhausting to be dragged out of bed at 3 a.m. simply to find reading glasses or that evening's newspaper, and then have to be at school for nine o'clock next day. It was exhausting in a different way to pretend to people that she had a normal home life.

At first local people occasionally asked about Aunt Eifa: did she still take her long cliff walks? Quite a familiar figure on that path, and it was strange not to see her striding along in her mackintosh. Maeve mumbled something about her aunt having had a bout of flu, but said she had almost recovered from it now.

When she told her aunt about the questions, her aunt pointed with her stick to the hall cupboard, where the outdoor coats hung. With a feeling of near-despair, Maeve put on the long mac. It had a stale smell, like bread left out of the tin for too long, but Aunt Eifa jabbed at the window and the cliff path with her stick. Maeve, studying her reflection in the long hall mirror, understood and was horrified. She was not only to shield her aunt's illness from everyone, she was to become her aunt – to take the long, solitary walks, so that no one would suspect that Eifa Eynon was helpless.

During the weeks and then the months that followed, Maeve wondered about asking someone for help – a teacher, the vicar, a doctor – but she did not know what kind of help could be given, and she was afraid of being taken away from Cliff House and made to live with strangers. And every time she thought about all this, she remembered how furious Aunt Eifa would be, and how much worse life would be afterwards. Even if Aunt Eifa was taken to a hospital and Maeve was sent somewhere else to live, Aunt Eifa would find a way of spoiling life even more for Maeve.

At intervals Maeve remembered that this could not last for ever. One day she would be free of this grinding dreariness.

It was a week before her eighteenth birthday when she realized there was a way out.

TWENTY-ONE

Michael said, 'I refuse to believe there's no way out.' He stared angrily round the dim stone room of the bell tower.

'There isn't, though. I'm the practical one, remember, and I've looked and searched, and I can't see anything.'

Part of Nell was glad beyond belief to have Michael with her, but she was also appalled, because it meant they would both die. If that happened, her beloved Beth would be on her own. This thought was so unbearable she pushed it away, and said, 'I keep hearing voices inside the sea sounds.'

'I heard them as well a minute ago. Like singing.'

'Yes. Are we imagining it? Which is worse – hearing ghost voices or thinking you're hearing them – or hearing the sea creeping in?'

As she said this, the whispering seemed to come closer.

I sang on the night I died . . . I waited for help to come, but no help came . . .

I'm not hearing it, thought Nell, shivering and wrapping her arms around her body. It's the sea. Water does create odd resonances.

All I had for comfort as death approached, was my family's song . . . The people here called it the devil's song . . . They did not understand the old Welsh that some call Primitive Welsh – the ancient Brythonic tongue . . . They said if you listened to it, it could draw the soul from your body . . . But it felt as if it was a hand holding mine . . . It felt comforting . . .

Nell stood up and walked around the room, stamping her feet loudly on the stones to cover the sounds. The heels of her boots rang out sharply on the stone floor.

Michael said abruptly, 'Do that again.'

'Do what again?'

'Walk across the floor like that.'

'Why?' asked Nell, doing as requested.

'The sound changes. The floor's different in that corner.'

'Is it? Yes, it is. There are wooden planks over here. Thick, heavy ones – almost like floorboards.' Nell stared at the floor. The planks covered almost a third.

'Who would put down a wooden floor in a place like this, with the sea and the damp and everything?' said Michael.

'It is odd. Any wood in here would warp and rot over the years – even without the sea washing in twice a day, the damp would be ruinous.'

They knelt down to look. There were ten planks altogether, each one about eight feet in length and about two feet wide.

'But I can't see that they provide any means of escape,' said Nell.

'There wouldn't be a trapdoor beneath them, going down into the cliff? No, of course there wouldn't; I'm straying into the realms of children's adventure stories.' Michael stood up, but Nell remained where she was, studying the wood.

'You've got an idea,' he said, after a moment, hardly daring to voice the thought.

'Yes, but I can't get hold of it. There's something in my mind, but I can't— Oh, yes I can, though!' She sprang up and grabbed his arm. 'Michael, listen, this might not work, but it's worth trying. If we could prise up one of those planks and get it on to the stairs, we could lay it across the gap where the stairs have crumbled away.'

He stared at her, not instantly understanding, then said, 'Creating a bridge to the top of the tower?'

'Yes. It wouldn't get us out, but I think it would get us above the water level when it comes in.'

'Let's look. Is there enough light?'

'I don't know . . . Oh, hold on, I've got a thing on the phone. Torch app. Beth downloaded it when she was experimenting. She said you never knew when things might come in useful.' She was already going up the stairs, switching on the phone-light. It was quite small, but it was surprisingly powerful.

'That's the sea mark,' said Michael, as they reached the collapsed section of stairs. Nell was directing the small light upwards as far as she could, letting it play waveringly over the section of the stair above them.

'There's very nearly an actual line, isn't there?' she said. 'It's way above the gap. But it's at the same level all across the walls – it must be the mark the water's left over the years . . . centuries, even, perhaps.'

She shivered, and Michael said, 'If we could get across this gap, we could wait up there – above the water level – until we're found.'

'They'll send out search parties, won't they?'

'Yes, of course. The Swan will do that if no one else does,' said Michael. 'I told the receptionist that if I hadn't traced you by about six I was going to call the police anyway.' He looked upwards again. 'If we could get up to where that window is – perhaps up to the bell chamber – we might even find there's a phone signal.'

'We haven't got much time,' said Nell, as they went back down the steps.

'Then we'd better get started. How do we prise the plank up? Think, my love – you've already said you're the practical one of the party.'

'Several of them have lifted a bit anyway,' said Nell, surveying the floor. 'I don't know what we can use for the actual prising, though . . . Oh, unless the iron staves on the stair wall would do it. Some of them must be loose and we only need one.'

After a couple of unsuccessful attempts, they managed to work one of the staves free. It was a thick, sturdy length of iron, one end tapering to a sharp point. But their first attempt to lever up the planks simply split the rotten sections of wood. Nell swore, but moved over to another piece.

'It's oak,' she said. 'It'll be heavy to move, but there should be sections still intact. Oak's very thick and dense.'

'Only you would know something like that. And,' said Michael, smiling at her in the wavering light, 'only you would say it at such a time.'

'I do love you,' said Nell, irrelevantly. 'Very much. Have I ever said?'

'Yes, but I can bear hearing it again. Try this plank here – no, let me do it.'

'It's all right, I've got it. You'd make a total pig's breakfast.'

'I thought you loved me.'

'I do, but it doesn't mean I think you're the world's greatest DIY expert.'

This time the oak plank came free and, when they lifted it, it stayed in one piece.

'And it's only slightly rotted at that edge,' said Nell, as they manoeuvred it around the narrow twists of the stairs.

It was more difficult than they had expected to position the oak across the gap so that it fell squarely and securely on to the other side, but eventually it dropped heavily and firmly on to the undamaged stairs on the other side, although it did so with a crash that echoed all round the tower, and sent up clouds of dust. Nell gasped and coughed, then, through the reverberations came a faint thrum from above, then the sound of something tapping against a hard surface.

Michael said, 'That seems to have disturbed the bell's mechanism, doesn't it? I expect some of it's still in place, even if the bell itself can't sound any longer.' He glanced at Nell, and said, 'But we don't give a stuff for whom it's tolling, because it isn't bloody tolling for us.'

But when they went back to the ground-floor room for another plank, Nell pointed to a corner of the room, where a trickle of water was seeping through the stones.

'A second plank would have been good,' she said. 'But I don't think there's time.'

'Nor do I. The one we've got should be wide enough to walk across.' He took her hand and they went back up the stairs.

'Will you go first, or will I?' said Nell.

Michael hesitated, then said, 'I will,' and Nell knew he was afraid of the makeshift bridge giving way. If he fell through to the ground, he would probably break his neck, but at least Nell would be left to make another attempt with more planks, and she might get to safety.

She said, softly, 'If I hadn't loved you before, I'd love you now for saying that.'

'Nell, I'd walk over broken glass barefoot for you,' he said, very seriously. 'Going across a plank of oak is nothing.' He looked at her. 'We're being very emotional, aren't we?'

'Yes, but in the circumstances, I think we're allowed.'

'If I say, "See you on the other side", will it sound like a metaphysical farewell?'

'Yes, but it's better than bad jokes about walking the plank, so say it anyway.'

Michael said it, then gave her a swift, hard kiss. 'This is only a matter of about six or seven steps – two or three seconds per step. I'll be on terra firma in thirty seconds maximum. You'll be there with me in another thirty. A minute for the whole operation. Here goes.'

He stepped on to the oak plank and Nell shone the phone-light, seeing that there were several of the iron staves in the left-hand wall.

'Can you use those for extra balance?'

'I'll try.'

He began to walk slowly and carefully, and Nell counted the steps. At four she dared hope he would make it. At five he seemed to fumble his grasp on one of the staves, and she saw it had worked loose. Her heart came up into her mouth, but Michael put the flat of his hand on the wall for balance, and went on. Even so, it seemed as if hours slid by before he stepped off the plank and called back.

'Easy as a walk in the park. The staves all felt firm except that last one, so avoid it. But don't rely on any of them too much – just use them for balance. What about the light?'

'If I throw the phone across will you catch it, then you can shine it for me?'

'Let's not risk it. It would be appalling if I missed.'

'Well, if I prop it up in my pocket I think there'll be enough overspill . . . Yes, there is.' Nell slung her bag over her shoulder and across her body, and reached for the first iron stave. She would not think that the plank might not bear a second lot of weight, because if she did not do this – if she remained here – she would certainly drown. The sea was coming into the lower room now – she could hear it and she could smell it. But all she had to do was take these six steps. Michael was waiting – he was holding out both his hands. He would not let her fall.

The world shrank to the dark stairwell and the stench of the sea, and to the rough feel of the iron staves in the wall. Nell managed not to look down, or even to think that on her right-hand side, within a few inches, was a black gaping hole that went all the way down to the ground. Three steps. So far so good. The plank creaked, but it did not move. Here was the stave that had shifted when Michael grasped it; she avoided that one. She was almost there. Four steps. Five. She was nearly within reach of Michael's waiting hands. She would not leap forward though, in case it dislodged the oak. With the thought, it shifted slightly, and Nell's heart leapt into her mouth. She felt it move again, and instinctively threw her body forward. There was a split-second of nothing, of no feeling, then Michael's hands closed around both of hers, and he was pulling her on to the stones beyond the gap.

Behind her the plank slid from its position, and crashed all the way to the ground. The sound was an impossible, painful explosion within the enclosed space, and the old stones shuddered and sent out clouds of black grit and dust. Splintered stones flew upwards, and above them came another shiver of sound from the bell.

But Nell was standing on firm ground and Michael was holding her against him. She clung to him, half sobbing, never wanting to let go of him. But, eventually, she managed to say, 'Sorry. Drama queen act. Very uncharacteristic.' She found a tissue in her pocket and mopped her tears, angry to find her hands were shaking.

Michael took the tissue from her and completed the mopping up. His hands were not entirely steady either, but eventually, he said, 'Are you all right to go on up? Because—'

'Because the sea's already got in,' said Nell.

They could both see the dull green light on the stair wall, and hear the slapping sound of the waves below them.

'Yes. Onwards and upwards,' said Michael.

'The plank falling made a terrific crash, didn't it?' said Nell, as they began cautiously to ascend. 'In fact, the window . . .'

She stopped, staring towards the narrow window, which was almost level with them.

'What's wrong? Nell, we need to get up to the bell chamber . . .'

Nell said, 'The stone figure. Can you see it?'

'Yes. It's a bit grisly, isn't it?'

'It's moving,' said Nell. 'The head's just turned round and it's looking straight at us.'

For a dreadful moment, neither of them spoke. From where they stood they could see the stone figure outlined against the darkening sky, and they could see the carved face and the eyeless sockets. They could see that it was moving – that it was leaning forward as if wanting to peer in through the window.

Nell backed away against the stair wall, a clenched fist thrust into her mouth, her face white. Michael grabbed her hand, preparing to pull her up to the relative safety of the bell chamber – prepared to carry her if he had to.

But the stone face was still turning – surely in another few seconds the terrible figure would be inside the tower with them.

There was a massive tearing sound – the sound of something hard and old splintering: bones, thought Nell, with horror. Bones being cracked apart, human muscle and nails and nerves tearing . . .

The stone face was changing – great lumps of rock were falling from it and plunging hundreds of feet to the sea.

At her side, Michael said softly, 'Dear God, look at that.'

Beneath the pitted stone face were human bones. They were old and yellowed with time, but they were intact. There was the brief impression of slanting cheekbones that would have caused the eyes above them to be narrow and mysterious, then the impression was gone, and there was only an empty skull from which all humanity had long since fled.

Michael's arms were around Nell as the last piece of stone fell away, and there was a glimpse of sloping shoulders, and of hands with long fingers that might have been crossed on a breast, in the traditional position of final repose.

Then the stone figure and what it contained fell away from the tower, plummeting down through the thickening twilight to the sea. For several seconds there was only a rushing sound, then an immense crash reached their ears. The water on the stairs churned furiously, throwing up massive waves of spray. They both flinched and clung to one another, waiting for the seething waves to calm down.

'It's stoppped,' said Michael, at last.

Nell was still shaking, but she said, 'It was the plank falling that dislodged the stone figure, wasn't it? It disturbed the bell, and there was a . . . a tremor of sound.'

'That figure had probably been loosening for years. It might have broken away at any time.'

'You saw . . . what was inside?'

'Yes,' he said.

Nell was still staring at the window. There was a faint dark glint of the sea beyond. Was the briefly glimpsed figure out there now? She said, 'What's that line about people along the coast not being able to die except when the tide's out? And that they can't be born until it's in?'

'It's *David Copperfield*,' said Michael. He was looking towards the sea as well. 'The line you probably mean is, "He's a-going out with the tide". Mr Peggotty said it.'

Whoever was inside that grisly stone tomb will do that later, won't he? Or she? Go out with the tide?'

'Yes.' Michael frowned, and looked up at the stairs. 'But for now we have to get up to the bell room. The water's still rising.'

Nell half expected that more steps would have crumbled, or that stone rubble would block their way, but although there were the remnants of birds' nests and an unpleasant sensation of crunching on tiny bird-bones, this part of the tower seemed to be intact.

They reached the head of the stairs and stood for a moment looking towards the bell chamber. Light streamed in from the side openings. It was a gentle half-light – not yet night but no longer full daylight – and there was something normal and comforting about it. It's going to be all right, thought Nell. We'll be safe up here and we'll get out. She glanced at her watch and saw with a shock that it was still barely half past five.

'Do we go in there? I mean – do we need to?'

'I think we'd better. The open sections might mean we'll get a phone signal. It's bitterly cold, isn't it? I should think the four winds of heaven whip through here.' Half to himself, he said, 'And all the winds with melody are ringing.'

So he had heard the strange singing earlier, as well. Nell thought they might discuss that sometime, and then she remembered the deep, lonely sadness in the singing and thought they might not.

As they stepped into the bell chamber, Nell caught her breath.

The chamber was lined with the same stone as the rest of the tower, but up here it was somehow cleaner and more wholesome. There were four apertures through which the bell would have sounded; they were rectangular, with arches at the tops, and sills near the stone floor.

Along one side was the bell mechanism: much of it wood, some of it metal. It was dull and pitted with age, and patches of rust showed on the metal. Nell made out the wheel of the mechanism, with a few strands of rope attached to it.

But she accorded all this only a brief glance, because it was the bell itself that dominated. It was far bigger than she had been visualizing – or was it? Those sullen thrummings earlier on had certainly been made by something immense and powerful. The Rede Abbas bell – the bell installed centuries ago by the Glaum family, used by the long-ago monks until the tower became unsafe – still had an aura of immense power. It was about five feet in height and probably three feet across, and the bronze of its outer casing had long since been dulled by verdigris, which lay across it like a disease. But it hasn't smothered it, thought Nell. It's mute and it's dimmed by age, but it's not quite dead.

Because she was finding the sight of the bell disturbing, she said, a bit too loudly, 'The mechanism looks in surprisingly good condition. They'd have operated it from below, wouldn't they? There was probably a room off that bit of collapsed stair. And there'd have been a rope attached to those wheels on each side of the bell. When the wheels were rotated, the bell would tilt and the tongue would bang against the sides.'

'I know it's intimidating,' said Michael. 'In fact I think it's one of the most intimidating things I've ever seen, but there's still a kind of dark, powerful enchantment. This is an alchemist's laboratory and a necromancer's cave, and I don't think I want to know what's behind the scenery.' He glanced uneasily at the bell and the shadows that clung to its base. 'In fact I definitely don't want to know what's behind that particular piece of scenery,' he said.

'You cling on to the gothic trimmings,' said Nell, slipping a hand through his arm. 'I'll focus on the realities, because if I start thinking about necromancers and whatnot I'll descend into a gibbering panic.'

'Before either of us starts gibbering, let's check for a phone signal,' said Michael, reaching for his mobile.

'Anything?' said Nell, watching him.

'No.'

'Me, neither.' Nell had to fight hard against bitter disappointment. She stared angrily at the massive weight of the bell, and suddenly said, 'There might not be a phone signal, but there could be another way we can send a signal.'

Michael turned to stare at her, then comprehension showed in his eyes and he looked back at the bell.

'How do we do it?' he asked. 'Because I don't think we'd actually manage to move it, do you? And, in any case, isn't it mute or whatever the term is?'

'If,' said Nell, looking round the room, 'we could find a long enough section of wood or steel or something, we might be able to bash it against the inside of the bell. What's that beneath the headstock?'

'It looks like a handle from one of the wheels. It probably rusted off years ago.' Michael picked it up and weighed it thoughtfully in his hand. 'It's quite heavy.'

'If we could fasten it inside the bell, it might act as a clapper. Would those wheels still rotate, I wonder?'

'There's a length of rope over there,' said Michael, who was exploring. 'We mightn't get both to move, but we might get one. The handle from the other wheel's here, as well.'

They managed to tie the two handles together with a frayed length of the rope, then Nell said, 'Which of us is going to climb on top of the bell to push this down into it?'

'I'll do it,' said Michael, in a tone firm enough to preclude argument. 'It looks as if I'll have to crawl along that section of wood directly over it.'

'The headstock,' said Nell.

'I don't care what it's called, as long as it stays put.'

It did stay put, but when Michael started to edge along it, it shuddered and creaked, and at one point a section broke away and fell against the bell itself. A sullen hum filled the chamber, and Nell clenched her fists, and tried to think that even if Michael fell it would only be a couple of feet to the ground. But he reached the hunched shape of the bell without mishap.

'And there's a kind of funnel where the original clapper would have been,' he said. 'I think it's wide enough to take these handles.'

Nell waited, not daring to speak; after several unsuccessful attempts, Michael said, 'I think it's in place. I've tied the end of the rope around the headstock section, and I think it'll hold. I'll have to crawl all the way back, though, because I suspect if I try jumping down I'll twist an ankle or fall against the bell or something. Pray this length of wood doesn't split halfway along.'

'OK.' Nell was looping the longest piece of rope around one of the wheels, so that they could pull on it and rotate the wheel, which would then tilt the bell. As Michael reached her, she said, 'I think the rope's long enough to stretch to the stairs. It would have been better if we could have got a rope down into the room below – assuming there is a room – and worked the wheels from there.'

'If there was a room on that collapsed bit of stairs, it would have been below the water level, though.'

'Oh, so it would. But even so, we should try to get as far out of hearing as possible,' said Nell. 'If this works, the chime could be at eardrum-splitting level.'

'You've been reading *The Nine Tailors*,' he said, smiling.

'Dorothy L. Sayers knew her stuff.

They payed out the rope slowly, backing away to the stairs as they did so.

'Four steps down,' said Michael. 'Five, six – this is as far as we can get it. We're still well above the water level . . .' He broke off, and Nell glanced down the stairs and saw with a shudder the slopping dark water on the stair. 'Is this sufficiently out of ear-splitting range?'

'It'll have to be,' said Nell.

'Ready?'

'Yes,' said Nell, and Michael pulled on the rope.

At first nothing happened. The wheel remained stubbornly still, and Nell began to think the rope must have slipped off. Then Michael pulled more insistently, and this time there was a deep, slow creaking, as if something immensely old was struggling to move. The wheel moved gratingly, but only by a couple of inches.

'And the bloody bell's not moving at all,' he said angrily.

'Try again.' Nell put her hand on the rope with his, and this time the wheel moved more surely. There was a shiver of movement and a scraping sound as if something was being torn from its roots. Then slowly, agonizingly, the bell began to tilt.

'More!' cried Nell, and they pulled the rope yet again. There was a faint brazen growling, then the huge old bell broke free of its moorings. As the pulley wheel jerked it unevenly up, the old metal handles began to rap against the insides.

At first the sound was small – almost hesitant – but when Michael and Nell plied the rope again, the wheel turned more steadily, and the bell swung more widely. The makeshift clappers hammered against the sides, and the immense bronze structure magnified the sounds a hundred times over. Discordant clangings began to fill the chamber – dreadful fractured sounds, as if something was being dragged from a deep, rusting darkness, screeching as its roots split. It was like being at the heart of a giant squealing nightmare.

But it had to be endured, and it had to be repeated if they were to attract attention. When Michael said, gaspingly, 'Are you all right to go on?' Nell nodded, and brushed a hand across her streaming eyes, before grasping the rope more firmly.

The dreadful clanging discordance streamed out of the bell tower and across the countryside.

TWENTY-TWO

The moment Maeve heard the clamour of the ancient bell, she knew it to be a death knell. She knew that somehow those two had managed to get up to the bell chamber and they had activated the bell. They would be heard and rescued – probably very soon – and they would tell what had happened. Miss Eynon imprisoned us in here, they would say. They would be believed – people would believe a man who was a doctor. Maeve would have no defence, no explanation for slamming the door on Nell West and Michael Flint and leaving them to drown. If she thought for a hundred years she would not find an excuse, and in the end they would take her to prison, and during the investigations they would find out all the other things she and Eifa Eynon had fought to hide.

Prison. Even the word was like a blow across her eyes. Fear scalded through her in a sick, sour flood, and within it was a bitter irony – the irony of knowing she had avoided prison all those years ago and of how clever and resourceful she had been.

No one had ever suspected what she had done that day. No, that was not true. This house knew what she had done. Andrew might know, too. He might have watched on that long-ago night – the night just before her eighteenth birthday. The night when Maeve had finally known she could not go on with the dreary, drudging half-existence. That she could no longer stand Aunt Eifa's constant demands, her incessant banging of her stick, her endless complaining and criticizing. Aunt Eifa's entire left-hand side was dead, encased in stone, but Eifa herself was not dead. She was not fully alive, though. Maeve sometimes thought that she, herself, was not fully alive, either. She would leave school in a few weeks, and what would her life be after that?

She was to wonder, later, if she might have been a little mad that day, because a sane person would surely have simply asked for help from a doctor. Also, eighteen was regarded as adult. People left home at eighteen; they worked and supported themselves. Maeve could get a job – earn money. But when she tried to think how she would get a job in Rede Abbas she had no idea. There was no industry, only a few shops, a couple of pubs, a handful of offices that employed girls. As for leaving Cliff House – she could not do it. She could not leave Andrew.

Aunt Eifa had been particularly troublesome and spiteful that day. She rapped on the wall with her stick all the time, wanting a cup of tea because the breakfast bacon had been too salty, then a hot-water bottle because it was cold, wanting Maeve to read to her because she was bored. But when Maeve took in the tea, the hot-water bottle, the newspaper and the book they were reading, her aunt waved them fretfully aside.

In the notebook she kept to hand, in her laborious script, Aunt Eifa wrote that she was thankful Maeve would be leaving school in a few weeks. She would have more time to see to the running of the house, then, and perhaps it would be run properly. Maeve sat down in the kitchen, the old clock ticking maddeningly, and thought about being shut up in this house with Aunt Eifa for years – with no school each day, where at least there was some companionship and interest and where she could pretend that one day her life would be better.

It would never be better. Aunt Eifa could live like this for years and years. Or could she?

It was then that the idea came into Maeve's mind.

She did not waste any time – if it was to be done at all, it might as well be done quickly. That was a line from somewhere, wasn't it? Probably it was Shakespeare; it usually was.

She carried the cassette player with the recording of 'Thaisa's Song' down to the music room. The music had terrified her aunt – Maeve was almost sure it had caused her stroke. If the door to Aunt Eifa's room and the door to the music room were both propped wide open, and if the player's volume was turned up to maximum . . .

It might not work, of course. If it did not, nothing had been lost.

She waited until the light was fading, and the strange twilit half-world that shrouded the coastline brought the sea mists clouding in. It was the hour when the ghost-faces looked out of the mirrors. Maeve generally ignored them, because she knew they were only her own reflection, fuzzy from the damp glass, but tonight they seemed different. Did Andrew look at her out of the mirrors? Was Theodora with him?

Maeve set down the cassette player, and pressed Play. The tape began to whirr, and the music and the voices – her mother's voice and that out-of-time shadow voice – poured into the room. The sounds were chilling, even to Maeve who had been prepared; they held a cold sadness that twisted and writhed with the drifting sea mists beyond the windows.

Who is this, knocks on my tomb?
Asks where and what I am,
Who is this who calls to me?
I cannot see nor hear.

One of the windows must be open because the thin old curtains were stirring as if something behind them was struggling to take shape. Maeve glanced at them uneasily, but she did not stop the tape.

I cannot see, I cannot hear
Who knocks upon my tomb.
I cannot speak, I cannot reach
The one stands by my tomb.

As the song reached the line about the one standing by the tomb, she heard the cry from Aunt Eifa's room – a dreadful strangled cry, then a kind of dull crash. Maeve clenched her teeth, and stayed where she was.

The one stands by my tomb, my love,
Can never save me now.
For the sea will be my grave, my love,
And you will be my own.

The cry came again, but it was weaker now. The tape reached its end; it whirred for the last silent seconds, then stopped. There was no sound from the adjoining room. Maeve was shaking violently and she felt as if cold damp fingers had wound themselves round her neck and pressed against her throat. She sat like that for half an hour, waiting, listening. Surely, oh surely, it would be over now. Stupid, said a voice in her mind. You'll have to go into that room eventually. You'll have to know.

Despite her resolve, she was trembling so much she had to hold on to the furniture to get across the room, and it was still some time before she could enter her aunt's room. She had no idea what she would do if the plan had not worked – if her aunt had not had a second stroke. It might be that the first one had not been brought about by hearing 'Thaisa's Song' at all – it might have been coincidence.

But when she stepped into the room she saw at once that it was all right. Eifa Eynon was lying back on the pillows, one hand flung out as if she had been trying to reach for her stick, but the stick itself lying on the floor where it had fallen – that would have been the clatter Maeve heard. Her eyes were wide and staring. Maeve forced herself to feel at the neck and then the wrist for a pulse – she knew how to do that. There was nothing. She was sure of it. But she placed her hand over the left side of her aunt's chest to see if there was a heartbeat. Again, nothing. One more test, thought

Maeve, and held a small mirror against Eifa's lips. If there was still breath – air – in the lungs, the mirror would mist. It did not. Maeve sat down in the chair by the bed, almost falling into it because her legs were about to give way. It's all right, she thought. She's gone. She's dead. But I didn't kill her, I really didn't. All I did was play a piece of music. But because of that she's dead and I'm free.

The doctor's surgery was closed for the evening, so Maeve shut the door of her aunt's room and sat in the music room, listening for a sound. She did not go to bed that night – she did not dare. Instead she remained in the music room, dozing occasionally before the fire, once getting up to make herself a cup of tea. Twice she stood outside her aunt's door, pressing her ear to the wood. Had something moved then? Had there been a faint slither of the bedclothes? No, it was only the wind snatching at the trees outside.

At half past eight next morning she telephoned the surgery. Aunt Eifa had resisted having a phone in the house for a very long time, but Maeve had finally overruled her. She was glad she had done so.

The doctor's receptionist asked how she could help, and Maeve said, 'Could the doctor come out to Cliff House, as soon as possible, please? I think my aunt is dead – I think she died during the night, and I don't know what I have to do.'

The doctor came half an hour later. Maeve left him in Aunt Eifa's room, and when he came out he patted her shoulder and said they would have a cup of tea together. Over the tea he said she had been perfectly right and he was extremely sorry, but Miss Eynon was indeed dead. He thought she had been dead for several hours – that she had had a cerebrovascular accident – what doctors called a CVA – which had been fatal. Yes, in layman's terms it could be called a stroke. It was very possible that she had had a smaller one at some previous date. Had there been any signs of weakness or tremor? Blurred vision? Difficulty with speech?

Maeve did not know what to say to this, so in the end she said she thought there might have been something of the kind a few years ago. Her aunt had been very dismissive of all illnesses, though, and she had never dwelled on any weaknesses. They had moved her bedroom downstairs a few years ago because she had troublesome arthritis in her knees and she found the stairs difficult. But she had not made a big thing of it.

The doctor nodded, and said it might have been an earlier, smaller stroke that had caused that problem, rather than arthritis.

'Now then, Maeve, in some cases of sudden death a post mortem's required,' he said. 'That's if death is due to some illness that hasn't been treated within the preceding two weeks or, more particularly, if the cause of death isn't clear. But that's not the case here. It's perfectly obvious what killed Miss Eynon. Still, if you do want a post mortem, I can request one.' But there was an unmistakable dismissive note in his voice, as if he was telling her it was not needed.

The idea of a post mortem frightened Maeve. Supposing they found something that made them question the diagnosis of a stroke? Supposing it was possible to tell if a person had died from fright? She pretended to think for a moment, then said she did not think her aunt would have wanted the fuss and upheaval of a post mortem.

'So if you're sure that's all right—?'

'I'm absolutely sure. I'm perfectly ready to sign the death certificate right away.'

The vicar asked, in a very kind way, whether Aunt Eifa was to be buried or cremated. What had her wishes been?

'I don't know,' said Maeve, who had not thought about this. 'But she was rather old-fashioned. I think she would have preferred a traditional burial. Can you do that, please?'

'Of course.'

Eifa Eynon was buried in the new cemetery on a weeping grey morning. The cemetery was quite a long way from Rede Abbas; Maeve would probably not be able to travel there very often.

But it could not matter to Eifa Eynon where – or how – she was buried.

Everyone said Maeve was very brave. It was a shocking thing for such a young girl to be suddenly left alone in the world, but presumably she would not be penniless. Old Miss Eynon had most likely had a nice bit of money tucked away in the bank. And the girl could sell Cliff House. It was quite run down and it was too near to the coastal erosion area for most people's liking, but she would get a fair price for it and she could move somewhere smaller.

Maeve had no intention of selling Cliff House. She did not want to move anywhere. She wanted to stay with Andrew and the memories. But the doctor had said and the vicar had agreed that she must see if her aunt had left a will. The doctor introduced her to a solicitor in Rede Abbas. The solicitor said it was almost certain that, as the only relative, Maeve would inherit everything anyway, but it would make things easier if there was a will. If he had that, he could apply for probate, and Cliff House could be transferred to Maeve. It was a good thing she was eighteen, because that meant she could own the place in her own right. Otherwise, a trust would have had to be created for her. It sounded very complicated to Maeve, but clearly it would be less complicated if there was a will, so a search had to be made.

Aunt Eifa's papers were stored in an old desk, which had been locked ever since Maeve could remember. She had no idea where the key was, and if her aunt had ever told her, she did not remember. But the desk was the likeliest place for a will, so she hunted for the key. She searched one room each day, and it took a very long time, but no key turned up. By now it was three weeks since the funeral, and the solicitor had phoned a few days ago, asking what was happening. Maeve gave up the search for the key and forced the desk open with a kitchen spatula. It splintered the wood slightly, but it could not be helped and she did not think the desk was especially valuable.

Eifa had made a will. Of course she had. Maeve thought she would have considered it untidy and irresponsible not to have done so. It was inside an envelope marked, 'Will: Eifa Eynon'. It was handwritten and it did not look very official, and Maeve flattened it out to read, trying not to compare the clear, vigorous script to the angry semi-formed scribbles of the last four years.

The will was very short, but quite clear. It said that everything of which Eifa Eynon died possessed was left to her niece, Maeve, who lived with her at Cliff House. The address followed in full, then there was Eifa's signature and the date. It was as simple as that, and Maeve thought it was enough for the house to become hers.

But slotted in with the will was an envelope, addressed to Maeve, also in Aunt Eifa's writing. As Maeve opened the envelope and drew out the two sheets of paper inside it, the room suddenly seemed very quiet and still. I don't want to read this, she thought. I think I'll have to, but I think it's going to be something I'll wish I hadn't seen.

'You will find this, Maeve,' Eifa Eynon had written, 'a long way in the future. I hope it will be a very long way.

'My will is in this desk – and, if you are reading this, you will have found it. You know where it is anyway, because I told you. I told you where the key of the desk is, so I have no fears this will not be found.'

But she didn't tell me, thought Maeve. She must have meant to, or she thought she had done it and forgot. Or did I forget?

'The will is one I wrote for myself, using a form from the post office,' Eifa wrote. 'I had no intention of paying a solicitor to perform such a simple task, and things are quite straightforward.

'Cliff House and any money I have when I die is to come to you. There is, though, a request I make, and it is a very serious and solemn one.

'Our family has a flaw. Not a sickness, exactly – perhaps a taint. There have been a number of words for it down the centuries, but I believe the medical term is catalepsy. It means a very deep coma, which resembles death; it has been said that it mimics death, and that it mimics death so exactly that it can deceive doctors. Several of our ancestors suffered from it and were found to have been put in their graves alive. I do not know the details and I do not know where the taint originated, but the stories are handed down, and I believe them to be true . . .

'No, that is an understatement. I *know* them to be true. For that reason I am telling you what happened on the night before my mother's funeral.'

Maeve turned reluctantly to the second sheet of the letter.

'My mother left instructions for me, in the same way I am doing for you, Maeve,' Eifa wrote. 'But her instructions for me were different, because that was a different world. She was born in the 1890s, and in those days people did not deal with sickness as we do now. The rich consulted doctors, but people in villages like Rede Abbas seldom did – often because they could not afford to, frequently because they were afraid of them, sometimes because they did not trust them. My mother had lived in this village all her life – she had no real knowledge of medicine, other than homely, handed-down knowledge – indeed she had very little knowledge of the world beyond Rede Abbas. She thought of doctors as people far above her, to be ranked alongside the vicar, even the squire. Oh yes, Maeve, in my mother's day there were still squires, and people tugged their forelocks to them. Even in my day there was old Squire Glaum, the last of his line, rattling around Glaum Manor alone. I remember people saying, after he died, that at least he had not lived to see his family home despoiled and bulldozed to dust.

'But my mother knew about the taint in our family and she feared it very much. She regarded it as deeply shameful, something about which no one must know. When she became ill, believing she was dying, she told me that when she died her body must be left overnight in the church. Before the funeral and the burial I must open the coffin secretly, to make sure she had not woken. If I had any suspicion at all that she might not be dead, I must prevent the burial. I had to promise – she made me fetch her Bible and promise with my hand on its cover.

'I was seventeen, innocent and naïve. Like my mother, I had never left Rede Abbas. There were only the two of us – my father had died when I was very small – and it did not occur to me to question anything she said. It certainly did not occur to me to suggest we enlist the help or the advice of a doctor. In fact, the nearest doctor was in St Mary Abbas and I had only ever seen him once.

'So I did what she asked. I asked for her coffin to lie in the church before the funeral, and that night, very late, I crept out of this house and stole along to the church. I had no idea what I should find, or how I would know if she were dead, but I had promised on the Holy Bible to open the coffin, and I would keep that promise.

'Removing the coffin lid was far more difficult than I had expected. St Mary's is an old church and, although I am not a fanciful woman, as I worked, loosening the screws, I could have believed that eyes watched me from the shadows.

'Even when the screws were all out, the lid would not budge, so I used a thin-bladed chisel to lever it up. That was even more difficult – it's possible that some form of carpenter's glue had been used; but in the end I managed it and I lifted the lid clear.

'She lay as I had seen her when they carried her from the house – pale and still, her hands crossed on her breast, her eyes closed. I remember I stared down at her, and thought – I think it's all right. No one who lives could look so remote. I can leave her in peace. I reached for the lid, which I had propped against the bier, intending to replace it as neatly as possible.

'Two things happened.

'A dull, menacing sound seemed to shiver on the air – a rhythmic beating, a coppery sound, almost like a monstrous bronze heartbeat. It struck terror into me, for I guessed it to be the old, dead bell, out on the cliffside.

'My image of a massive heartbeat seemed to have been a true one, because after a few moments a tremor passed over my mother's face, and her eyes opened.

'She stared straight up at me, but the dreadful thing – the thing I have remembered all these years – is the stark and mindless terror in her expression. There was no recognition – no understanding of who I was or that I was about to rescue her; but if she had known she was nailed into her coffin, it would account for the terror and the – I must write it – the stark madness that held her.

'Her hands came up to me, curved like an animal's claws, and raked at my face. Her nails dug into my skin and I flinched and tried to draw back, but it was already too late – both her hands had seized my throat and closed tightly around it. I have wondered since what she was seeing – whether she was seeing a denizen of some dreadful after-life bending over her, and was determined to fight it off.

'The pressure of those fingers on my throat was unbearable. Blood pounded agonizingly in my head, and darkness shot with livid crimson streaks closed over me. I struggled to get free, but she had the strength of real insanity, and I could not prize her fingers off. My own hands, flailing blindly, pushed at her and one of them closed around the chisel I had used to lever off the lid.

'What happened next was instinctive, entirely without intention, and has haunted me for my entire life.

'I grabbed the chisel and struck out at her with it. I can hardly bear to write it, but it is what happened – it is as clear in my mind as it was the night it happened.

'The chisel went into her. She let out a bubbling cry of pain or fear, or both, and the throttling grip relaxed at once. I fell back, gasping for breath, feeling air rush gratefully into my lungs. It was some moments before I could stand sufficiently straight to look into the coffin again, and this time I knew there could not possibly be any doubt. The chisel had entered her throat – it had dug straight into her windpipe and thick dark blood had poured out. But it was already drying and darkening, that blood; it lay in clotted pools around her neck. Her head had fallen back, the eyes open and staring. She was as dead as last week's mutton. And I had murdered her.

'I closed the coffin and replaced the screws and nails. Then I went back to Cliff House and the funeral and burial took place the next day. I was there. I prayed and joined in the hymns, and I stood by the graveside as the coffin was lowered into the ground. And no one ever knew what had happened.

'But now you understand why I have lived the life of a recluse, why I have kept the world away from this house, and why I have never sold it. I could never risk anyone looking into the family's background – looking into papers, title deeds, land transfers – finding old letters, references to our ancestors, anything that might bring the taint to light, and that might, as a result, lead back to what I did. People are curious. They ask questions – they uncover truths and lies and secrets.

'So I ask you to do all you can to preserve the secret of what I did. The world has changed a good deal since I committed that murder, but I do not think the world – any world – will ever look kindly on a young woman who was brought up by a murderess.

'There is one more thing.

'It is almost certain that doctors these days can no longer make the mistake of pronouncing death where death has not occurred. It is probable that by the time I die they will have better tests, better knowledge, and that our family's strange flaw will be recognized, and no more tragedies will occur.

'*But that is something else I dare not risk.*

'If – when – I die, you must ensure the doctors use all their knowledge to make certain that I am dead, that it is not the family taint. If you have to, you must explain about the taint. Ask for tests to be made. I read there are certain procedures now – something to do with provoking responses from the throat, also the eyes. I do not know the details, but doctors will know.

'I trust you to do this, Maeve.

'And even after these tests have been performed and death is definite, please arrange cremation rather than burial. I would rather that than being put alive in the grave.

'You are a good girl, and I trust you.

'Your loving Aunt Eifa.'

Maeve had wanted desperately to put her aunt's letter down to insanity – to believe that the family taint Aunt Eifa had referred to was not this catalepsy thing, but quite simply madness.

She thought she might have done so but for one thing. The baby the long-ago Thaisa had borne. The child Andrew had found in Quire Court, and who he had written about in his journal from that part of his life.

'It lay on its back,' he had written, 'the head straight, as if the eyes had been staring upwards . . . The hands and also the feet were raised in grotesque supplication . . . The child had not been dead when it was put into the grave . . .'

Not dead when put into the grave. And, three weeks earlier, Aunt Eifa's coffin had been lowered into the grave, and the soil sprinkled over it, and the grass turfs replaced.

If Eifa had been buried alive it was worlds and light years away from playing a piece of music in the hope that a second stroke would snuff out her life. It was monstrous, a nightmare, not to be thought of. Except that Maeve knew she would think of it; she knew it would haunt her for the rest of her life. Because it would be her fault.

She would give the will to the solicitor, but she would burn the letter, and she would go through Cliff House, from cellar to attic, and she would burn every scrap and every fragment of paper or photograph or document that might lead anyone to delve into the history of her family. She would burn the recording of 'Thaisa's Song', as well. It must never be played, ever again, because that, too, could revive memories, suspicions. It could waken forgotten curiosity.

When she had dealt with all that, she would do what her aunt had done. She would shut out the world and she would bar the doors of the house to everyone, and she would live her life without anyone knowing what had happened.

It would have been all right. Seated in the music room, the memories all about her, Maeve knew it would have been all right if it had not been for the revival of the medieval Revels – if it had not been for the search for 'Thaisa's Song'. And if Nell West and Dr Flint had not come to Rede Abbas.

The bell was no longer sounding – the clamour that Eifa Eynon had heard all those years ago as she prized open her mother's coffin had stopped. Did that mean those two had been rescued? Yes, of course it did. It could not be very long before people came to Cliff House to question Maeve.

I can't bear it, she thought again. She went out of the music room, and walked slowly round the house, looking into all the rooms, feeling the ghosts and the memories reaching out to her, feeling the tragedies and sadnesses pressing in.

Eifa, and Eifa's mother, whom Maeve had never known. Maeve's own mother, who had been here, and found 'Thaisa's Song'. She had not destroyed it after all – in the end she had not been able to sever the fragile link to her mother and to Andrew, so the tape was still in her wardrobe. Was it still playable after so many years?

There were things that must be done – done now and quickly. Memories to be destroyed. Clues to be burned. After that . . .

She worked quickly and efficiently. She did not think she missed anything. Then she sat down at her aunt's desk and reached for pen and notepaper. A very brief note was all that was needed.

As she laid down her pen, she thought Andrew was in the room with her, watching to make sure she got everything right.

TWENTY-THREE

'She took an overdose,' said the police inspector to Michael and Nell in the comfortable, reassuring coffee room of The Swan, much later that night. 'She was lying on her bed when we finally got into Cliff House. We haven't got forensic reports yet, of course, so we don't know exactly what she took. There's no note, but the obvious explanation is that she was so horrified at having trapped you both in the bell tower – at realizing you had escaped and she was likely to be arrested – that she took her own life.'

'How immensely sad,' said Nell, softly.

'It would have been sadder if you and Dr Flint hadn't got out,' said the inspector.

'That's true. And,' said Michael, 'we're immensely grateful to your men for responding to that wretched bell. Could you tell them that? It's a brilliant rescue service you've got here.'

'All part of the job, Dr Flint.'

'I shouldn't think I'll ever forget climbing out through the bell chamber into that helicopter,' said Nell.

The inspector smiled. 'I shouldn't think Rede Abbas will ever forget hearing that bell sounding, Mrs West. You'll go down in local legend.'

Michael said, 'I suppose Maeve Eynon was mad? Because there was no possible motive for her to imprison either of us in there.'

'We don't know what she was, or what her motive might have been,' said the inspector. 'Most likely we never will. There'll be a post mortem and an inquest, of course, and we might know a bit more by then. But myself, I think she was severely unbalanced. And she'd lived in that old house by herself ever since she was a girl. No friends, no work, no companionship.'

'That's the saddest part,' said Nell.

'Oh, yes. But enough to send anyone off the rails, I'd have thought.' He got up to go. 'It's very late, and you'll be wanting to get some rest after your ordeal, so I'll say goodnight. Are you able to stay on for the inquest? We've got your statements, but it might be useful if you were on hand.'

'We should get back to Oxford tomorrow,' said Michael. 'But if you think we'll be wanted, we could come back for the inquest.' He looked questioningly at Nell, who nodded.

'I'll let you know when it will be – probably a couple of weeks. One curious thing, though,' said the inspector. 'After we got you out, and after we found out what had happened, we went up to Cliff House, as you know. It was well after eight o'clock, and the Dusklight Concert had started an hour earlier – in fact it was almost ending. And the curious thing was that when we found Miss Eynon, she seemed to have been burning a number of things. Mostly papers and some old books, but there was also one of those old cassette tapes. You remember them? They gave place to CDs, of course, but they were very popular twenty or thirty years ago.'

'Yes, certainly.'

'The actual tape hadn't burned entirely,' he said. 'It had partly melted, but there was a small label next to it with the wording just about readable.'

Nell said, 'Was it by any chance "Thaisa's Song"?'

'Yes, it was, although how you know that—'

'A lucky guess,' she said. 'It's the music the festival people were trying to find for tonight, isn't it?'

'So I'm told. Gerald Orchard turned half Rede Abbas upside-down, and the choir were routed from their beds at crack of dawn today,' said the inspector. 'But from the times we've got, it looks as if Maeve Eynon was burning that tape just as the choir were singing "Thaisa's Song". She took the overdose immediately afterwards. The song would still be going on. Coincidence, I daresay, but even so, it's odd, isn't it?'

'Yes,' said Nell. 'Yes, it's very odd.'

'I daresay there've been odder things, though,' said the inspector. 'I'll bid you both goodnight.'

Later, in their room, Michael said, 'Would you like to have heard "Thaisa's Song" at the concert?'

'Not really. In fact I definitely wouldn't have wanted to hear it. I have,' said Nell, thoughtfully, 'got quite a lot to tell you about "Thaisa's Song".'

'I've got a few things to tell you about Quire Court,' said Michael. He paused, then said, 'Neither of us has mentioned the remains of that body we saw inside the stone figure yet, have we? I don't suppose we'll ever know who it was. But we haven't talked about it.'

'Do you want to talk about it?'

Michael considered for a moment. He was lying on the bed after taking his second, very hot, shower since they had reached The Swan. Nell thought they might both be slightly obsessive about showering for the next few days; it was as if the smell and the feel of the bell tower would never leave them.

'I don't think I could dredge up the mental energy to talk about stone figures at the moment,' said Michael. 'All I want to do is crash out here, and sleep for about a week.' He raised himself on one elbow and looked at her. 'On the other hand,' he said, thoughtfully, 'if you're going to be crashing out next to me, sleep could perhaps be delayed. For half an hour or so . . .?'

'Or even a bit longer than that . . .?'

'Well, yes. In fact, certainly yes.'

'And,' said Nell, coming over to the bed, 'we don't have to set off at break of dawn tomorrow, do we?'

Michael grinned and held out his hand to her.

They drove back to Oxford, resolutely not discussing what had happened while Beth was with them.

Beth, who only knew that her mother and Michael had been delayed and missed the Dusklight Concert, which she said had been lavish, was delightedly recounting all the things she had seen, and what people had said, and how brilliant it had all been.

'I'd really like to go back,' she said. 'Did you say you had to anyway, Mum?'

'Either Michael or I might have to in a few days' time, but it would only be a quick visit. It might even be there and back the same day.'

'Oh, OK.' Beth appeared to accept this, then said, 'Are we going back through that same bit of Oxford again? Where we saw that old house?'

'I shouldn't think so. We only took those side roads to escape the snarl-up of rush-hour traffic. Why?'

'Um, I just thought I'd like to see the house again.' Beth seemed about to say something else, then caught her mother's eye in the driving mirror, and subsided into the absorbing pastime of texting everyone who had been at the Rede Abbas hostel.

Michael had been reading the notes Nell had made that morning about Andrew's journal. As he finished them, Nell pulled in to a motorway service station for a late lunch, and when Beth went up to the counter to collect a pudding, Michael said quietly, 'What do we make of all that "buried alive" stuff you found in Andrew's journal? Andrew wrote about Adolphus Glaum and Theodora's mother being found still alive. Your notes on that part were pretty comprehensive. How much credence do we give it?'

'Some,' said Nell. 'There might have been a form of catalepsy; it might even have been an inherited condition, although I don't know if it's something that can be inherited – that's a grim thought, isn't it?'

'Was there a link between the Glaums and the Eynons?'

'There could have been. The Glaums sounded quite roistering. Bastard children and *droit du seigneur* all over the place, I shouldn't wonder. And catalepsy certainly used to fool doctors into certifying death. I don't think it could happen now. Or, if it does,' said Nell, with a shiver, 'I don't think anyone knows about it. It's certainly fuelled at least a dozen gothic tales, though, hasn't it?'

Michael said, 'Dumas's ill-starred Abbé Faria and George Eliot's *Silas Marner*. And all the way to the farcical end of the scale – Charles Dickens' Mrs Snagsby in *Bleak House* being carried upstairs like a grand piano.'

'Not to mention full-frontal modern-day horror splattering its gore across Blu-ray and Multiplex,' said Nell, gravely. She looked across at the food queue. Beth had reached the front, and Nell said, 'I hesitate to drag you into the present, but I wonder how well Jack Hurst's got on with the shops.'

'So do I.' Later tonight – or even tomorrow, when there was a bit more distance between them and the tower – Michael was going to tell Nell about finding that fragile little body. He had tried to imagine how she would react, and he had a worrying suspicion that she might be all right about working there during the day, with people coming and going, and the ordinary, daytime sounds of the

Court itself, but that she might feel differently about being there at night – about actually living and sleeping in the building.

'I should think the worst's done by now,' he said. 'Didn't Jack say you might be able to move into the new flat in about a week?'

'Yes, but builders tend to be purveyors of false promises. We'll probably be greeted by utter chaos.'

'One thing we will be greeted with is some research results from Owen,' said Michael, who had been checking his phone for messages. 'There's a very exuberant email from him here, saying he's deciphered quite a bit of the diary I found in the storeroom.

'The equivalent of the Chaucer manuscript in the baked bean carton?'

'Yes. Owen still thinks it's genuine, but he's going to talk to Brant next week. He's managed to decipher several sections of it, though, and – oh, this sounds really good – he says he's plundered the Bodleian, although we hadn't better ask how he got in there outside their normal hours—'

'If he's found Brother Cuthwin I don't care if he's committed blackmail and felony in every library in Oxford,' said Nell.

'He has found Brother Cuthwin!' said Michael, in delight. 'He says he's unearthed an interpretation or translation made by a nineteenth-century monk – might that be your Andrew?'

'More likely Brother Egbert,' said Nell.

'Oh yes, the scholarly monk. Anyway, Owen says he's only got about a tenth of the diary, but he's put that alongside the Cuthwin papers, and he thinks there's enough for a fair résumé of the on-goings at Rede Abbas in the sixteenth century.'

'Intriguing.'

'And he says can he come to supper as soon as possible to relate his discovery?'

'Assuming there's light and heat at Quire Court, he can come for whatever meal he likes,' said Nell, as Beth came happily back with a huge plate of chocolate fudge cake. 'I can't wait to hear about Brother Cuthwin.'

Quire Court, when they reached it, was not engulfed in Nell's prophesied chaos. The two shops had a pleasing air of being ready to take furniture, and there were clean scents of new paint and timber everywhere.

'Looking good,' said Nell, standing in what was now the large showroom. 'In fact, looking pretty terrific. It's much more spacious than I was visualizing.' She ran her hands over the smooth walls and peered into the display alcoves. 'I can't wait to get the stuff out of my house and properly set out.'

'It's utterly good,' said Beth, who was pattering round the rooms with pleased curiosity. 'Is my bedroom ready, d'you s'pose? Not that I want to sleep in it while it's all like this, but still.'

'I'm going to sprint upstairs to look,' said Nell. 'You two stay here.' She thought Michael made an instinctive move to come with her, but she said, 'I'll only be a moment,' and he nodded as if he understood, and said something about checking the storerooms where Jack Hurst had been working over the weekend.

Nell had not acknowledged, even to herself, that she was nervous of the attic where she had found Theodora's fear-driven note.

'*If anyone finds this, please pray for me, for it will mean the dead bell has sounded and I have suffered Thaisa's fate . . .*'

The attic room was quiet and untroubled. The scribbled message was gone, of course – Jack Hurst and his sidekicks had obliterated it with new plaster and timber beams and struts. Nell placed the flat of her hand experimentally on the section of wall where Theodora had written that message, but there was no impression that anything sad or frightened lingered. This was a relief; Nell had already decided Beth could not sleep in here if anything felt wrong. But she did not think Theodora's ghost had ever lingered here. And yet what about the flickering lights, and the sounds – the rhythmic slap of wet mortar against brick; the blurred figure that seemed to move across the shop, and then to vanish? And the faint singing – had that really been 'Thaisa's Song', or had it come from beyond Quire Court anyway?

Probably she would never know what had happened to Theodora and Andrew, thought Nell, and went back downstairs to where Michael was saying something about the old storeroom not being quite finished, and the door had better remain closed because the floor was still up.

'I have to say,' said Owen Bracegirdle, the following evening, 'that when you two stumble on a mystery, you do so in spectacular fashion.' He brandished a sheaf of notes at them.

'Cuthwin,' said Nell, smiling.

'Cuthwin, indeed. And,' said Owen, 'reading him felt remarkably like uncharted territory, because I suspect no one has read him for a hundred years – if, that is, anyone has read him at all since he found his way into the Bodleian.' He shuffled his notes. 'The transcribing seems to have been the life's work of a nineteenth-century monk at Rede Abbas monastery.'

'Brother Egbert,' said Nell. 'I found some references to him in the local library.'

'He seems to have made a scholarly and diligent transcription,' said Owen, judiciously. 'I think he tweaked a fair bit of the actual phrasing and words used, so although it's a bit Victorian-sounding, it's nicely clear, and we can put it alongside the journal Michael found in the shop – you do know about that by now, I suppose, Nell?'

'The child's grave? Yes, Michael told me earlier.'

'Ah. Are you all right about it?'

'Not yet, but I will be eventually,' said Nell, who was not in fact entirely sure about this.

'It's all very sad, but don't forget it was a long time ago—'

'And in the dark backward and abysm of time,' murmured Michael, looking across at Nell. 'Owen, are you going to read your notes aloud?'

'If that's agreeable. And from what I've deciphered so far, all I can say is I'm afraid it's all likely to be true. It was a brutal age,' he said. 'It isn't dated, by the way, but Brother Egbert seems to have assigned the early mid-1500s to it.'

'The year 1538,' said Michael, at once. 'The same time as the journal.'

'I think so. The sections that I think are the relevant ones are after the monks had a visit from Cromwell's Commissioners. That seems to be when Thaisa – our diarist – left.'

'And came here to Quire Court?' Nell glanced at Michael and knew they were both thinking about the child's body. Thaisa's child?

'It sounds like it. Myself,' said Owen, 'I think Thaisa was bundled out of the way because she was the Abbot's bit of fluff, or the illegitimate daughter of somebody in a high place, but that's theorizing without data.'

Nell said, thoughtfully, 'We've got a kind of shared knowledge in all this, haven't we, but it's fragmented. I know some of it, mostly the nineteenth-century stuff from Andrew's journal. But I know about him meeting Theodora Eynon and how that lecherous old Squire Glaum was killed – and put in the tomb alive. Pure Edgar Allan Poe. And then they came here to hide out. But I don't know anything about Thaisa.'

'I know a few slivers about her because of the sixteenth-century book we found here,' said Michael. 'But I only made out a couple of sentences. So read on, Owen.'

Owen nodded in appreciation and acceptance of the wine with which Nell topped up his glass, and began to read.

TWENTY-FOUR

'This morning,' Cuthwin wrote, 'we heard that Father Abbot and Thaisa had been captured in Oxford and are being brought back to Rede Abbas to face punishment. Brother John has learned that Master Cromwell's Commissioners believe Father Abbot to be guilty of simony.'

> 'They say,' said Brother John, 'that Father Abbot sold absolution to Edward Glaum and received properties in the Town of Oxford as payment. I do not believe it, though. Father Abbot denied it when he took Thaisa to Oxford and, whatever else he might be, he is no liar. The Commissioners may want a scapegoat – a reason to close down our house and take our few valuables. If so, they would have found it easy to persuade the villagers to their side. They were already in awe of the Commissioners, and they would be fearful of offending them.'
>
> 'More to the point,' said Brother Angus, 'they would be fearful of incurring the wrath of the King.'
>
> Angus is right. These days no one wants to incur the wrath of Henry VIII.
>
> As for Thaisa, none of us dares voice our thoughts as to

> why she should be part of Seamus Flannery's punishment, although I suppose most of us know. But I shall not write those thoughts, for I do not know who may read this. Also, I am mindful of the fact that, 'He who soweth discord among his brethren' is listed as one of the Lord's hates, so I do not gossip.

Owen looked up briefly from his notes. 'It is, of course, clear from what I've read that Cuthwin was the worst gossip you could meet outside of a tabloid newspaper.'

'Never mind what he was, let's hear what he has to say.'

Owen nodded, and resumed.

> We intend to bargain with the Commissioners for the lives and freedom of Father Abbot and Thaisa. Brother John, who is apt to be pernickety about details, says it is a dangerous ploy, and asks what we are to bargain with. We have not told him how we concealed the most valuable items before the Commissioners' visit. As Brother Angus said at the time, our few treasures could not add much to the King's coffers.
>
> The ciborium and the patens are in the vegetable gardens, beneath the onion patch. I know exactly where they are, since I was the one who buried them. It took an entire afternoon and I stank of onions for days afterwards, but at least we can retrieve them.
>
> Then there is an altar bread box and a communion chalice concealed in the gardener's fishing equipment, although the bread box may pose a difficulty, because when Brother Francesco last looked, it was being used for storing mealworms.
>
> In addition, a gilded monstrance is hidden beneath the floor in a privy, but we are hoping it will not be necessary to disinter that.
>
> If we can free Father Abbot and Thaisa we will take them to a place of safety – perhaps some remote village, where they might pass unnoticed. Brother Angus says Seamus Flannery will never pass unnoticed anywhere, but we cannot heed Angus's gloomy prognostications.

> We took it in turns to watch for the arrival of the prisoners, using the high window overlooking the cliff path. When finally

the procession came into sight, dusk was falling and great swathes of purple and violet lay across the countryside, but even through the thickening dusk we could see that the two Commissioners rode at the head of the procession.

'Six horses,' said one of the younger brothers, whose sight is keener than most of us. 'Three of them pulling drays, and I can see two figures tied up on the drays.'

The thought of Seamus Flannery – arrogant, disdainful, fastidious beyond description – bound and helpless on the floor of a common dray was appalling. The thought of Thaisa – small, fragile-boned, possessed of that bright inquisitive intelligence – being similarly treated was unbearable, which is, I know, an absurd word to use, because it had to be borne. And Thaisa herself was having to bear it.

We had thought the villagers would take their prisoners to the church, or to Glaum Manor, where Commissioners had lodged, but we saw with incredulity that the flickering torchlights were snaking a way down the cliff path. It was Angus who said, 'Dear God, they're going to the bell tower.'

'Surely not?' I leaned forward to see better.

'Angus is right,' said John. 'They're going towards the old tower. It seems strange, but does not affect our plan.'

'We go down to the tower to confront them?'

'We do,' he said.

As we walked through the night, I believe most of us were caught between terror and despair. (I write that with some hesitation, since despair is a sin, so I shall do penance later.)

I could almost believe none of what was happening was real – that we had somehow entered a dark nightmare. The bell tower, when we reached it, was lit by flickering lights, and it was strange to see it like that. As we drew nearer we saw that the door was propped open and that inside were the two Commissioners and some of the villagers. They had wedged torches into crevices in the stones, and the light flared upwards, bleeding through the entire building, and glowing from the half-window and the bell chamber.

We slowed our steps, and looked uneasily at one another,

because we could hear, very clearly, the shouts of what I can only describe as triumphant hatred.

Angus said, 'There are more of them in there than I had expected.'

'Can we confront so many?' I asked, worriedly. I was as determined as anyone to rescue Father Abbot and Thaisa, but the prospect of reasoning with such angry men was daunting.

'We can,' said John firmly, and led us forward.

I shall never forget the sight that met us. The room immediately inside the tower is small – the tower was built to house a bell rather than people, so there is not very much room. But the Commissioners and at least a dozen villagers were crammed in there, many of them standing on the stairs leading up to the bell chamber. And at the centre . . .

I was aware of a curious feeling of gratitude to Seamus Flannery and Thaisa for both looking so defiant. They were dirty and pale, but neither looked cowed or frightened. Seamus was unshaven and unkempt, like a vagrant who had come in from the roads. Thaisa's hair streamed over her shoulders, and her eyes, which are narrow and long, glowed with anger.

When we reached the door we saw that Job Orchard, the stonemason, was there. He is a great hulking figure of a man, his arms and shoulders muscular from years of wielding the stonemason's hammers and picks. In front of him were two massive pieces of carved stone. At first I could not make out what they were, then three of the village men dragged Thaisa forwards and began to lift the stones and horrified comprehension came.

At my side, John said, 'Our plan to bargain for their freedom will not work.'

'I see that. They are too angry,' I said.

'And too many,' put in Brother Angus.

We were all staring at the stone shapes, but John recovered himself sufficiently to say, 'Brother Francesco – you are the youngest, the fleetest of foot. Run as if your life depended on it to Glaum Manor. Bring Squire Glaum here at once – at once, you understand? There must be no time lost.'

Francesco, an intelligent boy, did not question. He was off, fleeing through the night, his robe flapping like birds' wings. The darkness swallowed him up.

'They may listen to the squire,' said John, frowning. 'If they do not—'

'Brother, forgive me, but what do they intend?' said Angus.

John said, 'They are going to imprison Thaisa inside those stones. Can't you see how they're fashioned in the shape of a human figure. Job Orchard must have been chiselling them out unbeknown.'

'I still don't understand—'

'It's a form of the punishment meted out to women who lie with monks or priests.'

'But what—'

In a voice of anger and distress, John said, 'They are going to wall Thaisa up alive.'

As we stared at one another in horror, the night began to fill up with sounds of hammering, and above them we could hear Seamus Flannery cursing his captors, swearing with a fluency that scalded my ears and my mind with the passion and hatred it contained. And yet in my own mind I was swearing as well, with just as much passion and hatred.

Then Brother John pointed towards the seaward side of the tower, where Orchard and two of the others had clambered on to the ledge of the half-window. The darkness made it difficult to see clearly, but ropes swung out and Orchard seemed to be attaching them to something inside the tower. Then Orchard himself sat astride the ledge, so precariously that I thought he might fall. I tried to suppress the hope that he would.

The massive stone pieces were being hauled into place against the tower's side – Orchard seemed to be chiselling some kind of fastenings into the stones. The hammering rang out again, but now, with it, came dull, menacing sounds from the bell.

'They've disturbed it,' said Brother Angus, looking upwards. 'It's angry.'

'Angus, it's only a lump of bronze and copper,' I said. 'It doesn't possess intelligence.'

'Doesn't it?' said Angus, softly.

It was a relief to hear Brother Francesco returning, and see the portly figure of Edward Glaum with him. The squire was panting with the exertion of running, but he still exerted authority and I felt a green-shoot of hope.

He nodded briefly to us, took a few seconds to regain his breath and his dignity, then strode to the tower. It was clear that either Brother Francesco had explained everything or that the squire understood it for himself. In a ringing, angry voice, he said, 'This must stop. You cannot commit these atrocities – I won't allow it.'

One of the Commissioners said, 'You can't stop anything, Squire. This is the King's justice. The girl is a monk's whore and a witch. The monk himself is a heretic – a transgressor of his own laws and a fornicator.'

The other Commissioner said: 'We have Master Cromwell's warrants to execute them both. Do you want to see the warrants, Squire? And do you really wish to oppose Thomas Cromwell and King Henry?'

'In any case, you are too late,' said the first. He pointed to the upper parts of the tower, and that was when we saw that the massive carved stones had been hoisted against the wall, just outside the narrow window. In the leaping flares of the torchlight from within the tower, silhouetted in profile against the night sky, was the outline of a female – a larger-than-life figure, macabre and brooding.

From inside the figure we heard Thaisa's voice.

At first I thought she was screaming for help, but as her voice wove through the night, I realized she was singing the ancient song she had brought when she came to the monastery as a tiny child.

None of us ever understood the words of that song, except to know they were strange and that there was something pagan and almost inhuman about them. Whether she sang because she believed the words might summon some kind of power to rescue her, or whether she did so simply for comfort, and even as a defiance, I had no idea then and I have no idea now.

The song affected Squire Glaum the worst. He gasped, then said, 'It's the gypsy's song. Dear God, it's the song her mother sang the night she – the night she and I . . .' He sent a slightly shamefaced look at me and at Brother John, then said firmly, 'The night Thaisa was conceived.'

'Ah. Yes. I see. We never knew,' said John, a diplomat to his toes.

'We never question such things,' I said, wanting to ally myself with Brother John's words.

'Thank'ee,' said the squire, and mopped his face. 'Alluring creatures, those gypsies. Not quite like other people. Let them stay in my meadow every year. Then Thaisa was born. Did all I could for her. Tried to keep her safe.'

There was the sheen of tears in his eyes, and I said, 'Squire, we will reach her. Somehow we will.'

'I don't think you can,' said the squire, pointing to the waves already lashing around the tower's base. 'Even if we can fight back Cromwell's men and the others, it will take hours to break open that thrice-damned figure. Job Orchard's a good stonemason.'

'And,' said John, in a voice of extreme pity, 'the tide is coming in fast.'

'But we can't just let her die,' I said.

'I think,' said John, with deep sadness and anger, 'that she is probably dead already.'

It was the squire who said, harshly, 'Pray God she is.'

Today we heard Squire Glaum is to install a new bell in the tower, with an inscription which will read:

'Bestowed on the good people of Rede Abbas, that they may pray for my family's darkness to one day be lifted, and the dead be truly dead and at rest. In loving memory of my daughter Thaisa.'

I do not know, however, how long Cromwell's Commissioners will suffer it to remain.

I am glad Thaisa did not live to see what happened to her beloved Seamus after that night.

We saw it, though. We did not dare disobey the command to attend, and we walked down from the monastery as the great bell chimed – Edward Glaum's newly cast great bronze bell.

We watched as Seamus Flannery was brought out, and chained to the stake driven into the ground in the village square. The charges against him were read out – simony was among them, and also heresy, but I could not hear the rest, partly because the wind was snatching away the words, and partly because . . .

But I cannot write what I felt. I will say only that I was too overcome by emotion to listen. I do know, though, that they offered him a gentler death – the axe rather than the flames – if he would admit to his errors and take the King's Oath.

Seamus laughed. He said he was innocent of everything except loving another human creature and, as for the King's Oath . . . From respect to the man who was our Abbot, I do not write what Seamus Flannery actually said there, other than that he cursed the Oath, Thomas Cromwell and Henry Tudor.

The men lit torches from a brazier standing on the edge of the square, and orange and scarlet flames leapt into the air. As they roared up, Seamus began to struggle, and then to scream. His hands – the sensitive, well-formed hands that we had so often seen clasped in prayer and that must have caressed Thaisa Eynon, seemed to clutch at the air, as if the flames were solid things that could be grasped and pushed away.

I thought I would be sick or faint, but then, at my side, Brother John murmured a prayer.

'*Eye hath not seen, nor ear heard, neither hath it entered into the heart of man the things which God hath prepared for those that love Him* . . .' He reached for my arm. 'He's almost there, Cuthwin,' he said. 'He's almost there.'

As he said it, the figure at the centre of the fire sagged, and it was over.

There was an unexpected aftermath to Seamus's death.

As the fire burned its way out, and we watched to be sure that what remained of our Father Abbot would receive a proper Christian burial, a woman stepped from the crowd and approached us.

Without preamble, she said, 'My name is Madge, and I was with your Father Abbot and the young girl, Thaisa Eynon, in Glaum's Acre in Oxford.'

'Yes?' John spoke tersely, I suspect to hide his emotion.

Madge said, 'There was a child that died. He was buried there.'

'Yes?' said John again.

'The boy's sister survived,' said Madge.

There was a brief pause, then John said, 'There were twins? Thaisa gave birth to twins?'

'Yes. I managed to hide the little girl when the house in Glaum's Acre was broken into – when your Father Abbot and Thaisa were dragged away.'

'Where is the babe now?'

'Safe. At my lodgings. Thaisa told me to bring her here. She said there was a woman who would look after her – a woman Thaisa said had brought her up, and who would be kind. A clifftop house, she said. And the Brothers of St Benedict on hand for schooling.'

John and I looked at one another. 'The Widow Eynon,' I said, eagerly. 'That's who Thaisa meant.'

'Of course. And this is Thaisa's daughter – we shan't have lost her entirely. The Squire won't have lost her entirely.'

'Thaisa wanted her daughter to be safe,' said Madge. 'She wanted her to grow up here, where she had grown up. She wanted to think of her family continuing, and to know that all its goodness – and also all its flaws – would be handed down.'

'And also,' said John, softly, 'its music.'

TWENTY-FIVE

For a long time none of the three people in Nell's sitting room spoke.

Then Nell said, 'I'm not sure I'm going to be able to bear remembering any of that. But I needed to know.' She looked at Michael. 'That was who we saw when the stone figure broke away from the tower? It was Thaisa. They walled her up in that figure, and she was there all these centuries.'

'Yes.' Michael's eyes were shadowed, but he said, half to himself, 'So there was a sister – a twin sister, who was taken back to Rede

Abbas.' He sat up a little straighter, as if pushing back the clustering shadows, and said, 'Owen, it's all tremendous. You've done a marvellous job.'

'More to come though, dear boy. I just have to tackle the remainder of the diaries.'

'We'll look forward to hearing them,' said Nell. 'But I do wonder what became of Andrew and Theodora.'

'We'll probably never find out.'

But next morning brought a gleeful email from Owen, bearing an attachment.

> Nell and Michael – I almost broke the keyboard on my computer in my haste to send this to you. It's from the contact I have at the Bodleian – I told you how helpful he was in giving me access to Cuthwin.
>
> Anyway, he was interested in the research – I didn't tell him about Thaisa's diary, of course, we'll save that for a massive and dramatic announcement when we're sure of its authenticity – and he delved a bit more. In some dusty and long-forgotten file, he's found a letter that seems to have accompanied Egbert's submission of the Cuthwin translation. He's scanned it and sent it to me, and I'm forwarding it to you.
>
> It was originally sent to a Bulkeley Bandinel – I do know that sounds impossibly Dickensian, or even Sheridan-ish (Sheridonian?), but he was a real person, a Reverend Doctor, Dean of New College, no less, and head librarian at the Bod for almost fifty years. Brother Egbert seems to have been a contemporary of his, and certainly knew him, because in 1858 he sent his translation of the Cuthwin papers, together with a covering letter. It's that letter I'm attaching. Read and rejoice!
>
> Owen.

Nell, too, almost smashed the computer's keyboard to get at the attachment. For a sickening moment she thought her computer's software was not going to recognize it, and she spent an agonized minute calling down curses on pdf files, Adobe Readers, and every other form of technological tool.

Then the attachment opened, and there it was.

My dear old friend,
At long last my *opus magnus* is completed, and I send it to you so it can be part of your august and scholarly collection.

Deciphering Brother Cuthwin and transposing him into more modern terminology has been an absorbing and even an emotional experience. Such brutal times our forebears lived through! If you have time, do glance through the pages so that we may discuss them when next we meet – which, please God, will be soon.

It was, though, disturbing to read Cuthwin's description of how a young girl was walled up in an old bell tower which is still standing in Rede Abbas today. Sadly, that girl does not seem to have survived, and after working on that section I asked our own Father Abbot to hold a Mass for her, which we duly did, choosing St Theresa's Feast Day.

However, there is a strange echo from that story, which reverberates down to our own time. You may recall I wrote to you about a young novice, Brother Andrew Fergus? Such an intelligent, sensitive young man, and the finest Precentor I have ever known – a real love for, and understanding of, music. (A somewhat robust life before he entered St Benedict's, I believe, but I do not know any details, and it does not matter.)

We had to charge Andrew with the task of accompanying a young local girl to safety following a most unfortunate altercation here in our village. Brother Ranulf, Father Abbot and I felt Andrew was the best person for this, being recently come to St Benedict's and therefore worldier than the rest of us who have been cloistered for so many years.

It was the purest chance and God's mercy that we heard how a group of local people, incensed by what they felt to be an injustice, brought Andrew back and actually imprisoned him inside the bell tower. It was not thought there was much chance of reaching him before the tide came rushing in, but of course we had to try.

You may picture the scene, my old friend. Myself, along with Brother Ranulf, our infirmarian, Brother Wilfrid, and Father Abbot himself, went out to the tower. A storm-tossed night it was, with strange keening voices in the wind and even the impression of the great bell sounding from the tower. That could not be so, of course, for the ancient bell, known as the Glaum bell, was silenced during Cromwell's dissolution of the religious houses. I believe it only sounded a few times, in fact, before the Commissioners removed its tongue, saying the inscription was ungodly.

And yet as we went through the darkness we all heard sonorous chimes from the Glaum bell, and we exchanged uneasy glances. I found myself remembering the inscription on the great bell of Schaffhausen Minster. You remember it, I am sure, from our studies and travels.

'*Vivos voco; mortuos plango; fulgura frango . . .*' 'I call the living, I mourn the dead, I break the lightning.'

When we reached the tower, it was to find that the villagers, may God grant them forgiveness, had imprisoned Andrew in the old bell-ringing room, boarding up the doorway. The sea was already starting to gush in and the lower room was several inches deep. However, Brother Wilfrid, a robustly built person, managed to wade up to the ringing chamber, and shouted to us to help him. There was Andrew, helpless behind nailed-up boards, and it took our combined strengths (which without Wilfrid would have been puny), to break through to reach him. He was in a pitiable state, shivering, icily cold and barely conscious. As we carried him down the stairs we feared he had fallen prey to delusions, for he broke away from us and began scrabbling beneath the waters filling up the ground-floor room. When Wilfrid and I attempted to take him through the door, he began to shout that someone was trapped under the floor.

'Theodora,' he said. 'Theodora is down there. We must get her out.'

We stared at him, for Theodora Eynon was the young girl he had taken to Oxford. We did not entirely believe him, but he was so insistent, and so fierce in his struggles, that we had to help him.

'Even if Theodora is down there,' murmured Father Abbot to me, 'she will long since have drowned – the water is already knee-deep.'

We could not stop Andrew in his frantic search, and it

was a nightmarish time. The tower was dark, save for Brother Ranulf's oil lamp (which kept flickering to almost nothing); all of us were drenched to the skin, and the water was rising. Still, we plunged into the waters with our hands, but I know we were all close to giving up. As Father Abbot said, even if Theodora was there, she must long since be dead.

Then Wilfrid shouted that a section of the floor felt insecure, and at once Andrew was at his side, both of them plunging their hands into the black sea, all of us thigh-deep in the lapping waters by that time.

Wilfrid had found several planks of wood laid on the tower's stone floor, and by dint of working furiously and applying all his strength, the plank finally came away with a dreadful wet sucking noise. Above us the old bell mechanism stirred restlessly.

'Don't listen to it,' said Father Abbot, as I flinched. 'The best we can do is get the girl's body out for decent burial now. That may be of some comfort to Andrew.'

'If,' I said, softly, 'she is there at all.'

But she was. Wilfrid plunged his hands down again, and moments later he and Andrew were dragging Theodora free of the dreadful grave fashioned for her, and lifting her above the water level. Water streamed from her, and her hair hung over her face and neck in strings.

'But Andrew – my poor good friend – she is certainly dead,' said Wilfrid as we carried her outside.

Andrew said, 'No. You don't understand. She has . . . I believe she has her family's taint. Their sickness.'

'Taint? Sickness?' We had reached the start of the cliff path, and were about to climb up above the high tide level.

'Andrew,' I said, 'Wilfrid is right. She must have been dead for some time.'

That was when Andrew Fergus said, 'No. She has catalepsy.'

And Theodora opened her eyes.'

Nell had hardly finished reading this, when the morning post arrived, slapping through the letterbox loudly.

It was a large envelope with the frank of Corby & Sons, Solicitors.

The new lease, thought Nell. I've really done it. I really do have those two shops – Michael and I have them jointly. She considered this and realized she was smiling.

Corby's had indeed sent the new lease, suitably and officially sealed, with Nell and Michael's signatures at the foot.

With it was what Nell thought was called the Abstract of Title – the summary of all previous activity and ownerships or lessees of the property in question. She sat down at the kitchen table to flip through this. She had looked through her own lease when she took the single shop on, but this now included Godfrey's shop. Curious to see if the monks figured anywhere or, indeed, if Edward Glaum and Seamus Flannery's names were listed, Nell began to scan that part of the document.

She got as far as 1860. Because, in that year, the lease of Godfrey's shop had been assigned to two people for 'business purposes'. Their names were clearly listed.

Andrew Fergus and Theodora Fergus (neé Eynon). Purpose of business: Bookshop.

'I'm so glad,' said Nell, as she and Michael drove away from Rede Abbas after the inquest on Maeve Eynon, 'that Andrew and Theodora finally got together. I think a bookshop was exactly right for them. And I'm more than glad that the wretched inquest of that poor creature, Maeve Eynon, is behind us.'

'Yes. Suicide while the balance of the mind was disturbed. A predictable verdict. Poor old Maeve,' said Michael. 'I suppose she was the last of the family.'

> From: Olive Orchard
> To: Daniel Goodbody
>
> Daniel –
> I thought they gave Maeve Eynon a very nice funeral, all things considered. I've just heard, though, that she left specific instructions that she was to be cremated. However, in view of the curious circumstances of her death, the coroner refused to grant a cremation order. It seems a shame her wishes could not be followed, but it can't make any difference to her whether she's cremated or buried.

Don't forget we still have to have that drink!
Olive

'The traffic's a bit snarled up, isn't it?' said Michael, as he and Nell drove back to Oxford. 'We're a bit later than I bargained for.'

'Me too. That's why I'm taking these side roads. It might avoid some of the snarl-up.'

'Isn't this,' said Michael, presently, 'the road where Beth photographed a house with a maple tree?'

'It's that turning there. We don't need to take it – we can go straight down.'

'No, let's take it.'

'Why?'

'Only so I can tell Beth I saw the house.'

Nell nodded, and indicated left.

'It is lovely,' said Michael, as they reached the house.

Nell had slowed down. 'It's for sale,' she said, suddenly.

'Wasn't it for sale before?'

'No.' Nell was seeing that her memory of the house had been exact. The big windows, the impression of book-lined rooms, gentle sunlight, companionship . . .

'It says the keys can be borrowed from the agents,' said Michael, looking at the 'For Sale' board.

'It'll be massively overpriced.'

'Oh yes.'

'Mortgages and things,' said Nell.

'Royalties from book sales and things,' said Michael.

They looked at one another.

'Shall we at least borrow the keys and look round?' he said.

Nell thought about the money it would take to buy this house. She thought about the money that had already been outlaid for Quire Court, but then she thought the shops might do extremely well, and she remembered that the antique workshop weekends were already amassing bookings. She remembered Jack Hurst observing how the newly created flat over the two shops would command a high rent.

She went on looking at the house, thinking that within its rooms would be a great deal of happiness.

Within its rooms would be Michael and Beth.

Michael said, hesitantly, 'We could think about it, and borrow the keys another time.'

Nell reached for his hand. 'Let's borrow the keys now,' she said.